LOVE'S
REDEMPTION

Kimberly Kaye Terry

Romantic Suspense

New Concepts   Georgia

Be sure to check out our website for the very best in fiction at fantastic prices!

When you visit our webpage, you can:
* Read excerpts of currently available books
* View cover art of upcoming books and current releases
* Find out more about the talented artists who capture the magic of the writer's imagination on the covers
* Order books from our backlist
* Find out the latest NCP and author news--including any upcoming book signings by your favorite NCP author
* Read author bios and reviews of our books
* Get NCP submission guidelines
* And so much more!

We offer a 20% discount on all new Trade Paperback releases ordered from our website!

Be sure to visit our webpage to find the best deals in e-books and paperbacks! To find out about our new releases as soon as they are available, please be sure to sign up for our newsletter (http://www.newconceptspublishing.com/newsletter.htm) or join our reader group (http://groups.yahoo.com/group/new_concepts_pub/join)!

The newsletter is available by double opt in only and our customer information is *never* shared!

Visit our webpage at:
www.newconceptspublishing.com

Love's Redemption is an original publication of NCP. This work has never before appeared in book form. This work is a novel. Any similarity to actual persons or events is purely coincidental.

New Concepts Publishing, Inc.
5202 Humphreys Rd.
Lake Park, GA 31636

ISBN 1-58608-741-x
2006 © Kimberly Kaye Terry
Cover art © copyright 2006 Kat Richards

NCP books are available at special quantity discounts for bulk purchases for sales promotions, premiums, fund raising, or educational use. For details, write, email, or phone New Concepts Publishing, Inc., 5202 Humphreys Rd., Lake Park, GA 31636; Ph. 229-257-0367, Fax 229-219-1097; orders@newconceptspublishing.com.

First NCP Trade Paperback Printing: April 2006

Dedication:

This is dedicated to my daughter's Imani and Hannah and my husband Bill. Imani is in Heaven, and I'm blessed to have Hannah with me on earth.

Imani thank you for inspiring Mommy, and Hannah thank you for continually motivating me, as only a five year old can.... Mommy loves you both.

Bill you're my rock. I could never write a fictional hero half as wonderful as you are.

PART I
PROLOGUE

Glasses perched on top of her head, Dr. Maya Richardson searched in vain for the file she'd just had in her hand. It was one on those days where she didn't know if she was coming or going she had so much work in front of her. Maybe the file had fallen off her crowded desk. Lord knew she needed to come in early to clean and organize the pit she called an office.

"*Sesute*, there is something on the news I think you should see," her assistant said from the doorway. Dalia knew Maya would never find the remote in time, so she came into the office and turned the TV on for her.

"Authorities believe two victims of the *San Antonio Slayer* have been found outside loop 410 near Huebner Road. The police have described the male as Caucasian, 5'8", short blond hair, and brown eyes, and in his early 40s. The second victim is a Caucasian female, 5'10", red hair, green eyes, with a long jagged scar running the length of her lower face. Anyone with information on either of these two victims is asked to call the San Antonio Police department at…" the newscaster droned.

"Oh my God. Not Allison. Please don't let it be Allison." With trembling hands, Maya picked up the phone and dialed the number displayed across her small television screen.

"San Antonio Police department, how may I direct your call?" the brusque, disembodied voice of the department operator asked.

PART II
CHAPTER 1

She had the prettiest brown eyes Mark had ever seen. The minute his gaze wandered in her direction, he couldn't look away.

He bent to refill his water from the cooler, where he stood near the doorway directly in front of Lieutenant Hernandez's door. The woman sat waiting outside the office in one of the dingy chairs that lined the precinct wall.

Normally, he would have glanced at the small, huddled figure and looked away. He would have done the same thing again had she not glanced in his direction at *that* same moment, and he felt pole-axed.

Transfixed, he stared at her.

Damn.

She was gorgeous. Large, light brown eyes, slightly tilted in the corners, drew his gaze like a magnet. Her hair was tightly coiled into one long braid that nestled between her ample breasts. What drew his attention to her hair were the small curls that had escaped and, like musical notes, framed creamy, golden-brown skin.

But it was her mouth that caused the sharp clench he felt in his gut. She had a sinful mouth. Lush and full, it grabbed his attention and made something more than his gut clench.

When their gazes collided, a flash sparked between them before the woman glanced away and lightly tapped one small foot in a staccato beat on the old linoleum floor of the precinct.

Her face in profile drew his attention back to her mouth. Obviously lost in thought, she pulled her bottom lip into her mouth with her top teeth and slowly let it pop back out. His overactive male libido had him wondering what else she'd be able to grip with the same intensity.

"Hey Mark, check this out--Jean Luc here bet me that in his prime, Ali would have beat Tyson any time, any place, any ring," Jordan Phillips yelled out across the room.

"What?" Distracted and slightly flushed, Mark glanced across at his partner, reluctantly dragging his gaze away from the woman.

"All I am saying is if both men were in their prime, fighting in the same generation, then it would be no contest," Detective LeDoux answered in his heavily accented English. "And please, refer to me by my correct name. My name is Frances LeDoux, *Detective Frances LeDoux if you do not mind, not Jean Luc.*" With a huff, the short, bald detective turned back to his desk.

"Look, you two are always trying to get me in the middle of this dumb ass argument when you both know Joe Louis would have beat the hell out of Ali *and* Tyson hands down," Mark answered, his mind on the woman.

"Man whatever." Jordan laughed in his deep voice before he spun his large body around in his chair to continue his harassment of LeDoux.

Glancing back in the direction of the lieutenant's office, Mark uttered a low curse when the unknown woman was no longer there. He brightened considerably when he realized she must have gone inside Lieutenant Hernandez's office.

He figured now was as good a time as any to ask if forensics had turned in their report on the latest murder victim in his investigation. Mark stood and stretched, and casually walked over to knock on the lieutenant's door.

* * * *

Maya sat opposite Lieutenant Hernandez with her hands clasped tightly in her lap. After calling the police department she'd sat in numbed silence denying the possibility that the murdered woman the newscaster referred to could be *her* Allison.

The operator had taken her information, and then transferred her to the desk sergeant. She had been told two uniformed officers would pick her up to bring her into the station. After giving them her address, she replaced the receiver with a listless hand.

Now, as she sat across the desk from the lieutenant, all she felt was numb. Numb and cold.

Her gaze took in the small office. The walls were painted the same washed-out color as the rest of the precinct and filled with standard, government-issue furniture that could stand a good scrub down.

Maya rested her gaze on the lieutenant. He'd been kind to her from the moment she entered his office. His soft brown eyes were wide set and thickly fringed behind the round glasses perched at the top of his small, straight nose. His lips and cheeks were a natural pale shade of rose and provided a light contrast to his olive complexion. His mild demeanor and show of sympathy had put her at ease the moment she sat down in front of him.

"Dr. Richardson, thank you for coming in with the officers. As you know from the news, there have been a series of violent murders involving 'clients' of prostitutes in the city over the last six months," Lieutenant Hernandez told her directly. "We believe we've discovered two more victims. We're hoping you'll be able to identify the body of the latest victim."

She couldn't seem to stop the flow of tears at his statement. He handed her a tissue as she began to cry. A knock made him look away from her to the door.

"Yes, what is it?"

"Lieutenant, is the forensic report in on the slayer's latest?"

Maya glanced up with tear-stained eyes to see the detective with whom she'd made brief eye contact earlier enter the office.

"Come in Mark. Dr. Richardson, this is Detective Mark Halstan. Detective, this is Dr. Maya Richardson. Dr. Richardson has come in to possibly provide an identification for the female victim."

Lieutenant Hernandez waved him in to have a seat. The detective moved further into the office and shook her hand, holding it a little longer than necessary before sitting down.

"As a matter of fact Detective, I was going to send for you to escort Dr. Richardson to the morgue to identify the body," Lieutenant Hernandez said. "This is a very difficult process, and we will do anything within our power to help make it as painless as possible for you," he promised, returning his attention back to her.

"Thank you, Lieutenant Hernandez. From what I've learned in the news, I was under the impression the killer was targeting the 'clients' of the prostitutes and not the prostitutes--is that wrong?"

"Actually you're right. So far, the offender has targeted the *clients*. However, in the case of this female victim, we believe she may have interrupted the killer in the act, and she was then forced to kill her."

"How do you know?" Although saddened by the possible death of Ally, Maya was acutely aware of the close proximity of Detective Halstan. She instantly felt guilty, but the office seemed to grow smaller with his presence.

It wasn't only his physical bearing, although he was considerably taller and larger than either she or the lieutenant. He just seemed to take up more space than seemed necessary.

Overlong sable brown hair barely reached the collar of his shirt. His dark blue eyes were deep set and stared at her from beneath lashes no man should have. His mouth held a hard edge of sensuality around the corners. The beauty of his face was saved from perfection by the slight crook in his nose, which only served to make him even more appealing. There was no denying he was one of the most gorgeous men she'd ever seen.

Uncomfortable with the direction of her thoughts, Maya glanced guiltily away, blaming her grief and confusion for her errant thoughts.

"The projection of the bullet, and where the shell casings were found near the victims, indicate your foster sister was likely to have been a small distance away when she was shot."

"Lieutenant, you said the victim had interrupted the killer and '*she*' had then been forced to kill her as well. Do the police believe this person is a woman? I assumed the killer was a man. Isn't that true for most serial killers?" Maya couldn't bring herself to actually say Ally's name as the victim in connection with the murder.

"While it's true for the majority, women do make up a small percentage of this population. To be honest with you Dr. Richardson, we don't have a good working profile on the killer, to make a determination either way, but the evidence at present suggest the slayer is female. Once we have a profile, we *will* make headway into this investigation." The lieutenant promised grimly.

"If you're ready, Dr. Richardson, we can go. Lieutenant?" Mark asked both Maya and his commander, as the interview came to a close.

"Yes, and afterward, Dr. Richardson, would you be able to come back to the squad room in order to answer a few questions?" Lieutenant Hernandez asked, coming from around his desk to walk the pair to the door.

"Of course, anything I can do to help. I'm more than willing." She shook the lieutenant's hand.

"It's going to be okay, Dr. Richardson. Detective Halstan will take good care of you." He grasped both of her hands between his, and patted them.

"Thank you, Lieutenant Hernandez, I appreciate your concern."

When the detective ushered her out of the office with his hand resting lightly on the small of her back, she felt electric warmth tingle through to her skin the minute he touched her. She was caught off guard, and she casually stepped out of reach of his hand as they walked down the hall, uncomfortable with his touch, and more uncomfortable with the spark it had given her.

* * * *

Mark steered Maya toward the open doorway to the squad room. "I'll be right back," he said and walked to his partner's desk in the open bay room.

"Jordan, I'm leaving to take Dr. Richardson over to I.D the female victim we turned up yesterday. I'm not sure when I'll be back."

His partner stole a glance at Maya as she waited for him in the doorway. With a low whistle he answered, "Man, take all the time you need. How does she know the victim anyway? She doesn't look as though they were 'colleagues,' know what I mean?" Once again, his partner glanced over at Maya.

"They weren't. From what I understand they were foster sisters. Probably grew up in a group home together somewhere. I think that's where the similarities end. I just met her in the lieutenant's office, so I'm not sure of all the details myself. After she's identified the body, I'll ask her a few questions and go from there. I'm not sure what time I'll make it back in, so don't wait around for me."

"Later on, partner," Jordan answered. Mark walked back toward Maya and together they left the squad room.

After they reached the elevator, he motioned for her to precede him, following closely behind her. Once inside, he punched the button for the basement-parking garage.

"I'm assuming a uniform came to pick you up?" He asked, as they silently rode the elevator to the garage.

"Yes. I was at Imani House when I called the station. It was a relief they came to pick me up. I don't think I'm in a frame of mind to drive right now."

They were the only two occupants in the slow-moving elevator, and when it came to a lurching halt, Maya fell against his chest, and he immediately wrapped his arms around her waist to steady her.

"I'm sorry," she apologized, and tried to move away from his light hold. Mark tightened his clasp on her body fractionally before allowing her to step away from him. When she darted her eyes in his direction, he hoped she wouldn't look down and see his body's reaction to the small contact.

As the elevator made it to the basement level, he led her to his late model Expedition. He opened the back hatch and threw in his gym bag after helping her into the passenger side.

He felt guilty over how he was handling his attraction to her. He knew she was terribly upset and worried. He knew it, felt guilty as hell about it, but couldn't stop himself from crowding her. "Dr. Richardson, when we're through with everything, where did you want me to take you?" he asked, seeking more neutral ground.

"Detective, please call me Maya. I was working when the officers arrived to take me to the precinct. I'm the director of Imani House. Are you familiar with it?"

"Please call me Mark. Yes, in answer to your question. Isn't it the halfway house for ex hookers--uh sorry, for former prostitutes?" he covered, maneuvering out of the parking garage and into traffic.

As she settled against the soft leather seat, he caught the sidelong glance she threw his way, before she answered. "Actually, there's more to it than that. We have a variety of programs, mainly designed for women to help them transition from prostitution to a more stable way of life."

"Sorry if I offended you. It sounds like a great place for them to go when they want to get off the streets and get their lives together." He backtracked, smoothly recovering from his gaffe. He then drove the short distance from the downtown precinct to the hospital.

After pulling into the underground lot of the hospital, Mark found a space to park. Turning off the ignition, he turned in his seat toward her. A curl had escaped her tight braid, and he barely resisted the urge to tuck it back behind her ear.

"The coroner is expecting us. Are you ready?"

"Yes. I may as well get this over with. Maybe it isn't Ally after all." She waited for him to come around to the passenger side and allowed him to open her door.

They walked the short distance to the entry before Mark stopped short and turned her around to face him. "I don't know if you've ever seen a dead body or not. With this possibly being your foster sister, it's going to be a shock, so take a deep breath, and I'll be right there with you."

He saw the fortifying breath she took, as she straightened her shoulders, before with a silent nod, she allowed him to lead her into the morgue.

Not until the attendant had drawn back the white sheet did Maya glance down, and when she did, her body bowed over in obvious pain.

"Oh my God, oh my God, it … it's her, that's Ally," she told him, covering her face with her hands.

After motioning to the attendant to close the drawer, Mark moved closer to her and encircled her shoulders with his arm, turning her away from the sight and out of the room.

Her golden brown complexion had a distinct greenish tinge to it. The eyes staring up into his were large and dilated. The distant hint of blood vessels near the surface of her skin stood out in stark relief against her complexion.

Once outside the doors, he turned her fully into his arms, as uncontrollable sobs racked her small body.

"Are you okay? I know that was hard to see. Would you like to sit down for a minute?" He had known this woman for less than a few hours, yet it was tearing at his heart to see her cry so hard. As she cried, the only thing he could offer was the comfort of his arms around her body. He rubbed her back and whispered soothing words, allowing her to cry until he felt her body calm down, and the sobbing wane to an occasional sniff.

Without her asking, he offered his last remaining Kleenex and watched as she wiped her face and eased her body away from his embrace.

"Thank you, Detective, but I'm okay. If it's all right, could we go now?"

"Of course. We don't have to go back to the precinct. There's a coffee shop nearby where we could talk. A little less formal, but we'll still get the job done." He told her and they left the morgue and walked back to his vehicle.

Once inside, Maya eased her head back against the cool leather headrest and closed her eyes. "That sounds fine, Detective. I could use a cup of coffee right now."

After giving her one last sympathetic glance, he eased out of the parking space and headed toward the café.

CHAPTER 2

Mark maneuvered his SUV with expert ease into a space directly in front of the popular coffee shop. Going around to Maya's side of the vehicle, he took her hand and helped her out before guiding her into the café.

"I haven't eaten since breakfast, so I think I'll have a muffin to go with my latte," she said, as she sat in the booth next to him.

"Sounds good. I hadn't realized it was getting so late. They have great sandwiches here if you'd like."

"I don't think I've ever been here before." Maya looked around the dimly lit interior of the inviting café. The walls were painted in grays and muted blues, a perfect contrast to the abstract prints that hung throughout the cafe.

The exterior had given the impression of a casually dilapidated building, but once inside, this illusion was quickly dispelled. To the left of the door was a horseshoe-shaped, fully stocked bar, flanked with a dozen or more high-backed wooden stools. To the right was a lounge area with a raised dais, where a woman sat strumming a guitar and singing softly for the small crowd.

There were several smaller tables and booths scattered throughout the café, giving it a casual put-together elegance. Looking up at him with approving eyes, Maya was going to make a comment when she noticed their waitress approaching them.

As she approached, the woman's smile considerably brightened as she caught sight of Mark. Smiling with interest in his direction, she took their orders, looking at him the entire time. With a slight smile, Maya's glance stole over the detective.

His close fitting shirt tucked into the waistband of faded jeans that hugged his muscular thighs. Not only was he handsome, but his body was the picture of male perfection. She had an inexplicable urge to reach out and touch his arm, if only to see if his bicep felt as strong as it looked.

Instead, she demurely sat with her hands clenched tightly in her lap. "Where do we start, Detective?"

"We can start by me reminding you to call me Mark," he reminded her with a smile. "And then why don't you tell me about Allison, who her friends were, where she hung out. Boyfriends, girlfriends, anything you can think of." He withdrew his notebook from his jacket pocket and flipped it open.

"Sure I can do that, but before we start I have a question. Do you know if Ally had a necklace matching this?" She pulled out a small pendant, suspended on a thin gold chain.

Leaning across the table, his fingers glazed the tops of her breasts as he took the pendant from her fingers. Her breasts tingled from the light contact. Gently he allowed it to fall back into place between her breasts.

"No, I don't remember a necklace being catalogued in the evidence room. I'll check tomorrow to make sure. You know, I kind of remember seeing these when I was a kid."

Maya remembered how she'd gotten the pendant and smiled in melancholy. "Allison and I became foster sisters when she was 5 and I was 7. We had both been in the same group home for girls, and bonded pretty quickly as only children can." She laughed sadly in memory.

Memories of Allison also brought on memories of Santa Lucia Hospital when she'd lost both of her parents in a tragic accident.

"My parents died when I was five years old. I survived the accident with only a small contusion. Well, physically at least."

"I'm sorry," he murmured in sympathy.

"Thank you." She paused before continuing, "My grandparents, who at the time I didn't know I had, wouldn't claim me. So I was left with social services and entered foster care. That's where I met Ally."

Taking a satisfying sip of coffee, she thought back to the dreary time in her life and of funny little Allison who had helped make life more bearable.

"At one point we thought we were going to be separated. Allison had been the one constant in my life for a long time and I didn't want to lose her. A few days after we were told we may be separated, she gave me this necklace. She had a matching one. She'd been saving it for a Christmas gift but decided to give it to me early, in case she couldn't later. She said no matter where we were, we would always be together as long as we wore our necklaces."

When he placed both of her hands into his much larger ones, she allowed his show of comfort. Taking a deep breath, she expelled it slowly and withdrew her hands as the tears she'd been shedding throughout the day threatened to fall once again.

"I've worn this necklace every day since she gave it to me," her voice sounded thick with the unshed tears clogging her throat as she fingered the small chain. "I replaced the original chain with a real gold necklace as soon as I could afford to. Ally always wore hers too. She said it was her reminder she had someone who loved her and she mattered."

"I'll check the evidence room as soon as I can and find out for you Maya. I promise you." He cleared his throat from the sudden obstruction he felt. "How long had your sister been a prostitute?"

Maya wondered, not for the first time, had she not shied away from what Ally had been doing to earn money, would things have turned out differently for her foster sister?

"When she was around 17, Ally became involved in prostitution. Soon after we'd moved out on our own."

She noted his surprised expression. "Ally and I didn't have the most positive, nurturing atmosphere growing up." She laughed sadly. "Drugs, violence, gangs, and prostitution were the norm for us. We never really had too many 'frills,' you know. We had the basics, and sometimes not even that. We were forgotten most of the time and seen as a burden all of the time. Ally wanted a lot of things she'd been denied all her life and finally saw a way to get some of them." She blinked her eyes several times in an attempt to hold back the pain of her childhood memories.

"I loved Ally. She was my little sister. I know she was only a couple of years younger than me, but she always *seemed* a lot younger. She only wanted the same things her friends had, and she thought this was the only way to get them."

Left unsaid was the guilt she felt. She believed Ally was her responsibility, and she'd let her down by not forcing her to stop her destructive behaviors.

"When was the last time you saw your sister, Maya? Did she continue living with you, or did she move out on her own?" As she'd been battling her personal demons, she focused her attention back to Mark.

"After I completed my Bachelor's, I received a full scholarship for grad school at UTA. By that time, Ally was 19, and I didn't want to leave her on her own; she was too young."

"You were young yourself. Did you ever get tired of the responsibility of having to care for Allison? It seems as though you had the responsibility of her care for a long time." Although he asked the question bluntly, she didn't feel as though he were judging her.

"I never felt she was a burden. We looked after one another. I couldn't imagine leaving her, because I knew she relied on me.

Besides, I didn't like the crowd she was hanging with, and I thought a new environment would be good for her," she insisted.

"Was it? Good for her?"

"At first. But within a few months, she'd found a similar crowd, and things escalated."

"How so?" Mark placed his pad down and signed the waitress over to order sandwiches and more coffee.

"She started smoking pot and drinking. I tried to talk to her about it, but she wasn't about to listen to me. By the time I'd finished graduate school, she was barely speaking to me, and I had no idea what was going on in her head." She ran frustrated hands over her face.

"That had to be tough," he murmured in sympathy.

"It was. She decided to move out, and I didn't see her for two years, and then one day she showed up at the help center where I was working." Maya tried to collect herself, but not before several tears had fallen unchecked down her face.

When her gaze eyes met his, raw emotion shone starkly in her eyes. "She looked awful. It hurt to look at her. Her hair was stringy and dirty. She was so thin, her bones looked like they were poking through her skin. She had a long red razor mark stretching across her face. I couldn't believe it was my Ally." She clenched her teeth together, her nostrils flaring, as she remembered the way Allison looked. She took a drink of her coffee before she picked the story up.

"I noticed right away she was talking really fast. She couldn't stay still, and neither did she keep eye contact with me. I knew she was high. She said she needed money, and wanted to know if I had any to spare."

After she paused, Mark prompted her, "Did you give it to her?"

"Yes," she admitted simply. "She told me she was staying with friends. I invited her to come home, but she wouldn't. She said she needed a little money to tide her over."

"Did you see her regularly after the two of you were reunited?"

"Unfortunately no. One of the last times I saw Ally was about two months ago. She said she wanted to clean her life up and was tired of living the way she was. That's the last time I spoke with her."

She wondered if she hadn't giving in and given her money, but had instead pressed the issue, could she have convinced Ally to give her program a chance? Unfortunately, she would never know if Ally had been serious. Considering the circumstances she died under, she doubted Ally had been ready to take that first step.

Signaling the waitress to bring the check, Mark reached in his jacket to pull out his wallet. "This is on me, please Maya."

She noticed for the first time how dark it was once they left the cafe. After he'd settled her into her seat and he'd gone to the driver's side, she turned in her seat to face him. "If you don't mind, I'd like to go home. I'm not really up to seeing anyone tonight. I think I need some time to myself tonight to take everything in."

After they'd driven away from the café, Mark reached a stoplight. The light cast a crimson glow on Maya's face, highlighting her fatigue. "Of course, just give me your address. How will you get to work tomorrow? Do you live close to Imani House?"

"Not too far away. It takes me fifteen or twenty minutes on the loop. I live in a converted older home with two other units. My neighbor, Dalia, is also my assistant at Imani House. I can get a ride to work with her in the morning," she told him, after giving her address.

"Why don't you relax for a minute and close your eyes. The traffic is kind of heavy; it may take us a while, and you should rest. It's been an emotionally draining day for you," he said as he turned on the radio. He immediately turned it back off.

She reached over and stalled his hand. "No, leave it on--it isn't bothering me. Music is soothing to me." She adjusted her body into the soft leather seat and closed her eyes, and was asleep within minutes.

* * * *

A few minutes later Mark glanced her way when he heard her light snores. After watching her for a few moments, he was disgusted with himself when even her snores turned him on.

He turned his attention back to the congested highway. Rolling down his window, he allowed the warm breeze to filter into the car. This was his favorite time of the year, the beginning of spring, when nature seemed to grant a new lease on life. It was the best time of year in San Antonio.

Having grown up and worked in San Antonio his entire life, Mark was intimately acquainted with most communities and knew his way around. After she'd given him her home address, he hadn't needed directions, already being familiar with the area.

When he glanced back in her direction, he noted that she'd barely stirred from her original position. However, instead of both hands resting under her cheek, the right one had slipped down into her lap where it rested upturned.

She looked so innocent with her hand nestled beneath her cheek and the other on her thigh. Her pretty brown skin had a healthy glow. Her lips were slightly open; the full bottom rim beckoned his attention.

Obviously, her mental exhaustion had warred with the caffeine she'd consumed, and the exhaustion had easily won.

Turning at the stop sign, Mark made the descent down the hill leading to her house. Within minutes, they were headed into the tree-lined community that had been one of the first to be established in the area.

He'd hidden his surprise after she'd given him her address. The area was not only an old established community, but was also a community known for its wealthy residents.

He'd reached her street when she began to stir. She slowly opened her eyes and softly yawned. She placed her hand on the side of her neck, and turning her head in the opposite direction, stretched her body.

Abruptly she turned back to him. "Oh Lord, I'm sorry. I must have dozed off. You're on my street! My house is the last one on your side." She self-consciously pat her hair, fingering the thick braid back into place, as he came to a smooth halt outside the brightly lit, brick, two-story Victorian mansion.

Even in the early evening light, he could see the flowers that provided a profusion of colors framing the walkway that led to her front porch. Abundant ferns framed the wraparound deck; the overall effect gave the mansion a warm and welcoming feel.

"You were tired, don't worry about it. How's your head? Does it still hurt?" he asked solicitously, as he turned his body toward hers. In the dimly lit interior, he was barely able to make out her features. Noting the exhaustion in her eyes, he turned the engine off and removed his seat belt. "Let me walk you to your door."

"That's okay, I'll be alright. It's a short walk to the door. I'll use my front entry, but thank you," she said, as she turned to open her door.

Before she was able to do so, he was there helping her climb down. Keeping his hand on the small of her back, he walked her the short distance to her front door.

"I wasn't aware there were any apartments in this area," he said as they made their way up the wide brick walkway.

"I own it. I have a hard time wasting anything, including space. So I converted it into three separate units." She reached into her purse and fished for her key.

"Allow me."

He reached down to take the key from her hand. After opening the first door, they were inside a hallway with two doors. She motioned him toward the one that was hers.

He turned around to hand her the door key. The overhead hall light starkly highlighted her tear-streaked face. Slowly the tears traveled down her face and swiftly gathered momentum. Without thought, he turned her into his arms.

Holding her tight, his intent was only to soothe. He spread his legs to reduce the height difference as he embraced her with one arm, while the other cupped the back of her head.

With both of her arms hugging his waist, she continued to cry uncontrollably. When her tears showed no sign of ceasing, Mark continued to caress the back of her head. Eventually, she went to unwind her arms from their tight hold around his waist until he reached around and prevented her from moving.

"I'm sorry. It's been an awful day. This is the second time today you've seen me like this," she shakily apologized.

"You don't have anything to be embarrassed about. It's been an emotionally draining day for you. My God, you just identified your foster sister's body."

As she gazed at him with her large beautiful eyes, still shimmering with unshed tears, his heart skipped a beat. He lifted her face and gently wiped the tears away from her smooth cheek with the rough pads of his thumbs.

She continued to look at him with her sad eyes and he leaned down to lift her chin and softly kiss her lips. When she made no move to stop him, he continued to kiss her with light touches that barely made contact with her mouth, making his way down her cheek, tasting her salty tears.

The moment his mouth touched hers he was on fire. What had begun in innocence, a simple desire to console, took on a life of its own. Setting out to comfort and soothe, the incredible softness of her lips sent blood rushing to his head.

Mark knew there was no way he was going to stop unless she asked. And he hoped to hell she wouldn't ask.

He deepened the kiss, and his tongue plunged into the moist recesses of her mouth in search of her warm, wet tongue. He pulled her bottom lip between his and drew on the lush rim, tugging it further and further into his mouth, causing a deep ache to pool directly in his groin. His hand traveled from her lower back to her rounded bottom to gently cup and caress the small mounds.

Her arms moved from the center of his chest to snake around to the back of his neck, tangling her fingers in the hair at the nape of his neck. Mark couldn't get close enough to her small sweet curves; the answering moan she gave him only heightened his response to her.

Gradually, the sound of a husky throat clearing made its way into his consciousness. Slowly breaking contact with the lush fullness of her lips, he lifted his head in frustration to glance around at the intrusion. A tall woman stood outside her door in a long floral housecoat wearing a deep frown, her lips pooched out in obvious disapproval.

Mark cursed low in his throat as he discretely adjusted Maya's clothes as well his jeans. He leaned his forehead against hers to give himself time to gain his composure.

As Maya too gained awareness, he saw the guilt and shame cross her face, and swore again. When he'd first kissed her, his only motivation had been to soothe, but it had quickly changed direction. He had every intention of kissing her from the first moment he set eyes on her.

But not tonight, and definitely not under these conditions.

His gaze swept over her swollen lips and downcast eyes. He didn't want her first intimate experience with him to be something she was ashamed of.

He turned to the unknown woman standing in the open doorway of her apartment. "If you don't mind, could we have a moment?"

The woman glanced at Maya with a questioning look. After being given a small nod, she turned away and said nothing as she returned to her apartment. He turned his attention back to Maya.

"Thanks for bringing me home. I'm sure that I'll hear from the police in the near future."

She'd probably said the first thing that came to her mind. He understood her feelings, but still wasn't about to allow her to retreat from the incredible experience they'd just shared. He wouldn't let her pretend it hadn't happened.

"Yes you'll hear from the police soon Maya. You'll be hearing from me even sooner. I'm sorry for your loss, I really am. Right now you need to go inside and get some rest. I don't want to add to your stress. But I *will* call tomorrow to see how you are."

With that, he kissed her softly on the corner of her mouth, his hand lightly caressing her smooth cheek before leaving.

Maya unconsciously placed her hand on the spot Mark had kissed, her eyes glued on his large frame until he'd climbed inside the big SUV and drove away.

When she finally let herself into her apartment, her first reaction was overwhelming relief. She realized how tense she was, and the beginnings of a migraine were returning with a vengeance.

She kicked off her shoes and tossed her bag on the overstuffed chair in the corner, and then made her way into the kitchen. Reaching into the cabinet, she took out a small package of her herbal tea that was touted as being designed for soothing the nerves.

Maya decided that she definitely needed her nerves soothed. With a weary sigh, she leaned against the counter as she waited for the other shoe to drop.

"*Mazyte Sesute,* where are you, dear?" Maya's assistant, friend and confidant called out. Or better yet, the proverbial other shoe.

She loved Dalia, but all she wanted to do was drink her tea and curl up in the fetal position and sleep. Weary and resigned, Maya reached for a second cup and placed it on the small table as she waited for her.

"So, who was the gentleman that you were involved in the lip-locking with, *Sesute?"* Dalia came into the large airy kitchen, and with long-standing familiarity, went directly to the pantry in search of a snack to go with the tea Maya was brewing.

"That was Detective Mark Halstan with the SAPD." Maya was well acquainted with Dalia's direct manner of speech, and her odd way of phrasing. Dalia had emigrated from Lithuania as a teenager and was now well into her fifties, and yet her voice still carried the lilting tone of her youth.

"Oh Maya, was the one from the television indeed your Allison?" Motioning for Maya to sit down, Dalia took over pouring the coffee.

"Yes, it was Ally. I wouldn't like to ever have to relive that experience. Detective Halstan was the officer who took me to identify the body." After filling her in on the details, Maya felt so worn out she thought she'd fall asleep at the drop of a hat.

"You are exhausted, Maya. You run your bath water, and I will clear these small dishes away. Go on, dear, and I will bring your tea in for you to drink as you relax."

"Thanks, Dal. I think I'll do just that," she told her friend with a weary smile. As she left the kitchen and walked through her house, she took pride in her surroundings. She'd inherited the house from the grandmother she'd never known. She'd also received a substantial monetary inheritance from her grandmother, which had allowed her to supply the initial funding for Imani House.

After the initial shock of her inheritance had worn off, Maya had fallen in love with her new home. She knew she would never feel comfortable in the sheer massiveness of the mansion; therefore, she divided her new home into three separate units, each one still large enough for a family to enjoy.

However, the most precious inheritance had been in the videotape and package that didn't really hold any monetary value. Not knowing what the videotape and package may contain, she had opted to wait before delving into its contents. Once she did, the tears had run unchecked down her face.

Her grandmother had begun by introducing herself as Catherine Elizabeth Rutherford-Spaulding, of the Atlanta Rutherford's, and that she was the mother of Elizabeth Chris Spaulding-Richardson, her Lizzy, and the proud grandmother of Maya Grace Richardson.

As Maya prepared her bath, she recalled how she felt as she watched the videotape of her deceased grandmother. Her Grandmother had told her that she'd wished she could have had the opportunity to meet Maya in person…

CHAPTER 3

"...*However, fate has decreed otherwise, it would seem. Obviously dear, if you're getting this videotape now, then I am no longer a member of this plane of existence and have gone on to my ' reward.'* She uttered a small half-hearted chuckle.

"*If the good Lord has any mercy, I am reunited with your mother, and we are finally together. Oh how I've missed that child. She was a precocious little thing, even as a baby. Why she was in such a hurry to experience life, she came almost two months earlier than they thought. Now back then, that was something to be concerned about. Babies didn't always make it when they were born so early.*

"*Well not your mother. She was not much bigger than your granddaddy's hand, but when she opened those big beautiful green eyes of hers, well we all knew we had us a fighter on our hands.*"

Pausing for a moment, Catherine began to pull her lower lip into her mouth with her top teeth before visibly catching herself.

"*As your mama grew up, she maintained that same fighter spirit. Lord have mercy, the disagreements that girl and I would have! She was what your grandfather would call an 'alpha female.' I thought she was just plain old stubborn. In all honesty it was a trait that most women on the Rutherford side seem to share. Maybe I didn't receive my fair share of that trait. If I had, then I would have been able to stand up to my husband on behalf of my only child.*

"*I won't try and defend myself, but I will say that it was a different era. Women didn't have the same options that they do today. But that's no excuse, Maya, and I won't use that way out.*

"*She was our only child. So, I guess you can imagine how very indulged your mother was. My goodness, there was nothing, and I do mean nothing, that she lacked.*"

An unhappy frown crossed her aged features.

"*The era that your mother was a young person in, the 1960s and 70s, were fraught with turmoil. The war, the civil rights movement, and the assassination of the president--yes it was definitely a tumultuous time in our nation. Your mother went to college up north against your grandfather's wishes. He'd wanted her to go to the women's Baptist college right in Savannah, but there was no way your mother was going to agree to that. No, that young hatchling was ready to test her wings to see how far and fast she could soar. Finally giving her his blessing, your grandfather 'allowed' her to go."*

She uttered a small chuckle.

"We didn't know it, but your father, who was the nephew of our gardener, had earned himself a full scholarship to this same college.

"Her visits became more and more sporadic as time went on. Your mother was very intelligent, but it took her a long time to graduate. She told us she couldn't decide on a major. Finally, she'd written us to tell us that she'd completed her degree in psychology.

"When it came time for your mother to receive her degree, we happily made the trip to see our baby girl cross the stage, there was no way that we were going to miss this!! When we got there not only did we see our baby cross the stage, but we also saw her cross the stage with you strapped to her back! When I got over the shock, I could not believe they had allowed her to do that. Your grandfather left in the middle of the ceremony.

"When it was over, I found him and convinced him to come back to the auditorium. We saw your mama at the same time that she saw us--and she waved us over, as though everything was as right as rain! 'Mama and Daddy' she said, 'I know this may come as a surprise to you, but I'd like to introduce you to my baby Maya Grace Richardson.

"And then she took you out of this native wrap thing she was wearing around her body, and handed you to me. You were absolutely beautiful. You had the prettiest eyes that I had ever seen, and so much hair!

"When I turned to your grandfather I noticed that his face had gone totally gray.

"I didn't know what was wrong. In my excitement, I hadn't noticed the one thing that your grandfather had zeroed in on. Although you were very light at the time, you were definitely not a white child. Your skin was a beautiful lightly toasted brown that had a gorgeous shining glow. I promise you Maya that is all that I saw when I looked at you. But not your grandfather. By that time your father had joined us, and your mother introduced him to us as her husband."

Pausing, she'd closed her eyes, as she placed her fingers against her mouth, before continuing.

"Your grandfather, in a voice devoid of all emotions, told your mother that he never wanted her or her 'spawn' to grace his

presence again. Your mother didn't say a word; she took you back and walked away. She and your father walked away to join their friends by the stage. Before she turned, I saw tears in your mother's eyes. She'd always been a daddy's girl, and I knew it was unbearable to her, what her daddy said. I never saw you or my baby girl again...."

* * * *

"Maya, I have brought your tea. I thought perhaps you could enjoy it as you take your bath." Speaking through the closed door, Dalia waited outside the bathroom.

Coming out of her reverie, Maya turned to the authentic, claw foot, scarlet tub and turned off the water taps. Opening the door, she motioned her friend inside.

As Maya was adding bath salts to her bath, Dalia walked over to her and gave her friend a tight hug before kissing her lightly on the brow. "Maya, I am going to leave you to your bath. You and I will talk tomorrow. If you need me for anything, please call me. I am so sorry about your sister, Maya. You will see that you will feel better tomorrow." She promised.

After she'd left, Maya slumped against the door. Peeling her body away, she undressed and slowly sank into the fragrant, steaming water. The water began to work its magic; Maya felt her rigid muscles start to loosen, as the combination of the water and heat made their way into every tense muscle and tendon.

She sighed and leaned back against the inflated cushion and allowed the day's events, and the warm bath, to wash over her. She loosened her hair and pinned it on top of her head as she picked up the teacup and took a sip. As she tried to relax, her mind refused to allow that to happen. Instead images of Ally's lifeless body on the cold impersonal slab in the mortuary played havoc behind her closed lids. Although they'd grown apart, in her heart, her love and commitment to her foster sister had remained strong, something that time or distance hadn't erased.

She finished her bath and dried her body. After she finished her nightly routine, she turned off the light and slipped under her quilt. She hugged her pillow tightly to her chest and fell into an exhausted sleep, tears staining her pillow.

* * * *

In another part of town someone else was also preparing for bed. Walking into the bathroom, the reflection that gazed back mirrored a small smile that disappeared as quickly as it appeared.

The mirror images reflected the olive-toned arm as it reached up and took off the cascading blonde wig, and then opened the cabinet to carefully place it atop its Styrofoam head. There it sat next to its three companions.

Staring long and hard at the reflection, a well-manicured hand opened a jar of cold cream before meticulously scrubbing all traces of makeup away.

Keeping skin smooth and soft was no easy task.

The carefully manicured hand began to vigorously scrub each and every tooth, making sure none were neglected, with excruciating slowness.

After completing the last tooth, the face that stared back was one that was quite different from the one that was presented moments ago. With a satisfied smile, the wig cap was tossed aside and both arms reached up to begin a deep massage throughout the much shorter tresses.

It had been quite a day at work. The investigators had found two more, after much careful and deliberate planning. One interesting tidbit was the apparent popularity of the male. He was known as quite the philanthropist around town.

Well, *his* damn benevolent days were over. It would take the idiots a while to find the latest that 'justice' had been dispensed to.

The woman had been an accident. Unfortunately it couldn't be helped.

If she had been allowed to escape, there was a chance, although *really slim*, that she would have been able to make identification.

That could *not* happen yet. The time was not right, not quite yet. There were still so many who needed to learn their lesson.

Jaime wondered what Aunt Meg would think. She'd raised Jaime from the time her sister had overdosed on cocaine. Aunt Meg and her lover were the reason Jaime was compelled to dispense judgment to those self-righteous pillars of society.

Walking into the bedroom and turning off the light, a satisfied smile settled across small attractive features, as the slayer quickly climbed into bed and within moments fell into a deep, content sleep.

CHAPTER 4

Monday morning, Mark was at his desk working before his customary 8 a.m. He'd been restless the entire weekend, at loose ends.

It wasn't as though he didn't have plenty to do in his off hours. He'd recently purchased a turn of the century Victorian farmhouse and had already clocked in most of his free time renovating it. Jordan often joined him, and the two would participate in traditional male bonding that only the presence of hammer and nails seemed to inspire.

"Hey, man, when did you get in?" Jordan went directly to the coffeemaker after entering the squad room.

Mark silently asked for a refill before answering. "A few hours ago. I needed to clear up a few cases. This damn case has demanded so much of my time, I haven't had much time to do anything else."

"Yeah, tell me about it. By the way, did the lieutenant get the DNA results back from the strand of hair they found on the female victim?" Jordan asked as he handed Mark the steaming Styrofoam cup.

Mark took a tentative sip before grimacing. "Damn, man, how long has this stuff been in there?" He set the coffee aside and went back to his files.

"Snob." Jordan laughed. "The night crew made it, I think. Man, what happened Friday with the doc? Did she make a positive ID?"

"Yes. It was her foster sister, Allison Hill. I asked Maya if she knew any of her sister's 'friends' but she didn't. It seems as though Allison kept a tight lid on who she hung out with."

"Maya, huh? First name basis? I guess the two of you got pretty acquainted." Jordan flopped his large frame in his chair and crossed his equally large feet on Mark's desk.

Mark rudely tossed his partners feet back to the floor and decided to ignore the question for the moment. He remembered the necklace that Maya asked about. "Jordan, do you remember seeing a necklace with a pendant on the female victim's neck? I don't remember seeing it on her body or in the evidence bag."

"I don't think so. Why?"

"Maya mentioned that she and Allison wore matching necklaces from the time they were kids. You know the type; they look like two halves of the same whole. I'll go and check in the evidence room later."

After several hours of nonstop work, Mark glanced down at his watch and noticed it was well after lunch. Thoughts of Maya had made their way fleetingly into his mind throughout the morning. He'd had enough, and knew if he didn't do something about it soon, he'd lose it.

Mark stood and looked at the clock. Jordan noticed him and said, "I didn't know it was so late. You want to go grab a sandwich or something? Man I'm starving. Chips and coffee can only hold a man so long."

"Go ahead without me. I need to follow up on something, and I'm not sure how long it's going to take. I'll catch up with you later."

"Do you need any backup?" Jordan volunteered as he stood and kneaded his neck, and then picked up his jacket.

"No I can handle it. I'll be back as soon as I'm finished." Mark didn't want to disclose the exact nature of his errand. "I'll pick something up to eat on my way back."

Before he left the station, he verified the address for Imani House, and as he went to his SUV, he felt an unfamiliar clench in his stomach. If he didn't know better, he'd swear it was nervousness. Which, he thought, was ridiculous. He never felt nervous about a woman, no matter how good she looked.

After he arrived at Imani House, the door opened and he came face to face with the nosy neighbor who'd interrupted his intimate encounter with Maya on Friday.

"May I help you, Detective?" she asked in a husky voice.

"Yes, ma'am. I came to speak with Dr. Maya Richardson on official police business. Is she available?"

"She is conducting group counseling at the moment. When she finishes, I will let her know you are here, Detective." The woman indicated the small waiting room that stood adjacent to a much larger room, where Mark could hear feminine laughter drifting from its walls.

"Thank you, ma'am. I'll wait here for Dr. Richardson."

Left alone, he drifted toward the slightly opened door. Moments before he'd heard muted laughter, now he was straining to hear a single voice that had already imprinted itself into his brain. Without feeling the least bit guilty, Mark watched through the pane and listened to Maya as she perched on the edge of a table at the head of the room, speaking to the gathering of women.

* * * *

"Before we wrap up, I'd like to thank everyone for the consoling notes regarding the death of my sister. This is a very difficult time for me, and I won't pretend otherwise. Your emotional support is really important to me, and I feel blessed to have such a group of courageous woman around me." Maya had to clear her voice several times as she thanked the women.

"Thank you all. I will see each one of you throughout the week for our individual therapy sessions, and see you all back here next Monday for group," she said, ending the session.

As the ladies began filing out, each one stopped to hug her. As she turned back to her desk to gather her paperwork, she missed seeing Mark slip inside the doors.

Closing the door, he advanced further into the room and leaned against the wall right behind her, waiting for her to notice him.

She made a visible start when Mark came into her line of vision. "Detective Halstan, I didn't know that you were here."

"I arrived fifteen minutes ago. When I saw the ladies leaving I thought your session was over."

"Did you find out anything new, Detective? About the investigation? Did they find my sister's necklace?" She asked with a hopeful look.

"Unfortunately, Allison wasn't wearing the necklace; it wasn't found on her by the crime techs."

Seeing the disappointed look on her face, Mark felt compelled to continue. "Do you know where she'd been recently living? Maybe she has it in her personal belongings. I'm sure that it meant as much to her as it did to you."

As he'd been talking, Maya had been leading him away from the room. "Why don't we continue this conversation in my office?"

Mark followed her as they walked through the conference room toward the kitchen. In the middle of the large kitchen standing before the butcher-block counter was a small dark complexioned man. He was humming and chopping vegetables on a cutting board, and brushing them into a gently bubbling stockpot.

The small man turned and smiled at the sound of Maya's voice. The wide grin slid off his face as soon as he noticed Mark. He turned back to his work, his shoulders stiffening and his singing coming to an abrupt end.

"If you are hungry Senora, then I will find something for you to eat. This is for dinner, but I will heat for you what the other ladies are eating for lunch."

"Jorge I would like for you to meet Detective Halstan. He's with the SAPD, and he's one of the detectives investigating the death of Ally. You may be seeing him around the House once in awhile. We were on our way to my office so that we could discuss the investigation." Maya's voice was gentle, as though she were talking to a child.

"Detective Halstan, this is Jorge Gonzalez, chef extraordinaire, to whom the ladies and myself of Imani House are blessed to have here to prepare our meals and help us make our house a home."

"It's nice to meet you, Jorge. Whatever you're making smells great." Mark cast hungry eyes in the direction of the pot.

Jorge stole a shy glance in Mark's direction. "Why don't you stay and eat? When Jorge cooks there is never a shortage; everyone is satisfied. I will bring a plate for you and the detective, Dr. Maya. Now you two may leave my kitchen." Shooing them both out of the kitchen, a smile returned to his face, reanimating his somber features.

Maya laughingly nudged Mark out of the kitchen and walked through the house with Mark close, his admiring glance taking in everything as they made it to her office.

"I've never been inside Imani House but I have to complement you on the overall feeling. You've put a lot of hard work and time in, and it shows. How did this all take place?" They'd reached her office and Mark cast approving eyes around the office.

Although files were scattered on the desk and her small trash could stand being emptied, the room reflected the same comforting feeling as the rest of the house. One large print featuring two little girls with curly hair in ponytails holding hands dominated one of the walls.

An entire wall was a built-in bookshelf. From what he could see she had very eclectic taste. There was everything from scientific and medical books to popular best-selling works that he had read. Hanging from a corner wall was large lush fern. As he was settling back in his seat a knock sounded on her door.

"Excuse me please, Mark. Come in," Maya called out.

Jorge brought in the promised lunch for the two of them. "Oh Jorge, thank you so much. It looks delicious."

With a smile he accepted the compliment. "Thank you, Dr. Maya. When you and the detective are finished, place the tray outside. I will pick it up." He gave a timid smile in Mark's direction before leaving her office.

"I wanted to thank you for the way you handled the situation with

Jorge in the kitchen. Jorge is the only male resident of Imani House."

"He was a prostitute?" Mark guessed.

"Yes he's a former prostitute. Jorge came to the U.S. as an illegal immigrant. He worked as a migrant farmhand, working seasonally, and moved often, trying to avoid the INS. He was approached by one of the other workers who told him he knew how to make more money without having to work sixteen hours a day. Once he started he couldn't stop. The money was better than his migrant work, and he was afraid of his pimp. He was known on the streets for being cruel to the young boys who worked for him, and the men that he catered to were equally sadistic."

Mark knew that to be true. In his days as a uniform officer, he'd brought in more than his fare share of beat up young men from the streets.

"Although he was afraid, he took the first step and came to me. He's been with us ever since, and is now employed here." Mark could hear the pride in her voice.

"I can imagine how hard that was for him to take the first step. Most don't."

"I know. In the time he's been here, Jorge's self-esteem has been restored. It's been an emotional uphill process, but he's getting there. Whenever we have a man enter the house, I introduce him to Jorge. When he sees the newcomer with me, it helps him to accept that he's safe and the newcomer won't hurt him."

After finishing his lunch, Mark set it aside to look across the room at the woman he was growing to admire with each passing moment in her company.

She was such an amazing person, and he'd bet his last dime she didn't see herself as special. Both her pride and commitment to her work were evident from the way she spoke. She cared for those under her care and it showed as she went out of her way to ensure their comfort and safety above all else.

Mark became aware for the first time how long he'd been there when he glanced at his watch and recalled his reasons for the visit.

"I admire what you've done here, Maya. I'd like to learn more about what you and your staff provide for the residents of Imani House when you have time. Have you found out anything more about Ally from any of your sources?"

"I haven't had the opportunity to find out where Ally had been staying before she was killed. Most of the women here are well connected with what's going on in the community, and I should be able to find out something that can help."

"Have you made any arrangements for her?" He referred to her burial as delicately as he could.

"Yes. When I came in this morning, I started making calls. Allison once told me she wanted to be cremated, so I'll honor her wishes once her body is released to me."

"That should be soon. The coroner has completed the autopsy, and you'll be contacted soon. In fact I'll find out when they'll contact you."

"Thank you, I would appreciate it."

"No problem." After a brief pause he continued, "Maya I've been doing some thinking. You have an insider's understanding of this community. Not only do you have the knowledge, you also have the trust and respect of the women as well as the men," he added as he thought of Jorge. "I'd need to speak to Lieutenant Hernandez, but I think that you could provide invaluable information that would give us some insight into the psyche of this killer. We've already established that the killer is either a prostitute, or is able to blend in with the other prostitutes."

"Exactly what are you asking, Detective?"

"First, that you please call me Mark, and not 'Detective,'" he asked with a beguiling smile. "Second, if you would consider lending the department your expertise by acting as an informal consultant. You'd be compensated. Anything that would help us is needed at this point. We've been batting zero." Mark held his breath, waiting for her response as he watched her consider his proposal.

"Most of the time I feel like I'm running to keep up in my normal day routine. Imani House takes a lot of my time and energy. But, anything that I'm able to do to help capture the person who killed my sister, I'll do. As far as the monetary compensation, it would be accepted on behalf of the House. It takes a great deal of money to keep the programs running and fully staffed," she said, accepting his proposal.

"Great. I'll speak with Lieutenant Hernandez, but like I said, we're budgeted for outside consultation." He let out a low breath in gratitude, relief coursing through him when she agreed to help. He wanted her aid and knew she could be valuable to the investigation. He also wanted to be around her as often as possible so he could get to know her.

"I'd better get going. I didn't get a chance to ask you, but were you able to get your car back without too much trouble?" he asked as she followed him to the door, bringing Friday night into the conversation to see her reaction. The flush on her golden cheeks gave him the answer he was looking for.

CHAPTER 5

"Thank you, I did. Dalia brought me to work, and I drove myself home."

Maya gave him a side-glance from beneath lowered lashes. She wondered at the sudden turn of conversation. Memories of the kiss they'd shared replayed itself with ongoing regularity in her mind, which made it hard for her to get any real work done.

She was the first to admit she wasn't used to the intense sexual thoughts she'd been having because of Mark. Instead of feeling guilty, she thanked God for them because they kept her mind occupied and away from thoughts of Ally.

She glanced at the man at her side, the one that was the cause for her errant thoughts, and instantly her nipples peaked when she saw the way he was watching her lips.

He was looking at them like he wanted to eat them. Before she could react, he bent his head on level with hers, took her chin between his fingers and boldly did what his eyes had been promising.

He ran his tongue along the seam of her mouth, encouraging her to open for him. After she obeyed his silent request, he took advantage and pressed his tongue deep into her mouth. With a deep groan, he settled her closer and deepened the kiss.

With a moan, she lifted her arms and wrapped them around his neck, standing on tiptoe to get closer to him. He withdrew his tongue from her mouth, only to lightly bite her lower lip. Maya shivered at the unfamiliar sensations.

She was restless, feeling like she couldn't get close enough to him, her body strumming hard with desire, making her shake.

He broke contact with her mouth, his breathing harsh as he rested his head close to hers and took deep even breaths. Bereft, she instinctively reached up to touch his mouth before bringing her hands back down to her sides, ashamed of her neediness.

He took her hands in his and brought them to his mouth. Closing his eyes he began to softly kiss each finger, rubbing the backs of them gently against his lips. Goose bumps tingled up her arms with his touch. The burgeoning sounds of the house began to slowly make its way into their temporarily private world, and he lowered their joined hands to his chest.

"What is this? This feeling, this whatever, I'm not even sure what to call it," she asked shakily, trying in vain to withdraw her hands from his much larger ones. Finally she stopped struggling, allowing him to keep them where they were, nestled between his.

"To tell you that I understand what this is between the two of us would be a lie. I can honestly tell you I've never in my life felt like this." He turned her back around to face him when she tried to turn away.

"I'm serious. I know it sounds like some type of line, but it's not. From the moment that I laid eyes on you when you were outside the lieutenant's office, I haven't been able to get you out of my mind, Maya." He wracked a frustrated hand through his hair, spiking it in all directions.

"I don't understand any of this," she admitted.

"Neither do I, but I'm not going to run from it. I won't rush you; I know that this is all new to you, and that you just lost your sister. I want us to have the opportunity to find out where this may lead. Is that fair? Can you give me that?" His expression was somber, his eyes asking questions she didn't have the answers to.

"I've never been involved in a long-term relationship before." With a laugh directed at herself, she continued, "Correction, I've never been involved in any *real* relationship before. I'm not sure if I know how, or even that I want to," she admitted.

"I find it hard to believe that a woman as beautiful and as intelligent as you are has never been involved in a relationship, Maya. As far as you not being sure that's what you want, I want it enough for the both of us. Please give us a chance to get to know each other better, and we can move at any pace you're comfortable with. Just so that we're moving together."

Maya smiled in response and gave him the nod that she knew he wanted. "I can't promise anything. But I would like to get to know you better, Mark. But I warn you most of my time is spent here at Imani House. It's important to me, and I would never sacrifice it for anyone or anything."

"I wouldn't try and come between you and your love of the work you do. I want a chance to be able to share you and we'll see that you can have both a relationship and Imani House." He gave her one final lingering kiss good-bye. "Tell Jorge I enjoyed the lunch. And speaking of food, would you like to go to dinner with me tonight?" The rough pad of his thumb caressed the underside of her full bottom lip as he asked.

"I can't tonight. One of my interns can't facilitate one of the group sessions, so I need to find a replacement, and I'm going with Dalia to the library to do a little research," she hated to admit. She felt ambivalent, wanting to take the time to get to know him, but knowing she had commitments and people who relied on her for their well-being.

"That's okay. Why don't you look at your calendar and I'll call you later. Then you can tell me what day you have open this week for dinner. I'll also talk to Lieutenant Hernandez about you consulting with us. I'll call you later."

Maya walked him back through the house and opened the front door for him to leave. He surprised her by pressing his lips to hers a final time before he left with a promise to call.

She touched her still tingling lips with the tips of her fingers, and watched as he climbed into his vehicle and drove away. When his car was no longer visible, she went back inside. As she turned around, she came face to face with Dalia.

"How long have you been there, Dal?" Maya wondered how much her friend had seen, as she glanced down to make sure her clothes weren't crazy looking and twisted.

"Not long, little sister. The detective found you, I see. Did he have more news for you about your Allison?"

The two women moved together toward her office and Maya updated Dalia. "Detective Halstan came to give me information about Ally. He has also asked if I would consider consulting on this case with the police department."

"In what capacity? As a psychologist?"

"I guess it's more on the line of a special consultant. Because the police believe this killer is a prostitute, Mark, that is Detective Halstan, believes that I may provide an insight that may help in completing the sketchy profile they have."

Dalia pretended not to catch the slip as Maya continued to fill her in on the details, and how she'd planned to fit consulting with the police into her already busy schedule.

CHAPTER 6

"*Mazyte Sesute,*" Dalia began, addressing her as she often did, as little sister in her native Lithuanian language.

Dalia loved Maya. She'd met her four years ago soon after Maya had bought the building that was now Imani House. At the time it was a safe house where Maya had spent time doing her internship while completing her PhD. Although the safe house had an adequate referral system, it didn't have funding or staff. Maya had changed all of that after she bought the building.

Dalia had real affection for Maya, who was responsible for affecting so many lives. Dalia had immigrated from her small village in Lithuania to New York thirty years ago and had been lured into prostitution. She'd worked the streets for years, before she knew she could no longer live that life. She'd gathered her small possessions and moved to Texas. Within months she'd met Maya and not only had she become the young woman's first client, she became Maya's assistant, and in turn provided aid for the new women in the program.

She continued to listen as Maya outlined the sketchy details of what she could provide to the police as a special consult.

"If anyone can give this insight they are looking for, then it is you, Maya. I pray this person who killed Allison is caught. How are you feeling today? We have not talked very much."

"No, we haven't. You know how it gets toward the end of semester. The interns need to make sure they have all of their hours added, and it becomes a madhouse around here. This reminds me, we need to recruit a few more volunteer counselors: one for the night shift and the other for the early afternoon." She avoided giving a direct answer.

"I will leave you to your work. We can talk more tonight on the way to the library," Dalia reminded her.

Looking up with a smile, Maya answered, "Don't worry, I didn't forget. It shouldn't take me too long to wrap this up, and then we can go."

With a small sigh, she picked up the phone to try and locate a substitute for the evening class that was scheduled to start after dinner. Looking at her watch, she knew if she hurried she'd be able to grab a bite to eat before she and Dalia made their way to the library.

* * * *

Mark made it back to the station in the afternoon from his visit with Maya. Jordan was there, working at his desk.

"Hey man, that was some errand. Did you get everything taken care of?" Jordan asked as Mark walked over to his desk. "By the way, the lieutenant was looking for you an hour ago. He wants to know the specifics about Dr. Richardson and her connection with the female victim. He said when you came in to send you to his office."

"Thanks, Jordan. I wanted to run something by him anyway."

"Yeah well you also got a shit load of messages. I put 'em on your desk for you to sort. Some woman kept calling, she must have called a dozen times, I swear. And she *would not* talk to anyone else but you. Anyway, I asked her name, but she wouldn't tell me, kept saying she wanted to speak to you." Jordan told him with a shrug.

Mark gave an answering shrug. These types of cases, because of the media coverage, often generated a lot of misinformation and general gossip.

It was crazy the way the public got involved in the ones that the news broadcasts followed, as if it were some type of reality show. Unfortunately, most of the leads they followed up on were unsubstantiated--a pissed off coworker or ticked off spouse.

Because Mark's name was the one related to this case on television or in the papers, many of the callers would ask for him by name, not willing to share their misguided information with anyone else.

As Mark was leaving the squad room, LeDoux came in and, spotting Jordan at his desk, headed in his direction with a smirk on his face. "Did you see the fight last night?"

Mark knew the ensuing argument that would take place and escaped, knocking on the lieutenant's door. The first thing that struck him when he entered was how clean the room was.

In all of his time at the station he'd never seen it as clean as it was today. Walls he'd thought were gray were white and sparkling. Glancing around he noticed the garbage can was not only emptied but it too seemed as though it had seen a good scrubbing. Looking back up, he caught the lieutenant watching him as he surveyed the room.

"Looks good in here, smells even better. What happened?" he asked, as he pulled up a chair.

"Nothing happened. The place needed to be cleaned, so I came in myself this weekend to clear up some files, and I decided to clean it up a little." The lieutenant pulled his tie away from his throat, as though it was too tight.

Changing the subject, the lieutenant asked, "I received your message about the positive ID Dr. Richardson was able to give on the female victim. Were you able to find out much else after you questioned her?"

"The two of them hadn't had too much communication during the last few years. Her foster sister would come around when she needed something, usually money. Other than that, Dr. Richardson didn't have a last known address for her, but she thinks she can find out through her own network, which is what I want to talk to you about, Lieutenant."

"What about?"

"Dr. Richardson has great insight into this population and a strong rapport with most of them. Even those who don't live there respect her, and I believe she could provide valuable information we may not have access to otherwise."

"That sounds like a good idea. The chief is starting to breathe a little too close down my neck since Hardcastle was murdered." The lieutenant mentioned the latest victim found along with Allison.

"Although the circumstances around his murder were less than ideal, his family is up in arms and wants to know what the police are doing about his murder. Like we're sitting around twiddling our thumbs or something. It would be nice if Santiago could back us up once in a damn while." The lieutenant's dislike of the chief was well-known. He considered him an opportunist who saw his current position as a mere stepping-stone in his political aspirations.

"What were you able to find out about the victim from Dr. Richardson?"

"I got some background information about her, but nothing current. Dr. Richardson is sure she'll be able to use her network to find out something about her sister's last known address, as well as who she was keeping company with before she was killed."

"Hmm." The Lieutenant murmured, "That's fine. I'll clear it with the department, but it shouldn't be a problem bringing Dr. Richardson on board. Bring her in as soon as she's available and we'll go from there."

After Mark finished the meeting with the lieutenant, the remainder of the day was filled with him and Jordan following up on leads. Looking at the wall clock, he decided to retire for the evening and pick it up tomorrow. He glanced over at Jordan and noticed he was checking out the time.

"I don't know about you but I'm tired. Man, it was a long weekend, if you know what I mean." With a satisfied smile on his face Jordan stood to stretch out his long body. "I'm going home for some much needed rest. What about you?"

"I don't think my weekend was as pleasurable as yours. I'm tired for an entirely different reason," he said with envy.

He knew it was too soon with Maya, but he wished he was tired for the same reasons Jordan was. However *his* fatigue was associated with his inability to get her out of his mind and go to sleep, unfortunately. "I'm leaving too; I'm going to make one more call before I go."

"I'll see you in the morning, partner." After saying goodnight, Jordan left Mark to make his call.

Picking up the phone, he decided to see if he could catch Maya at Imani House. It was late, and he suspected she was long gone for the night. As he waited for her voice mail to pick up, he was surprised when the phone was picked up on the fifth ring with her breathless, "Hello."

Surprised he once again looked at the clock. "Hi Maya, are you okay?" he asked. She sounded completely out of breath.

"Mark? Yes, I'm fine. Sometimes I have a hard time locating my telephone," she admitted with a light laugh.

"I didn't think I'd catch you still at work. I expected to leave a message on your voice mail." Mark settled back into his chair, an unknowing smile on his face.

"I'm usually at the House until around eight or so, sometimes later. Today was busy. I searched for a replacement for one of tonight's group sessions and I couldn't find one, so I conducted it."

As she spoke, Mark picked up on her need to help everyone. He wondered if it was at the expense of her well-being. He didn't want to voice his opinion on such short acquaintance, so he kept his observation to himself.

"At any rate, I'm finished for the evening and was on my way out when the phone rang." she finished telling him.

"I don't want to keep you, Maya. Lieutenant Hernandez thinks it would be a great idea for you to consult with the department on the slayer case, if you're still interested. But I know you have a heavy workload. I don't want to add to your burden."

"Thanks for the concern, Mark, but if I didn't think that I could handle it, I wouldn't do it. I may seem like a masochist, but I'm not.

I enjoy what I do. If I didn't I wouldn't be able to put in the time without having serious resentment issues, and I have none. Believe me, when I do begin to feel a little run down, I take a break.

"Honestly, I do. Although I'm the only full-time psychologist here, I do have a colleague who devotes some of his spare time here on a volunteer basis. Once in a blue moon, I'll take a day or two off, and he's happy to fill in for me."

"I'll take note. That's good to know for the future." Clearing his throat he continued. "The lieutenant wants to set up a time for you to come in so that you can be filled in on both the particulars of the case and police protocol, and we can come to a mutual agreement on what we'd like from you as a consultant." He tried to squash his guilt over his need to have her available by telling himself it was for the investigation.

"Give me the time, and I'll put it on my schedule."

He secured a promise from her that she'd drive home carefully and hung up. The smile on his face still there as he gathered his things to go home.

CHAPTER 7

"Listen, Maya, I expect this damn house to be clean when I get back, no fuckin' around this time. And get Ally to bed, and *your* ass better be in bed too when I get back--you hear?" Melissa would demand, as she slathered more mascara on lashes already thick and coated.

As she sprayed more hairspray and attempted to fluff her thin blonde hair, Maya would feel her glare. She'd call her a mutt. Maya particularly hated that name. She wasn't a mutt.

During that time Maya had grown increasingly afraid of Melissa's lover Danny. She'd caught him staring at her when she began developing. His stares made her nervous, and she'd then started hunching her shoulders and wearing oversized sweaters to try and hide her developing body away from his creepy stares.

Danny had just gotten out of jail for having sex with an underage child. He'd told Melissa he thought the girl was nineteen. Maya wondered at the time if Melissa had believed him. She'd been little more than a child herself, and she'd known he was lying. But Melissa was blind when it came to Danny.

"Damn," Maya said out loud in her empty office. "Will the memories ever get easier?" She asked on a weary sigh to no one in particular.

"Yes sir. I'll get right on it. As soon as I have updates, I'll let you know." Jaime gently replaced the phone on the receiver and settled deeper into the soft leather chair, staring out the bay window.

Spring was the best time in San Antonio, with the soft fall of rain. It was a time of renewal. Jaime looked out the window with a small, pleasant smile and thought back to a rainy day years ago. Just like today, it too was a day of discovery.

"Jaime, Jaime where are you? I've been calling you for the last two hours…" Jaime could hear Aunt Meg's voice halt outside the door, and then heard muffled cries.

She had to know what was going on behind the closed bedroom door. She had to know what had been going on for the last few weeks. Meg *knew* what Rick was doing on that cold rainy day. She had been the one to encourage Rick. She'd been the one to suggest it was time for Jaime to join the "family business." The bitch. She deserved what she got. If her man no longer wanted her, it was her own damn fault. She should have never let her lover rape her own sister's child in the first place. Jaime turned away from the window and stared gloomily into empty space. The carefree happiness of moments ago falling away, leaving a cold determination in its place.

* * * *

"Mark, we got a call from the uniforms. Looks like it might be the slayer," Jordan yelled out, and they donned their jackets, hiding from view the holsters that housed their weapons and left the squad room at a half jog.

"Looks like our girl may have hit again," Lieutenant Hernandez shouted out, coming out of his office.

"We're on our way, sir," Jordan called back as they were nearly out of the door.

Favoring the stairs over the slow climbing elevator, they took them two at a time in their rush to reach the underground parking lot. Tossing the keys his way, Jordan yelled across the roof, "You're up, partner." They'd started early on with both of them taking turns driving, and the tradition had continued throughout their partnership.

Driving through the streets at a fast pace, they soon reached the interstate and drove to the coordinates they'd been given.

"What do we have here, Davis? Is it our girl?" Mark questioned the crime technician who, with gloved hands, was placing evidence into a plastic bag, as he and Jordan approached the taped off scene. This was the same tech that'd worked the two last murders, and Mark knew he was familiar with the MO of the slayer.

"Yeah, it looks like the same. Down the road a bit we found an abandoned black Mercedes SLK 350 with an empty wallet on the passenger seat--no identification left inside of course to tell us who are victim is. The uniforms ran the plate and the car is registered to Guy Kross. We also have found shell casings from a .22 and evidence that the victim had been sodomized." He listed the familiar MO of the killer.

"Any witnesses?"

"Jogger over there discovered the body," Davis motioned to a female standing near the trees, hunched low, and petting an oversized Doberman pinscher. "She was taking her dog out for a run and let him off his leash. Dog went ape-shit and took off up the incline. She went after him just in time to see him pull out an arm."

"Oh hell. Not the kind of bone you want your dog digging up," Mark murmured.

"No kiddin'. She had her cell phone in her fanny pack and called 911," Davis finished.

"I'll go question her," Jordan volunteered.

"Fine. I'll check out our victim."

As Jordan walked over to the jogger to get her statement, Mark made his way over to the murder victim. As he came closer to the body, flashlight in hand, he shone its bright light on the ground to help light his path. The light allowed him to see small chunks of what appeared to be gelatinous matter on the ground. As he worked his way closer to the victim, he confirmed in his own mind the presence of brain tissue.

He and Jordan continued to work the scene until every piece of evidence had been collected and questions were answered. Finishing their task, they made their way down the incline toward their vehicle. As they drove back to the precinct, both men were exhausted, but knew their night wasn't quite over. They would have to file their report when they returned.

Soon after they arrived back at the precinct, they were called into the lieutenant's office. Not bothering to knock they walked into the office and waited until he hung up the telephone, running his hands thorough already disheveled hair.

"Yes sir, we'll be right on it. Yes of course. All my men are highly trained professionals. I have Detectives Halstan and Phillips on the case, and we've added the help of Dr. Maya Richardson to aid us in profiling this case, Chief Hardcastle. Yes she is, sir--fully qualified. We believe that she can bring insight into this case that we are not privy to. Yes sir, right away. We'll be bringing her into the station, today?" Looking to Mark he raised an eyebrow, and with his nod continued.

"Yes, we'll bring her in today. Yes I know that this isn't the type of media attention that we want or need. Okay yes of course we'll keep you updated on everything." Hanging up the phone he began to rub at his temples.

"What was the scene like?"

"From what we saw, it looked like it was the slayer, Lieutenant. There's a good chance that the victim may be Guy Kross, the owner of Kriss Kross apparel," Jordan answered, naming the owner of a franchise of adult novelty clothing and accessories.

"Just what this case needs is another famous, or if this is Kross, infamous name attached to it." Raking a frustrated hand though his hair, he turned toward Mark.

"What about Dr. Richardson, when is she coming in?"

"She's coming in tomorrow." Catching himself, he remembered his earlier conversation with her. "No scratch that, she won't be able to come in until Friday. But in light of this new murder, maybe she can work it out so that she can." Mark felt guilty knowing the tight schedule Maya tended to keep.

"That would be better. I've got the chief on my back enough already. Look, it's late. You guys go on home; you've been at it all day. We can pick this up in the morning."

"Thanks, Lieutenant, we'll file the report and head out." Mark answered as he and Jordan left the office. He was more than ready to go home, as he continued to review the complex case in his mind.

* * * *

It had been one heck of a day. Finally, left all alone in the empty room, Jaime happily spun around and around in the leather high-backed chair until dizziness called a halt to fun time.

Oh brother. It was just as well. With the end of the day came other responsibilities. Other duties called.

Jaime giggled lightly, remembering the latest that justice had been served to. That cross-dressing mother fucker's days were over. With another trickling giggle, Jaime remembered with glee how it felt to be the one to stick it to Kross. The fucker had squealed like a stuffed pig when his ass had been rammed with that stick. It was fine to be the poker, but they rarely liked to be the one poked.

With a happy sigh, Jaime reached down and retrieved the small leather briefcase beneath the desk before walking toward the exit. With one final look around to make sure everything was in order, Jaime turned the light off, and with a jaunty step, left the office, nodding to the late night personnel on the way out the door.

CHAPTER 8

"Hello, Maya?" Mark asked in surprise, expecting to receive her voice mail, "You're still at work?" he asked with real concern.

"Hi Mark." Her voice sounded tired and strained.

"No, I have my personal line at work transferred to my home at night, in case of an emergency."

Mark had been inundated with beloved 'tips' over the course of the last few days, and not one had proved beneficial. It was Thursday, and he and Maya had talked on the phone long into the early hours of the morning. They'd talked about their childhoods, the good and the bad. Both were surprised with some of their similarities.

"Sweetheart, you sound tired. I'm sorry to have to call you so late." He caught himself as he uttered the endearment, surprised at how it seemed to trip so easily from his tongue.

Forging on, he cleared his voice and continued, "I know you said you couldn't make it in tomorrow, but we've found another victim tonight. Lieutenant Hernandez wants to know if there's any way you would be able to come into the station tomorrow. We'd work around your schedule Maya."

"Another victim? Were you able to identify who it was?"

"We think we have an idea, but won't know for sure until we get the coroner's report."

"Sure I can come in, but it will have to be early if that's okay. I dropped my car off to be serviced, so Dalia will have to bring me in."

"I could pick you up and take you back to Imani House after we finish up. Then you wouldn't have to find a place to park. And I can take you back to Imani House afterward."

"Well if you're sure, Mark, that would be fine with me." Her relief came through in her voice.

He could also hear her exhaustion. "I'd better let you go. I'll see you soon, Maya."

"Goodnight, Mark."

After hanging up the phone, he shed his clothes and took a long hot shower, allowing the heat to loosen his aching muscles.

When he climbed into bed, he thankfully sank into the king-sized mattress. His thoughts alternated between the investigation and the way calling Maya *sweetheart* had seemed so natural, until he fell into a hard slumber.

* * * *

After Maya hung up the phone, she undressed. She tossed her well-worn familiar jeans into the corner chair of her bedroom and walked across to the smaller bathroom in the room to take a quick shower. After completing a shortened version of her nightly ritual, she walked back into her bedroom and went to bed, sinking her tired body into its welcoming comfort.

Before succumbing to sleep, her thoughts were usually of Imani House and her schedule for the upcoming day's events. Tonight her thoughts were on Mark, and the way her heart skipped a beat whenever they spoke.

* * * *

Mark arrived at her doorstep bright and early at 6:30 a.m. with two Styrofoam cups in his hand. He was dressed in faded jeans and a dark blue chambray shirt. Her smile of welcome poured over him like warm honey.

"Good morning, Maya, you look great. Are you ready?"

"Yes I am. Is that coffee for me?" She asked with a hopeful, appealing smile.

"I thought you might like it. I wasn't sure how you took it, I have cream and sugar in my SUV." He automatically took her oversized bag and slung it across his shoulder.

"Thank you," she said in response to both the coffee and his taking her briefcase. "I take both cream and sugar."

As they walked to his SUV, Mark shortened his stride to match her much smaller gait. "You like it sweet, huh?"

"That's the only way that I can drink it. Let me rephrase that. I prefer to drink it that way, but if desperate, I *will* drink it straight," she laughed.

She waited for him to open her side of the door and took an appreciative sniff of the heady aroma wafting from the cup.

"Ready?" he asked after climbing behind the wheel of his vehicle and starting the engine.

She glanced up after taking another sip and slowly bobbed her head up and down. "Sure go ahead, I'm fine."

"I know you have a really tight schedule, and I want you to know we appreciate your coming in today. It shouldn't take too long. We need to fill you in on where the investigation is so far, ask you a few preliminary questions and of course answer any questions you may have. I believe you'll be able to help us in this investigation." He said as he drove along the highway toward the precinct.

"I'm not sure how much help I'll be, but I'll do my best. And I do have some questions, but I'll wait until we arrive at the station before I ask. That way we won't have to repeat anything."

"That's fine. Any questions you have, I'm sure we'll be able to answer them. My partner may be arriving later, so I'm not sure if he'll make our meeting, but we'll be with the lieutenant, and we should be able to cover everything."

The remaining drive was held in companionable silence, as they finished their coffee. The warm San Antonio breeze vented through the lowered windows as he drove and helped the caffeine in rejuvenating them.

When they approached the station Maya noticed camera crews and news vans situated in front of the precinct. At the same time that she noticed this, Mark swore under his breath and made a U-turn, heading for the back entry into the underground parking garage.

"I was afraid that this would happen. Somehow, the media's found out about the slayer's latest victim before we've issued a statement." They both saw the television station van with a big number three on the roof.

Mark answered her unspoken question. "Last night we couldn't make a positive ID, but we believe that the latest victim was Guy Kross--the owner of the adult novelty chain. Somehow the media has found out, and that's not good." He said grimly.

He opened the backseat door and retrieved Maya's oversized bag before he opened the door for her. He placed his arm across the small of her back, his hand resting above the small indentation of her waist. He hoped to have averted the eyes of the waiting reporters, and was disappointed when he spotted the female reporter who'd pointed toward his retreating vehicle.

Mark quickened his stride and urged Maya to do the same. Just as they reached the stairs that would lead them into the sanctuary of the station, a bright light shone brightly in their faces.

"At this time the police don't have any comment to make, and when we do you'll be the first one we contact for the press conference." Mark rudely shoved the camera out of Maya's face.

"Detective Halstan, isn't it?" The reporter asked, directing the cameraman to get a close up them. "Detective is it true that the slayer has struck again? And is it also true that her latest victim was Guy Kross?" she asked, as the light from the camera continued to beam in their faces.

As the light shone, Maya ducked her head away from its relentless glare. When the reporter noticed her, she directed her gaze toward her new target and demanded, "Who are you? Are you connected with the case? Your face looks familiar."

"Look, we need to go. I already told you that as soon as we know more, we'll have a press conference. Now if you'll excuse me." Mark spoke in first person, trying to direct the attention away from Maya. He knew this reporter. Alicia Meyers was relentless when it came to getting her story.

The reporter snapped her fingers. "I know who you are. You're the director of Imani House, aren't you?" As Mark urged Maya to continue walking the reporter kept pace with them, redirecting the cameraman to get a close up of Maya.

"Dr. Richardson, what connection do you have to the case? Are you in any way involved with this investigation?"

"Alicia, I've already told you when we have more information we will let you know, and if you want any of your questions answered, I would suggest that you put the damn camera away and get the hell out of here."

Alicia recognized his tone of voice as nonnegotiable and shook her head at the cameraman. "Do I have your promise that you'll answer my questions when you have the conference?" She asked in a low voice, her hand touching his arm.

"As soon as we have the news conference, I'll let you know." Mark shook her clinging hand from his arm, not promising her anything.

She noticed both slights, the removal of her hand, and the refusal to make her any special promises. She glanced again at the small woman at his side with a speculative look, noticing how he held the woman close to his side with an almost possessive hold.

As she catalogued his dismissal of her and his attentive hold on the psychologist, Alicia's mouth stretched into an insincere parody of a smile.

"Well, that's all that I ask." And unable to resist, added, "On a personal note, call me sometime. You still have my cell number, don't you?" With a last lingering look, the reporter walked toward the waiting cameraman.

CHAPTER 9

Mark had seen the look in Maya's eyes as Alicia made her parting shot and wondered if he should say anything about the comment or let it slide as they waited for the elevator to open.

She seemed to have an inordinate interest in the cuff of her shirt, studying it as if it were a bug under a microscope. As he was opening his mouth to speak, she took the decision out of his hands as they entered the elevator.

"Do you have any idea how news of the murder got out?" she asked.

Mark stood close to her in the cramped elevator, stooped down to pull her chin up, and pressed his mouth to hers. He gave her small, yet thorough caress before he reluctantly freed her lips. After he released her, he took a small step back and answered her question.

"No, but there's a leak. Someone in the department is talking when they shouldn't, and I plan on finding out who it is. I'm not sure yet how information is getting out, but I'll find out."

From his peripheral vision, he noted the deep breath she inhaled after he released her. Her breasts rose and fell, as she cast him a sidelong glance. He needed her to grow used to his presence as well as his touch, and he took every opportunity that presented itself to touch or kiss her.

As they exited the elevator, he allowed his hand to rest on the small of her back and they entered the doors to the squad room, which was already bustling with activity. He led them to his desk where he put both of their bags down, removed his jacket and draped it across his chair.

No sooner had he turned around to face Maya, than the lieutenant's strident voice hailed him from across the room. Turning in his direction, Mark acknowledged his call and turned back to Maya.

"Looks as though the lieutenant's inside and waiting for us. No doubt the group outside has something to do with his early arrival. I thought that we'd have a few minutes to go over any questions that you have before we met with him. Are you ready, sweetheart?"

"Yes, but I need to take my bag with me. I have my notebook in there and I've jotted down some questions I would like to ask."

Lieutenant Hernandez was on the phone speaking in low tones as Mark and Maya walked into the office. After hanging up the phone he walked around his desk, his hand outstretched as he greeted Maya.

"Dr. Richardson, thank you for altering your busy schedule so we could meet. Detective Halstan says you had been scheduled to come in tomorrow, but agreed to come in today in light of the murder discovered last night. We appreciate you changing your schedule for us." After shaking hands, Lieutenant Hernandez brought a chair close to her and sat down with Mark following suit.

"The purpose of this meeting is to bring you into the investigation as a special consultant. Detective Halstan brought to my attention the potential aid you could give us in apprehending the slayer. Although I'm somewhat familiar with Imani House and the work that's done there, I don't know the specifics. But what I hope is that you'll help provide insight into this population."

The Lieutenant nodded in Mark's direction before continuing. "I'm sure Detective Halstan has informed you, but I would like to reiterate that of course anything you hear in this office is to be held in strict confidence."

"Of course," Maya agreed.

After her nod of acceptance he continued. "With that I'd like to fill you in on what we know so far, and we'll go from there. If and when you have any questions at any time, stop us, and we'll answer to the best of our ability. Alright?" he asked, just as Jordan walked in after a brief knock and took the last available chair, bringer it closer to the trio.

"Detective Philips, you're just in time. We're filling Dr. Richardson in on the case. Do you have anything to report?"

"The coroner gave the affirmative on our latest; it's Kross." Jordan reached inside his jacket pocket to retrieve the small black notepad that was every detective's staple. Flipping to the desired page, he ran down the information he'd gathered.

"Thanks, Jordan. Here's what we know or believe about both the killings, and the killer, Dr. Richardson. With the latest victim found last night, the murder toll comes to eight we believe to fit the slayer's MO As we told you, when you came in to identify your sister's body, we believe the slayer is a female and a prostitute. The first two victims were found in a neighborhood park known for men driving through looking to pay for sex. Both victims had been buried naked. However, the crime techs recovered condoms near both victims, both unused."

"Does that mean there was no sex involved?" Maya asked.

"The evidence doesn't indicate the victims willingly participated in a sexual encounter, but what it does show is that they had been victimized."

"Are you saying the killer raped the victims? Anally?"

Mark noticed the lieutenant's red neck and knew what was causing his sudden discomfiture. Maya held an aura of innocence draped around her that made you want to censure words that were too crass for her ears. Although she had asked the explicit question, he sensed the lieutenant was hesitant to confirm it for her. Picking up the story he continued in his place.

"Yes, that's right. The evidence shows the victims have all been raped with a blunt object."

"If you believe that this is a female prostitute, how is she able to overpower these men and rape them? If it's not consensual, how is she able to do this?" Maya asked.

"Each victim was shot with a .22 caliber handgun three times in the back. From the location of the bullets in the body, the crime lab had deduced that the victim had been turning away, either to take off his clothes or get a condom when the first bullet hit. The second and third shots were fired in the center of the back, after the victim had collapsed. After she killed each one, our killer took off the remainder of the clothing and put on her gloves. After she'd finished raping him, she dug a shallow grave and dragged the body into it and buried him."

Maya pulled her reading glasses from her bag and glanced down at her notes and circled two items before looking back up at the men.

"I have two questions for you. You said the first two victims were found at the same neighborhood park that was known for prostitution. I know which park you're referring to. Wouldn't *someone* have witnessed a body being buried? And to piggyback that question with another, if they hadn't seen it wouldn't they have at least heard the shots?"

"I'll answer the second question first because it may answer both. We believe the handgun had a silencer. In that area, people don't report it when they hear gunshots; it's not an unusual sound to hear. The first question is a little more complex. Occasionally we have sweeps. The city will "sweep" known areas for illegal activities to temporarily clear them out. With the recent retirement of our chief, we've had an acting Chief of Police. The acting chief was under pressure regarding the increase in crimes and decided to go on an all-out spree to clean up the city."

The lieutenant's dislike for the acting chief was clear in his expression and voice.

"One of the 'cleaned' areas was this particular park and for several weeks the area was patrolled at routine intervals, and the women who normally worked this park stayed away. It was during one of these times that the first victim was found. No one was around, so it wasn't difficult to disguise both activities: the sound of the gun and the killer digging the shallow grave," Lieutenant Hernandez finished.

"It also happened during the time when the park wasn't scheduled for patrol, during shift change. It kind of makes you wonder if this was coincidence or not," Mark interjected.

"We should probably focus on what we do know for Dr. Richardson's benefit," the lieutenant once again redirected the discussion.

"Have you established any type of motive? Do any of the victims have anything in common with each other except for their need to solicit women?" Maya aimed her query at Lieutenant Hernandez.

"That's a good question, Dr. Richardson. Out of the victims to date, only two have anything solid in common, and that happens to be our latest two men, excluding your sister. The two men were both successful businessmen, although in different areas. Robert Clemens, the victim found with your sister, was a respected real estate broker, while Guy Kross' businesses were all in the adult entertainment area. That's all we have so far on any type of connection between the two. Because the last two victims were publicly known, we should be able to find out more information about their lives, which will give us better clues into what their private lives were like," he finished.

"What we don't know is if our killer is an everyday working girl, or if this is something she's doing for the thrill. Whichever way she's playing it, we do know that she wears at least two different colored wigs: one a curly brunette and the other a long blonde piece. At two different sites, this has been the only physical evidence about her that our crime techs have been able to find." Looking up from his own notes, Mark's glance encompassed the group.

"We don't have much to go by, but what we do have is a start. I believe you'll be able to help us with your insight and connections with the women in this industry, Dr. Richardson. Any knowledge you provide will benefit this investigation; I don't have any solid perimeters for you to operate within. I hope that's not too loose of a framework for you to work with."

"No it's not, I understand what you'd like to gain from me, and I'll do my best to help in *any* way. When I return to Imani House today, I'll begin my quest to find out any information I can. I've already begun asking questions as to Ally's last place of residence, as well as who she'd been associating with."

"Great. This is the best way to dig up leads, Dr. Richardson," the lieutenant encouraged her with a half smile.

"I do have one other question before we continue. You mentioned that Ally had been found within a week of her death. How long between time of death and discovery for the others? I don't know about the other victims, but the last two had families and people that would miss them. Does this play a factor in your investigation?"

"We've uncovered the majority two to three weeks from the time of death. Based on the coroner's report, our victim last night had been killed within the last 48 hours, which is the soonest," Mark interjected.

"Why was this victim's discovery sooner?" Maya asked.

"A jogger and her dog discovered the body. This is important information. Because as you say, if our victims had close families, and based on what type of lives that the men led, they'd be reported as missing as soon as they didn't show up when they were supposed to. Your sister didn't have a report filed on her and neither did the greater majority of our other victims, including Kross, our man from last night. If the slayer is stalking loners or men without family members, which was our original thinking, it would be easier to see some type of pattern. This in turn makes life easier for us, because the closer you come to completing the pattern, the closer you come to finding the offender."

Jordan, who'd remained silent, added, "Either she's changed her mode or it never was her mode. We assumed based on the type of victims targeted that maybe she had been scouting out her victims, choosing them based on their anonymity. The only victim with a missing report filed, had it filed by his employer."

"Which leads us to the question: is our killer watching and then targeting certain men, and if so why did she kill both Kross and Clemens? Because neither one fit the type of her previous victims. And what, if anything, is the connection with Allison?" Mark questioned.

"Let me suggest we go into Dr. Richardson's expertise if we may. As we're all aware she's here despite a busy schedule," Lieutenant Hernandez rerouted the conversation.

CHAPTER 10

Maya glanced at her watch and was surprised to see the time. "I hadn't realized it was so late. Are there any questions for me?"

Jordan spoke up. "You work with women who've been in prostitution for a lot of different reasons. It's got to be hard for them to leave prostitution on their own; it almost seems like a drug."

"In the time I've worked with these brave women and men, I've found that most come from abusive homes where there was no father living in the home or the father that was present was abusive physically and or sexually to them or another family member. In an attempt to escape the abuse, they run away." She gave the handsome detective her full attention.

"You said that it seems like a drug. In a way it is. Drugs find their way into a person's bloodstream, destroying anything in their path. Prostitution is a behavior that does the same thing. At Imani House we treat it for the 'drug' it mimics. We know that it takes more than finding a 9 to 5 job to reclaim their lives."

Maya had strong feelings for the women and men who came to her, trying to recapture a life that had been stolen from her. Although she'd directed her response to Jordan, she could feel the collective stares of Mark and Lieutenant Hernandez.

Lieutenant Hernandez shook her hand at the close of the discussion. "Thank you for taking so much time out of your schedule for us Dr. Richardson. I hope we haven't put you too far behind in your day."

"You're welcome. And no you didn't. I hope I'm able to help. I'll be in touch with you whenever I find any new information," she said, and allowed Mark to lead her out of the office.

Once she and Mark were inside the elevator, she turned toward him. "Do you think the media are gone?"

"They should be gone by now; it's been a while. They can't gain access into the garage. How Alicia and her cameraman got through I have no idea, but I'll find out." He promised grimly.

As they were leaving the elevator and walking toward his vehicle, seemingly out of nowhere a bright light shone directly in Maya's face. Again.

"Hey what the hell are you doing?" Mark demanded, as the

cameraman evaded the arm he swung in his direction.

"If you'll give me a nice sound bite, I'll be out of your way, and I promise I'll make the police look good. It won't take long," Alicia pleaded.

"That's fine, Mark. I don't have a problem with speaking with the reporter." Maya spoke up, just as Mark was opening his mouth to shoot the channel eight reporter down. As she'd spoken, Maya had moved closer to Mark. She knew the best defense was always a good offense.

"Make it quick, Alicia, Dr. Richardson has given up enough of her time this morning, and she needs to return back to work."

"How is *she* involved in the investigation?"

Maya took marginal offense in the way the reporter talked about her as though she was invisible. "*She* can speak for herself. If you have a question about me, please direct it toward me."

"Fine. How are you involved in the investigation?" Alicia asked with a discernible bite.

Mark gave her silent approval to disclose her involvement with the police with a nod of his head.

"I have agreed to act as a special consultant to the police department," Maya answered nominally.

Wasting no time, the reporter nodded toward the cameraman as she spoke into the camera. "Good afternoon, viewers. This is Alicia Somers with channel 8 news and I'm here with Detective Halstan, along with Dr. Maya Richardson. We've just been informed that Dr. Richardson, who runs the halfway house for area prostitutes, is now a part of the slayer investigation." Turning toward Maya she aimed her question to her.

"Dr. Richardson what will you bring into the investigation that it is currently lacking?"

"I'd like to offer a correction by saying Imani House is not a halfway house. We are a privately owned and funded agency that provides not only a *home,* but also a wide variety of programs to aid those who wish to bring dignity back into their lives. Now in answer to your question, our collective prayer is that my knowledge in this area will provide aid in helping the police apprehend the person or persons responsible for these murders," Maya was confident and comfortable with her topic.

"And you, Detective? What do you hope to gain with Dr. Richardson?" the reporter quickly turned away from Maya and smiled at Mark.

"In what way do you mean?" Mark asked and raised his eyebrow.

Maya cast a curious glance his way at his response.

"What do believe she can bring to this investigation that it's obviously lacking?" She asked tersely.

"Dr. Richardson is an expert in her field. We hope to gleam any bit of information we can in the hopes of ending this before more lives are lost."

Continuing her brief interview, the reporter asked Maya few additional questions that required minimal answers. She soon brought the interview to close.

"Thank you for your time, Dr. Richardson--the piece will air on the five o'clock news this evening." After shaking her hand briefly, Alicia turned her full attention to Mark. "Remember what I said earlier, give me a call." Reaching out to touch him, her hand never made contact with the intended target of his face.

Catching her hand in midair he answered, "I think I'll pass on the opportunity. I'm sure I'll have other plans." Clearly irritated, the reporter left, heels clicking angrily on the cement.

Mark turned to Maya, "Let's go," and escorted her to his vehicle.

They'd driven for a while before Mark turned to look at her. She saw admiration and surprise in his eyes. "You handled yourself well during the interview with Alicia. Most people are nervous in front of a camera unless they're used to speaking in front of one," he complimented.

"Thank you. After defending my dissertation, I got over stage fright pretty well," she admitted with a laugh.

"I bet you did. I don't think Alicia appreciated your confidence." He laughed along with her.

"I don't think that's the only thing Alicia didn't appreciate," Maya couldn't resist adding, and it was her turn to be surprised when she saw the red stain his cheeks.

They drove in silence after that, with an occasional comment or question offered by Mark, until he pulled up in front of Imani House. He turned off the engine and was taking off his seat belt when Maya stopped him.

"You don't have to get out; I'll hop out and go inside." She placed her hand against his as he took off his seat belt.

"It's not a problem. Let me get your bag and take it inside for you." He turned her hand to cover hers before he reached his long arm in the backseat to retrieve her bag. Then he helped her out of his vehicle.

When they'd reached the front porch, Maya turned to Mark. "I'd better go inside; I have a ton of work to do. I guess I'll hear from the police when you need me?" she questioned.

"Yes, you'll hear from the *police* when they have a need for your expertise, and of course you should contact us whenever you have information for us. Now as far as you and I are concerned, you'll hear from me much sooner. I know you're going to be swamped today to make up for your late start, so do you think you'd be able to make time for me this weekend?" he asked with a hopeful expression.

"I think that I can make time for you. I already have plans for this weekend, what about next Saturday?" She smiled hesitantly.

"That would be great. I'll call you and we can decide what we'll do." Mark gave her a small, yet lingering kiss good-bye before jogging back to his vehicle and leaving.

With a half smile, Maya walked inside Imani House, an odd contentment settling in her spirit despite the sad event of Allison's recent murder.

CHAPTER 11

"I've been informed that because of the high visibility of this case, we're bringing in the FBI." Lieutenant Hernandez told the men without preamble.

The men were strategizing over the slayer investigation. Mark and Jordan were in conference with Lieutenant Hernandez more times with the slayer investigation than he thought they'd ever been with any other investigation during their tenure under his command.

"Who ordered this? No, let me guess the *acting* chief himself," Jordan both asked and answered.

"Hole in one. However, I'm sure I can count on my men to be cooperative and helpful professionals." The Lieutenant said with a lift of his brow, aiming his comment at both men. He knew he could count on them, but both were strong men with strong opinions and he knew of their distaste for working with the FBI.

"As far as Dr. Richardson is concerned, without compromising the investigation, she is to be provided with police help if she needs it. Her aid in this investigation may provide us with the break we need. Mark, it seems as though you have good communication with her, so we'll continue with you being her contact person for the department. Of course make sure she's aware she can call any of us when needed."

Lieutenant Hernandez saw the way Jordan's glance fell on Mark after his comment. He used the remaining time to go over plans for the current investigation as well as the decision on which detectives to delegate Mark and Jordan's other cases to. The slayer investigation had top priority, and the decision had been made to devote his two top detectives' time in its direction.

Mark and Jordan were the highest producers in their division, solving many of their cases with lauded efficiency. Lieutenant Hernandez was confident of the fact that the acting chief dare not pull Mark off the case. The Halstans, along with their close-knit peers, were known for making or breaking political hopefuls. With this knowledge in mind, the chief was careful not to commit political suicide by posturing and pulling the young detective from the case.

As he dismissed the two detectives to their own work, he sat back and pulled out his notes, a pensive look on his small features as he went over the information the detectives had on the case, his eyes narrowing in thought.

* * * *

Mark knew Jordan had questions. "Okay, what do you want to know? You've been staring at me since the meeting this morning with Maya and the lieutenant, and I can guess why," he said, no longer able to take his partner's stares.

"How 'bout we grab some lunch and talk. It's been a long morning and I didn't get much breakfast." Jordan asked, not denying his curiosity.

"Let's go."

Jordan took the familiar route to their favorite café. Once inside, after they had given their order to the waiter, Mark took a long drink of water and waited for the inquisition from his friend.

"So man, what's going on? With you and Dr. Richardson?" Jordan asked bluntly.

Mark knew better than to play dumb. He valued Jordan's opinion as his partner and as a friend. He and Jordan had been together in the academy and had graduated from uniform to plain clothes together. As friends and partners they'd shared a mutual respect for the police force and commitment for their job.

Clearing his throat Mark began to speak. "I'm sure you know something's been going on between me and Dr. Richardson." At Jordan's nod, he continued, "When she first came to the precinct, I saw her outside the lieutenant's door waiting to go in, and man I swear it was like--Damn!"

"What do you mean, 'damn'?"

"That was it, Jordan. Nothing else can describe it. I felt like I got sucker punched, and I hadn't even gotten a clear look at her. At first I saw this figure kind of huddled in the chair, and I thought she was a kid. She looked so damn little sitting there. But then she turned toward me, and I felt like someone hit me. I have *never* felt like that in my life--you know?" he asked his friend in an abstracted voice.

"I mean she's gorgeous. Those eyes and those lips--man what I think about when I look at those lips...." Catching himself he looked at Jordan. "I've dated beautiful women before, but there's something different about her. She's gorgeous and I don't know if she knows it, or she just doesn't think about it too much, like she doesn't care."

As the waiter returned with their lunch, both men took a moment to take a few bites before Mark continued the conversation.

"Maya puts out a different vibe. From the moment she speaks, you can feel that she's interested in what you have to say; just in the way she looks at you. I met her under pretty rough conditions, and yet that *still* came across. When I went to Imani House I saw her in her counseling session, and it was even more obvious. Man, she has a beautiful soul."

"Damn, Mark, I don't think you've ever waxed poetic like that. She's made an impression on you in a short time. What's the problem? She not feeling the same way?" Jordan asked as he took a long swallow of the sweet tea the waitress had refilled.

"Not a problem. More like maybe a concern. There's no way she's not feeling this chemistry. There's no way this feeling is one-sided," Mark insisted.

As he paused and took a healthy bite of his BLT, Jordan asked, "Is it because she's black? Is that the problem?" Jordan asked bluntly.

"Hell no. I mean yes. She is black but that's not a problem. At least not for me. Why? Do you have a problem with it?" Mark and Jordan were close and their discussions had ranged from politics to religion with no issues. If one of them had a differing opinion, it was handled with good nature; they ribbed each other and let it go.

On the issue of race, Mark always felt they saw eye to eye on most topics. But as a white man, he knew he'd never be able to understand or see the world through Jordan's eyes as a black man.

"Man I don't have a problem with interracial relationships. You know me, I'm an equal opportunity lover." Jordan laughed. "But everybody doesn't feel the same way. I see it like this; we're on this earth for a blink of an eye. Grab love where you can, and don't worry about anybody else's hang-ups."

"Now who's waxing poetic?" Mark laughed, relieved with Jordan's assessment. It wouldn't have altered how he felt about Maya, but it was good to know how his friend felt.

"Maya and I have touched on the issue, but we haven't gotten too deep with it. So to be honest, I'm not sure how she feels about it," Mark admitted.

"Yeah, I can see that. I mean the relationship is new, kind of in the honeymoon stage. You're busy trying to get to know her, and she's doing the same. Everything else will come with time. The deeper you get into the relationship, the quicker reality starts to kick your ass," Jordan laughed, as he finished his sandwich.

They ate in companionable silence before Mark continued. "My problem is with her work. She has this *incredible* commitment to Imani House, and I think she has a hard time separating herself from it. She's already warned me her priorities are always going to be there first."

"Well if the relationship deepens, I'm sure things will shift. But this is all new, right? I mean it's not like you're in love or anything, you know?"

Mark was taking a long swallow of his drink when Jordan spoke, and being unprepared, the question made him choke on his drink.

Jordan jumped up and thumped him hard on the back. "Damn man--are you okay?" he asked after Mark regained his composure.

"I'm fine, thanks," he choked out. He could feel the heat spread throughout his face as realization dawned. He couldn't believe it. It was too soon. There was no way he could be falling in love with her this soon.

The waiter returned to ask if they needed anything and Mark asked for the bill.

Not realizing the cause of his partner's near choking accident, Jordan continued. "Yeah, like I was saying, give it some time. This is new to the both of you and time will tell."

"Yeah, you're right. We'd better head back." Leaving money on the table for the bill and a healthy tip, they left the café.

As Mark drove home later that evening, he remembered the interview Alicia Somers had conducted with Maya. He drove faster so he could catch a glimpse of her on the late news, as he thought back over his conversation with Jordan.

* * * *

Imani House was quiet when Maya finished her duties at the end of the day. Time was approaching when her practicum students would finish their semester. Although some had agreed to stay on for the summer to earn an additional graduate credit, most would not be returning until fall.

Summer was the House's downtime. She was able to have less staff than at any other time because people were at their most content during late spring and summer, and her residents were no different. She needed fewer counselors because she held less counseling sessions.

Maya stretched her achy back and began to straighten her desk, placing important documents she was working on in her bag as she prepared to leave for the day. Turning off the light, she left her office and said goodnight to the night security officer as well as to Jorge and the few residents watching television in the dayroom.

As she drove home, Maya popped in a CD, eased back into her

seat and listened to the smooth vocals of Etta James coming from the speakers. Music always helped her relax on the drive home; time seemed to go by, if not faster, at least pleasantly. As she maneuvered through the near empty streets heading toward the interstate and home, she thought back on the current events in her life.

She hadn't had time to start her investigation for information today. Now as she was driving home she had time to think about what her first plan of action would be to gain the information she needed. Whenever she needed information she would put the word out in the community and it didn't take long before either one of her staff members or one of the residents would come through with what she needed.

Although this time there was a difference. This was more personal.

Maya could see the lights were on in Dalia's section of the mansion as she drove into her driveway. Finals were approaching and although her friend was a part-time student, she took her studies seriously.

Using the automatic garage door opener, she drove inside the garage's brightly lit interior. Turning off the ignition, she grabbed her bag and jumped off the raised platform of the jeep, landing sneaker-clad feet on the garage floor. Humming the tune she'd been listening to under her breath, Maya walked to the door, which led into her private entrance.

After she'd entered the house, she automatically turned on the light and didn't look up. Instead, she leafed through the mail on the side table. Because of thi, she accidentally bumped into a large vase filled with a beautiful arrangement of fragrant yellow roses.

CHAPTER 12

Maya's mouth formed a perfect O as she placed the unread and forgotten mail down to admire the beautiful floral display on the small table. A note sat beside the vase written in Dalia's hasty script. "These came for you this evening. I didn't want them to stay outside so I brought them in for you. From your detective, *Sesute*? Enjoy!!"

She smiled and took a deep breath before she began to hunt around for an accompanying note. Finding it tucked into the middle, she opened the small envelope and read the contents.

"I saw you on the news. You were wonderful. I'll bet that Alicia Somers will think again before she opens that big trap of hers and tries to make anyone else look foolish!!" The note wasn't signed, but she couldn't think of anyone who'd send her flowers, except for Mark. Although the wording seemed a bit odd, she smiled, as she once again took one of the delicate stems between her fingers and inhaled its lovely fragrance.

She had forgotten all about the interview and wondered if she could catch it on a later broadcast. As she glanced around the room, she noticed the red light blinking on her antiquated answering machine. The machine was old, but it served its purpose, and she had a hard time wasting money. She took off her Nikes and padded on stocking feet to hit the play button to listen.

"Hi Maya, it's Mark. I'm at home catching up on paperwork, but I wanted to call to see how your day went. It's after ten, and after I catch the evening news, I'm turning in. I don't want to call you at Imani House, because if you're still there, I'm sure you're busy and I already feel guilty enough for us taking up your morning. I saw you on the news, and you looked and sounded great. I'll give you a call tomorrow. Sweet dreams."

Maya was surprised he hadn't mentioned the flowers. She'd have to remember to thank him tomorrow. She picked the flowers up and carried them with her into her bedroom.

After she'd placed them on her dresser, she stripped out of her clothes, anxious to take them off, having had them on for over 15 hours. She was too exhausted to do anything else but take a quick shower and climb into bed. The last thought in her mind was Mark, and the unexpected turn her life had taken with him in it.

* * * *

The following week was a busy one for Maya as she planned to take time off on the weekend. She didn't know the last time she had and was looking forward to it.

She'd spoken with Mark often during the week and found herself more and more attracted to him. She believed what made a person interesting wasn't the outer trappings. The inside, the spirit of a person, is what called to her.

She liked the very way he spoke, how she could often hear the smile coming through. He would ask her questions about herself, and she could tell he was really interested in the answer. On Wednesday, they'd talked long into the night. She told him about her short stint in private practice during her days in graduate school.

"That didn't strike you in the least bit funny? Come on! I don't see how you do it. I couldn't have kept a straight face if someone was flipping back and forth like that, right before my eyes!" he laughed outright.

She'd been telling him of a client who had multiple personality disorder. The client was a middle-aged, overweight, white male, whose alter ego was a flirtatious young black woman in her mid twenties. Who was *very* sexually active.

"Mark, it's what I do." She knew she shouldn't laugh, but his was so infectious she couldn't help herself. "I'm a therapist. How would it look if I laughed? That could have seriously damaged his already fragile hold on reality…"

"But what about when he was giving you advice on how to please a black man in bed? That didn't strike you as funny?" She could hear him holding back another deep chuckle.

"I've learned to roll with the punches. I thanked him for the advice and went on with the session!" she said, tongue in cheek, desperately holding her humor at bay. She finally gave up and laughed out loud, right alongside him.

"I have to be honest, it would have driven me nuts, Maya." She loved his laugh, so deep and husky; the sound alone sent a quick jolt through her body.

They talked for a few minutes more and she caught herself yawning, and looked over at her bedside alarm clock for the time.

"You sound exhausted Maya, maybe we'd better end this. It's getting late. I could talk to you all night." He admitted in a husky voice and laughed again when she yawned for the third time in five minutes.

"So could I," she said and Mark laughed.

Eventually they were forced to hang up, and Maya couldn't remember the last time she'd enjoyed talking on the phone with anyone through the night as she had with Mark.

At lunch the next day, Dalia had come into her office to tell her she had a visitor, and moved aside to allow Mark, with a huge, overflowing basket in his hands, to enter her office.

"I hope you're hungry!" he said, a huge grin on his face as he looked around the pretty wicker picnic basket. He placed it down on her desk and gave her a casual kiss.

Between the kiss and the picnic basket, she didn't know which one caught her more off guard. "This looks wonderful," she said around the growl of her stomach. She groaned as she hungrily viewed the contents. There were dinner rolls, strawberries, assorted cheeses, and a bottle of nonalcoholic wine.

"I felt bad for keeping you up so late last night. Thought this would make up for it." Maya turned to him and had to quickly look away, overwhelmed with the gesture as she pulled out food and placed it on the picnic plates in the basket.

"It all looks so wonderful, I don't know where to start," she said on a shaky laugh. She felt a silly urge to cry. She didn't know what was wrong with her, but his showing up so unexpectedly, thinking of her with something so simple, made her want to bawl.

"I don't know about you, but I'm starved," he said, as he sat down in the overstuffed chair near her desk.

"Thank you so much for thinking of me," she said, and smiled when he gave her a sexy wink, as he picked up a piece of chicken and sank his even white teeth into the breast.

"Delicious," he agreed, licking his lips, and Maya had the feeling he was referring to more than the chicken he held in his big hands.

The impromptu picnic kept a smile on Maya's face for the rest of the day. By the end of the week she was looking forword to their upcoming date on Saturday with nervous excitement.

* * * *

Saturday morning arrived as a clear and cloudless day, perfect for gardening. Maya had gone into work early on Friday and worked through both lunch and dinner, wanting to get work out of the way. She knew she surprised her staff, including Dalia, when she'd informed them she planned to take the weekend off. With her day off she had plans to work around her yard and go out with Mark later in the evening.

She hadn't been out on a date for, well, it had been a long time since she'd been out on a date. Being honest with herself, she knew she wanted the day all to herself. Maybe it would help her rid herself of the jitters.

Even in late spring, San Antonio weather was warm, the temperature comfortable enough for her to put on old cutoff gray sweatpants and an old tee shirt. She laced up the short yellow work boots and grabbed a baseball cap to protect her eyes from the sun.

Before she headed to her garden, she grabbed her MP3 player and wrapped the elastic belt around her arm, looking forward to the day of physical labor, sunshine, and music.

CHAPTER 13

Mark had risen early to get a good workout in before he and Jordan worked on his house. He'd briefly spoken with Maya on Friday, and she'd confirmed the date for today. He'd decided that a safe bet would be the River Walk. The atmosphere was nice to walk around, and it had a variety of restaurants to choose from.

After throwing on sweats and running shoes he waited for Jordan to arrive. Just as he was attaching the house key to his laces, Jordan pulled up in his driveway.

They exchanged early morning grunts and stretched before setting off at a casual clip, warming their muscles before they picked up the pace. By the end of the fast-paced four-mile run, both men were exhausted and panting, and collapsed as soon as they made it into the house.

Mark went into the kitchen to grab two bottled waters, as soon as he caught his breath. He tossed one to Jordan and twisted off the cap of his before taking a deep swallow.

Jordan finished his in record time and placed the empty bottle on the table in front of him. "Man, what was that all about?"

"What was what all about?" Mark asked, as his breathing returned to normal.

"I don't know the last time I ran that fast for that long. The last time was with you, and you'd gotten into an argument with your dad about practicing law. Everything okay with the family?" Jordan asked, leaning back on the sofa and closing his eyes in exhaustion.

Mark answered, "Yeah everything's fine. I felt like having a good run, that's all. Why? Was it too much for you?" He returned from the kitchen and tossed Jordan a second bottle of water. Mark flopped down on the opposite sofa, and once again guzzled his water in record-breaking time.

"No, I can hang, buddy, any time any *pace*--don't worry about me. I was wondering where *your* extra energy was coming from. You think maybe it's from this date you have with Maya tonight?" Jordan asked straight-faced.

"What's that supposed to mean?" Mark asked as he rose from the sofa and took the four plastic bottles into the kitchen and tossed them into the recycle bin.

He knew Jordan was screwing with him, but he also recognized the truth behind his words.

Maya had been the last thing on his mind when he'd gone to bed last night and the first thing on his mind when he'd woken up this morning. It had been that way throughout the week. He'd found himself wondering how her day was going, and had to stop his hand more than once from reaching for the phone to give her a call.

They'd spoken on the phone almost every day that week, learning more about the other. Although most of their conversations had been short, a couple had lasted long into the night.

Mark had never been able to talk on the phone to a woman for that long. With Maya, he'd not even noticed the time, a definite first for him. In fact, she was the reason he ended the conversation. After yawning for more times than he could count, he reluctantly allowed the conversation to come to a close.

"I don't know, maybe you have some sexual energy to work off and running is your only option. Now me, I'm not having that problem right now. Sheila has been very *very* accommodating," Jordan gloated, referring to his latest girlfriend, and laughed at Mark's mumbled curse. "Speaking of Sheila, I need to pry my ass off this couch. You're not the only one with plans for the night."

When Jordan left, Mark looked at the clock and decided he had more than enough time for a soak in the hot tub he'd installed, knowing the hot water would relax his bunched muscles. With that in mind, he headed toward the tub with a smile of anticipation creasing his face, as he thought of the night ahead.

* * * *

Maya had been in her garden for most of the day, and before she realized it, the morning had given way to late afternoon. Calling it quits, she placed her gardening tools away and came face-to-face with Dalia when she closed the shed door.

"Hello, Maya. So this is what you have been doing with your day." Dalia wiped a smudge of dirt from the end of Maya's nose.

"Hi, Dal. Yeah, and it's been a wonderful reprieve from everything. It's been too long since I was in the garden; the weeds were taking over my rose bushes. And it helped eased the jitters about this date," she admitted, as they walked back to the house.

"What is there to feel nervousness for, *Sesute*? He is only a man, and the two of you will have a wonderful time."

"Well, it's been a while since I've been out on a date, Dal. I know I know, you think it's my fault," she said when Dalia's expressive eyebrows rose. "I haven't met anyone I've been interested in. And *definitely* not enough to take my time or mind away from Imani House--you know that."

"Yes, and I know this detective has caught your interest. Where are the two of you going tonight?" Dalia asked with a sly smile.

"To the River Walk. It's been awhile since I've been there."

"Have you decided what you're going to wear?"

"I haven't given much thought about it." She glanced at her watch and was surprised at the time. "Do you want to help me out?" she asked, smiling, knowing Dalia's secret desire to dress her.

Although Dalia abhorred everything to do with prostitution, her quirky sense of humor would assert itself when she'd say the only thing she missed was the dress up part.

She loved the extra high heels, the big hair and over the top makeup. Dalia said she couldn't wear her favorite type of apparel at Imani House because she didn't want to give the wrong impression to the residents or their sponsors. She didn't want them thinking it was a place for *current* prostitutes instead of *former* prostitute, she'd say with a husky laugh.

Maya knew Dalia didn't care for her standard uniform of jeans and shirt or the comfortable dresses she wore to work. Dalia once suggested she needed to show off her figure and wear something that fit for a change. Maya laughed when Dalia took her by the hand and said, "Let us go and see what's in this closet of yours."

After several minutes of searching Maya's closet, Dalia threw her hands up in defeat.

"Really *mazyte Sesute*, you are in dire need of a shopping trip as soon as possible. This is ridiculous. There is *nothing*, and I mean nothing in here that would be decent for your date with your detective, nothing at all," Dalia said in a disgusted voice.

"Oh Dalia, it's not that bad. Is it? I know I have a few dresses in there. I bought them this spring; let me take a look."

"Please do not tell me you are referring to these?" she said as she took out two lightweight dresses that hung side-by-side. "These are definitely not suitable for a first date Maya," she groaned.

"I guess you're right. I haven't had the chance to bring out my spring and summer clothes from storage. I've been so busy around Imani House I haven't found the time."

Dalia was in the middle of mumbling about how one should always make time for beauty when she paused in mid-mumble. "What do we have here, nestled in the back?"

Dalia took the plastic off the dress and smiled. "Now this, *Sesute*, is more of what I am talking about."

CHAPTER 14

"No way, Dal, I don't think so!" Maya tried wrestling the dress away from Dalia's clutching hands.

Looking down at Maya from her superior height with one raised eyebrow, Dalia deftly kept the dress away from Maya's grasp. "Allow me to see this dress, Maya. It is beautiful. Why do you not like it?"

"Dalia, I've never worn that dress! Arlinda gave it to me when she donated those other dresses for the auction we had last year for the House." Maya mentioned a friend from college with whom she'd kept in contact with who owned a small and very exclusive boutique.

When she'd opened Imani House, it was her friend who'd come up with the idea of an auction/fashion show fundraiser, and every year had helped her round up the necessary donations to help the auction be a success.

Maya wasn't sure if she had the nerve to wear it. She had never tried it on, had pushed it, along with the matching red shoes, to the back of her closet and forgot about them. Now as she looked at the dress and at the rest of her wardrobe, she knew she didn't have much choice.

"*Mazyte Sesute,* you will be beautiful in this, and I will help you with your makeup and hair if you would like," Dalia volunteered.

"Dalia, thank you. I would like that very much. But first I need to take a bath after being in my garden all day. I stink." She wrinkled her nose and laughed, heading to the bathroom.

After she'd finished taking a shower, she sat in front of the small padded stool of her vanity and willingly placed herself in Dalia's hands. After semi-drying her hair, Dalia used a few of Maya's own styling aids to moisturize it, and had allowed the strands to dry on their own and form into their natural curl pattern. She'd then pulled a few tendrils out, and laughed as they sprang back into small bouncy curls framing her face.

Maya didn't appear to be wearing any makeup at all. Dalia had only applied a light cream to powder foundation to enhance her natural glow. She'd gone on to outline Maya's full lips and fill them in with a shimmering bronze gloss.

Dalia had gone all out when it came to her eyes. Maya's lashes were already thick and dark, so when she outlined them with a soft brown pencil with layering shades of brown, it gave her slanted eyes an even more exotic look.

Maya was surprised and pleased with the overall job Dalia had done as she looked in the mirror of her vanity.

After her hair and makeup had been completed, Maya put on silky underwear and slipped the dress over her head. It fit as though it had been made just for her. The material of the dress clung to her rounded curves, the hem flirting at the top of her knees.

On the hanger the color was the most daring thing about the dress. But once Maya smoothed it over her body that notion was quickly dispelled.

Turning around, she looked at herself from all angles and felt a rare thrill at the image that looked back at her.

"Thank you, Dalia," she said as she turned away from the mirror and back toward her friend.

"Do not thank me. I polished the gem, I didn't create it." Dalia complimented her friend with a wink. "Those are one sexy pair of shoes, little sister. I feel for your detective; he will not know what hit him." Dalia whistled when Maya laced the ribbons on the small red shoes she placed on her feet.

"Do you think it's too much? I'm not even sure if I can walk in these things, although I do like the added inches." The spike-heeled sandals were a matching deep red color with satin ribbons that laced up the front, ending with a sexy bow near her shin.

Taking a few experimental steps around her bedroom, Maya was surprised at her ability to walk in the high heels with relative ease.

"No it is *not* too much, *Sesute*. You can never be too sexy! What is wrong with you?" Dalia laughed. "Listen Maya, you have a wonderful time. I will be waiting to hear a full report when you come home. I am going to leave, so that you may do any final preparations in private, before your detective arrives." With a hug Dalia left Maya to complete her final touches. She sprayed a natural light floral perfume to her pulse points as she waited for Mark to arrive.

Soon after Dalia left her doorbell rang, and as she turned to leave, her glance stole to the floral arrangement on her vanity. She made a mental note to thank Mark for the beautiful flowers, and with an excited tingle in her belly left her bedroom.

* * * *

Mark held a bouquet of flowers in one hand and a grin on his face when Maya answered the door.

"Please come in, Mark. I have to grab my purse," she invited after he gave her a lingering kiss hello.

It was then she noticed the bouquet of flowers he held. "Oh Mark, they're beautiful, thank you. You sure are spoiling me! Let me go and place them in a vase. I have one in the kitchen. I'll be right back," she promised as she accepted the flowers and went in search of the vase.

As soon as she returned, flowers in vase, he complimented her. "Maya you look stunning," he said.

"Thank you. You don't look too bad yourself," she complimented in return, her gaze settling over him. He wore loose, black tailored slacks with a small cuff at the ankles. His lightweight jacket was unfastened over a burgundy close-fit ribbed shirt.

As she was admiring him, he was doing the same to her. The deep red of the dress set off the golden tones of her complexion. The dress was tiny and clingy, and it outlined her curvy little body to perfection.

Mark's gaze traveled downward, and his eyes took in her small feet encased in the sexiest shoes he'd ever seen. They made her feet look like a small present. He wouldn't mind skipping dinner to start unwrapping.

The constriction in his throat had him clearing his voice as he complimented her again, before escorting her into a waiting late model Jaguar sedan. Once they were inside, he turned on the radio, and the sound of a bluesy saxophone filled the car.

Maya settled back against the soft leather interior and turned her body toward him. "Nice car. What happened to your SUV?" He watched her hands caress the cool, butter-colored leather seat.

"I wasn't sure what you would wear tonight, and I didn't want you to have a hard time climbing inside, so I borrowed one of my brother's cars. It's a lot easier to get into than my Expedition."

"Thank you. That was thoughtful." They sat in companionable silence for long moments until Maya spoke. "Are you and your brothers close? Allison was the closest I had to a sister, but I always wondered what it would be like to have had a real family."

"It was fun at times. At others, my brothers could be a real pain in the … butt. Overall we're pretty close." As he spoke, the love he had for his family came shining through in his voice and Maya felt a pang of envy.

When they reached the popular River Walk area, Mark parked in a secured lot not far away.

"It sure is a beautiful night," her voice was low and admiring as she looked around and smiled. Her lovely face lit with joy as they strolled along the lit path.

As Mark captured her hand in his, he knew the night held nothing in beauty compared to her. He wanted to tell her, but knew if he did, she'd think it was a line, and a corny one at that. Instead, he brought her hand to his mouth and placed small kisses on her knuckles before giving her pinky a final kiss.

"It certainly is," he agreed.

As they strolled along the walkway, Mark noticed the small steps Maya had been taking. Much smaller than her normal gait. "Are your feet okay? I remember you told me you don't go out too much and you were more comfortable in running shoes than heels. Those are sexy as hell, but they don't exactly look like running shoes."

"I'm fine. I wasn't too sure about them at first, but they're a lot more comfortable than they look. I'm walking a little slower to make sure," she said with a self-conscious laugh. "And you know, I think I could get used to heels. I feel like a giant!"

The top of her head was still inches below his shoulder, so he refrained from commenting on her height. After walking a while longer, they settled on a restaurant and decided to eat at one of the outside tables.

Looking across the candlelit table at Mark, Maya smiled. "It's been a long time since I've been here. Thank you for inviting me."

"Thank you for coming with me."

"Speaking of gratitude, I never thanked you for the lovely flowers you sent last week. They were beautiful." She smiled across the table at him.

"Maya, I didn't send any flowers last week. Someone sent you flowers? When did you get them?" Mark demanded, as unbidden, jealousy rose sharp at the thought of some other man sending her flowers.

"It was the same day as the interview with Alicia Somers. I thought they were from you, even though the wording was kind of strange." She recalled the odd phrasing. "I kept the note."

"I'd like to take a look at it if you don't mind. It's nothing to worry about; I'd just like to see it."

"I kept it in my jewelry box. You can read it," Maya agreed.

Soon they returned to their easy conversation, until the waiter appeared with their food. By the end of the meal, Mark felt as she were opening up to him and sharing more of who she was.

"What made you want to study psychology?" he asked, as the

waiter brought them coffee.

Before answering, she took a thoughtful sip. "I've always wanted to know what makes us behave the way we do. I guess I'm curious as to what makes us tick to put it in layman's terms," she laughed lightly. "Because of my childhood, it seemed fitting for me to try and learn what motivates behavior."

"That's one of the reasons I enjoy being a cop," Mark accepted the leather bound folder that held his credit card, along with the charge slip from the waiter. "I've always wanted to know why people do some of the things they do. What makes a woman snap and kill her husband after years of abuse? What makes a man beat up on someone smaller and more helpless than he is?"

"Was that why you chose to be a police officer rather than pursue law?" After Maya declined a second cup of coffee, Mark pulled her chair out and she rose from the table as they left the restaurant.

Hand in hand, they walked along the lit path of the River Walk. They passed several street musicians and paused to listen to them play, dropping money into open guitar cases or hats before continuing on their way.

"That was one of the main reasons," Mark picked up the thread of their conversation as they walked. "I also had a hard time seeing myself defend the same people who were abusers. My father's firm is one of the best law firms in San Antonio, and his services aren't cheap. But just because you can afford a good attorney, doesn't make you any better than the guy who beat up his wife and has to have a public defender represent him," he said in disgust, as he thought about some of the cases he'd seen daily at the station.

Maya opened her mouth to answer when her right foot buckled. With a small sound of distress, she stumbled against him, and he steadied her, both hands gripping her waist. "Sweetheart, are you okay?"

"I tripped on a rock, and it hurt my ankle," she said on a small hiss of pain. As she steadied herself, she took a tentative step and cried out again. "Oh my God, that really hurts!" Before she knew what was happening Mark had swung her up in his arms and swiftly strode away, toward the parking lot.

CHAPTER 15

"Mark, put me down. I can walk, really I can. And besides I'm too heavy to carry that far." At his incredulous look, she had to laugh at what she'd said. "Okay, strike that. With the way you're built, I'm sure there aren't too many things you couldn't handle."

When he laughed again, she thought of what she'd said. "Don't be a perve, you know what I mean. I can walk," she laughed despite the throbbing pain in her ankle.

"I'm sure you can, but indulge me, okay? And for the record honey, as small as you are, a 90-pound weakling could carry you and not feel it." He feigned pain when her small hand balled up in a fist and smacked him in the middle of his chest.

She gave up trying to convince him to put her down, and instead, laid her head against his chest with an exaggerated sigh.

It was no hardship for her to allow him to carry her. She knew her thoughts would set the women's movement back a few years, if anyone could hear them. But she liked the feel of his hard chest against her cheek. She felt protected and safe.

"Do you want to stop by the hospital? Do you think you sprained it?" he asked with concern etched in his voice and on his face. He'd adjusted the seat so she could have more room to stretch out her legs after he placed her carefully in the jaguar.

"No, in fact it already feels better. My ankle turned, nothing drastic. It'll be fine by the time you drive me home," she said, holding back a grimace of pain. She caught him looking at her throughout the drive to her house.

When they reached her home, he carried her inside before gingerly depositing her on the floor. "Can you walk inside okay? Or do you need me to carry you?"

"It feels better." He carefully watched her as he unlocked the door and helped her inside.

Maya flicked on the light switch in the entryway. "Could I offer you something to drink? Coffee?"

"I don't drink coffee this late, but if it means spending more time with you, I'd drink a whole pot. You sit down and point me in the right direction, and I'll do the rest."

She grinned and removed her shoes before leading him to the

kitchen. Once there, she told him where to find the necessary things to make coffee. She sat down at the table and messaged her tender ankle.

"Here, let me do that," Mark said and moved her hands out of the way as his long, strong fingers deftly took over the task of massaging her achy foot. Before she knew it, a moan had escaped from her closed lips.

At that moment, she looked down and caught the harsh look of desire stamped on his face, and felt her nipples tweak in response. He gently placed her foot down and captured her lips with his. He drew the lush lower rim slowly into his mouth before he allowed it to ease back out. "Baby, you taste so good," he groaned. He tore his lips away from hers and lifted her in his arms and strode from the kitchen.

"Which way to your bedroom?" he demanded in a rough voice, tearing his mouth from hers.

"This way," she pointed to the end of the hall and fell back against his chest when he headed in the direction of her bedroom.

* * * *

Mark was impatient with the feel of their clothes. He pushed the straps of her dress down to her waist, and leaned back to look at her heavy breasts in the black demi-bra. With a groan, he unhooked the front clasp and feathered his fingers across the light-brown colored globes, and felt his hands shake.

"Baby, you're beautiful. Please don't hide your face from me," he said when she looked away when he touched her breasts.

"I'm sorry. I'll try to slow down, but I've never felt this excited before," he admitted. "I want to explore every curve of your body. And I want you to do the same thing to me," his voice deepened, growing huskier as his need for her rose.

He didn't understand her shyness, and he lifted her head so he could look into her eyes. "We won't do anything you're uncomfortable with sweetheart. Any time you want me to stop, tell me. It won't be easy, but I'll stop. Okay? I promise you."

"Yes." When she agreed, he let out a long breath.

He kept his gaze on hers and captured one turgid nipple in his mouth. He suckled it while his other hand kneaded its twin. She arched her breasts more fully into his mouth. He loved her response to his touch.

He pulled away from her breasts and tore his shirt over his head, tossing it on the floor. Reaching between the two of them, he unbuttoned his pants.

He went back to work on her breasts, and after switching sides, greedily laved the other with the same attention he'd given the first. Her answering moan spurred him on to reach between them and lower her dress further down until it pooled around her hips.

The glow from the moonlit night accented her pretty brown body, and his breath caught at the picture she presented. Her lips were swollen and red from his kisses, her plump breasts and stiff nipples begged for his touch. Bra discarded, the only thing she wore was a sexy pair of panties, which barely covered her thatch of dark springy curls.

"You are so beautiful," he barely whispered past the constriction in his throat.

He pushed aside the silky material guarding her entrance and slowly drew his finger down her soft cleft. She arched her body in immediate response. Loving her reaction, he put his finger in his mouth and licked away her cream, his eyes never leaving hers.

When she groaned, Mark lowered his head; his mouth and lips replacing his fingers. At the first touch of his tongue, her body arched away from the mattress.

"Oh God. That's too much," she cried out on a low moan, writhing beneath him.

"Stay with me, baby. You can take it. Just let me love you," he pleaded as he held her hips down. She gasped again when his tongue made contact with her slick folds.

He then inserted a finger into her tight opening, and her walls instantly clamped down. He eased his finger out and tested the feel of two fingers, and nearly came when she gripped him even tighter. He couldn't wait to feel that same tight grip on his cock.

He leaned between her legs, and this time he pulled her panties completely off. He gently separated her folds. After he exposed her clit he closed his eyes in anticipation before capturing the small bud in his mouth.

Maya nearly screamed with the first contact of his lips on her clitoris. She looked down at the sexy image of his dark head between the V of her legs as she bit the inside of her mouth to keep herself from yelling out. But she was helpless to stop her body from jerking as he licked and sucked her in a place no man had ever seen, much less kissed.

She closed her eyes, and colors sprang against her closed lids as another spasm hit her hard, while he continued his intimate assault. The next wave sent her over the edge. She grabbed the sheets on either side of her hips as her body jerked, and this time she couldn't stop herself from screaming from the intense pleasure.

Spent, she could accept no more and could only lie limp against the soft pillows against the headboard. His hot tongue continued to caress her, until all of her tremors had come to an end. As he came to lie beside her on the pillows, he propped the side of his head in his hand and stared down at her with a tender look in his eyes.

"Sweetheart, no one's ever done that for you?"

Maya came back to herself and was a bit shamed at what she'd allowed him to do. She knew she was a grown woman and had nothing to be ashamed of, but there it was. She was embarrassed. "No. No one ever has."

"Look at me. It's not a crime, but I need to know something else. Has any man ever made love to you?" He gently lifted her chin to see her face better.

"I think you already know the answer. I've never made love to anyone. I've never felt comfortable enough with anyone to share my body with them," Maya told him, feeling vulnerable and exposed. She was telling him more than she'd ever told another man--allowing him inside her body and her mind. The thought scared her.

"There's nothing wrong with that. I've got to be honest and say words can't describe how it makes me feel that I'm your first. That you trust me." He kissed her, and she could taste her essence in his mouth.

She touched the dark hair that fell into his eyes, before resting her hand on his chest. Taking a deep breath she came to a decision. "I want you to make love to me, Mark. Fully. I'm not afraid."

Mark sat up and removed the rest of his clothes without hesitation. Before he discarded his slacks he reached over and extracted the small square foil package from his pocket.

"Are you sure about this?"

"I trust you."

Those three words mobilized him into lifting her small body up and over his. Her face was pressed deep into his chest, as he ran his hands through her hair, loosening the pins, allowing the thick mass of curls to tumble down around her shoulders and back.

"Thank you." He paused and placed the side of his face against hers, pressing a kiss against her temple. The caress so sweet and spontaneous, Maya felt her heart expand in her chest.

He lay her back down against the lightweight brightly patterned quilt. With leisure, he made his way up her body, pausing to deliver a hot kiss and sweet caress along the way.

When Mark reached her face, he took it between his hands and seized her lips with his, and then sucked her bottom lip. Damn he loved her mouth. It was so plump; it was like sucking on a juicy grape.

He cupped her breasts as he kissed her, kneading and caressing them as he tugged on her nipples. His hands traveled down the length of her body, along her sides, back toward her belly, before resting at the small triangular thatch of curls.

Separating the folds, he massaged the small nub with featherlight touches that had her arching her body closer to his. He glided one of his big fingers in her vagina. As he started playing with her clit, he pushed another finger into the small wet opening. He loved the sound of her responding groan.

She was stretched taut as her inner muscles clamped down on his finger, clenching and releasing it in pulsating spasms. His body hardened more as he thought of how it would feel to have that tight grip on his cock.

"Sweetheart, I want your first experience with me to be good. Trust me?" He pleaded, and was satisfied when she nodded.

Using the pads of his fingers to scrape up and over her clit, the palm of his other hand pressed down above her pelvic bone in orchestrated rhythm with his thumb, as Mark prepared her for what he had in store for her.

It wasn't long before her frantic movements against his hands reached the point of no return. Head thrown back, she uttered a keening moan that grew in tempo and endurance, culminating into one long wailing sob of release.

After her body had calmed, he turned her to place in front of him, as she was boneless in her repletion. One of his hands cupped her quivering mound, and the other cupped the fullness of one breast. As he held her shaking body tight, he felt as though he had experienced the orgasm along with her.

"God, baby, you're beautiful." He groaned on a long breath, holding back the cum stealing up from his balls.

"Thank you. I can't believe how good that felt. But what about you? This may be my first time, but I know you didn't get much out of it."

He kissed the back of her neck, and her body's response to the simple caress gave graphic testimony he'd only given her a sample of what was to come.

He picked up the foil package from the nightstand and tore it open with his teeth, never taking his eyes away from her. Her eyes followed his hands as he rolled the condom down the long, thick length of his cock. He rolled her beneath him, and inch by inch pressed into her welcoming warmth.

Her body received the stiff, foreign rod until he hit the thin barrier, and her small whimper made him come to a halt.

"It's okay, baby. We'll go real slow. I'll take good care of you. I promise." Testing the strength of the barrier, he rocked back and forth in shallow, rhythmic strokes.

He took both of her hands in his and placed them high above her head as he forged ahead, tearing through her maidenhead. When she uttered a cry of distress, he covered her mouth with his and held his body still, allowing her to grow used to the unfamiliar fullness in her body.

Eventually her muscles relaxed, and he felt her slick sheath tighten once again on him. "Are you okay?" he asked on a groan. When she nodded, he couldn't hold back anymore.

Their tongues clashed as they met, their mutual touch so hot, he pinned her hips to the bed, and with a groan, deepened his strokes, rocking the bed with his strong thrusts. When she moaned, turning her head helplessly on the feather pillow, he licked his fingers and reached between them, found her clit, and tortured the small nub until she broke, sobs wracking her small frame.

"Oh God, Mark. Oh God. What are you doing?" She begged and panted at the same time.

He could feel the orgasm start in his balls as soon as she screamed her release. As he glided in and out of her, his thrusts growing stronger and stronger, he rocked into her steadily, until finally, he threw back his head, his neck muscles standing out in stark relief. "Maya, Maya!" He yelled her name on a long harsh groan as he came.

He collapsed on top of her after his shattering climax. He rolled onto his back, putting her on top of his chest as he snuggled her against him. Rubbing his hand over her head, he smoothed it away from her face and placed small kisses at the top of her head. After a few moments, he could speak again.

"That was wonderful, Maya. Thank you." As soon as the words left his mouth, he didn't feel they were adequate enough to express the feelings their lovemaking had given him.

When she didn't speak, he realized something was wrong. It was strange and new to him, but he felt as though the two of them had their own private wavelength, able to sense and detect things about the other no one else could.

He turned her around so they were facing one another in order to get a better look at her facial expressions.

"Maya, I want you to know what we shared was beyond anything I've ever experienced. I know you're not very experienced in this, so I want you to understand this was unique and special, and you have nothing to feel shame about, okay?"

"I know I shouldn't feel shame, and I don't. I'm 30 years old, Mark, and although I'm probably the last living thirty-year-old virgin in the city…" She stopped and rephrased her statement, after he gave her a small grin. "I *was* the last thirty-year-old virgin. But although I'd never had sex before, I knew the mechanics. I never thought it would feel like this. I need a minute to adjust. Which is kind of hard to do when the cause of all these feelings is staring me in the face," she laughed shakily.

"I understand your feelings, baby. Why don't I go and get a small towel and help you wash up." He delivered a small kiss to the corner of her mouth before he left the bed. Although conflicting feelings were ripping through her, that didn't stop Maya from admiring his round muscular butt as he unashamedly padded naked to the bathroom, discarding the spent condom when he passed the small trashcan.

When he returned, he washed her with the warm towel, concentrating on the small area where she was bound to be the most sore. After he finished, he lay down beside her, pulled the quilt over their cooled bodies, and closed his eyes. His last waking thoughts were of the woman who lay in front of him; glad she'd come into his life.

CHAPTER 16

In the morning, as he opened his eyes, Mark reached blindly in front of him expecting to feel Maya's small, warm body. Instead, his hand closed around empty space. With a disappointed groan, he raised his body from the bed and scratched his bare chest.

A tantalizing smell made its way through the bedroom, and as he looked around, he spied his slacks from the previous night and left the bed to put them on. After locating his undershirt, he walked out with it dangling from his hands.

As he walked into the kitchen, he heard Maya laughing in response to another familiar voice's husky comment. Before he could retreat, the owner of the voice had already spotted him.

Mark stood in the doorway and saw Dalia's gaze take him in, from the bottom of his bare feet up to his bare chest. In his hand dangled the undershirt, which he'd neglected to put on.

With a mental shrug, he forged into the room and walked over to Maya. He pulled her slight frame up and with her toes barely reaching the floor, gave her a very thorough, very hot morning kiss. "Good morning, baby," he said, and set her back down before he turned his attention to Dalia.

"Good morning, Dalia," he said with a small grin.

"Good morning, Detective."

"Please call me Mark."

"Good morning, Mark." Dalia acted as though it was nothing out of the ordinary to see a half-naked man in Maya's kitchen.

Turning to Maya, she said, "I thank you for the coffee, and I will speak with you later." With a meaningful look, Dalia snatched up the small baggie of coffee grinds and left them alone.

Mark had casually walked away, pulled the T-shirt over his head, and adjusted his pants. He made his way toward the brewing coffee and poured a steaming cup. He took a healthy swallow before turning back to Maya.

"When I reached out this morning, I was hoping to feel your warm body. And when I didn't, I followed my nose to the kitchen smells. I didn't know Dalia was here until it was too late. Had I known, then I would have put more clothes on." He was trying to gauge her feelings, wondering how she felt about last night. But she wasn't giving him any clues from her expression.

"I'm sure it's not the first naked male chest Dalia's seen. But I'm not too sure I'd like her to have a repeat viewing of yours."

The telling comment registered in Mark's brain. He didn't think she knew what her words showed, but he did. Satisfied, he placed his cup down on the table and walked over to where she stood in front of the marble counter. He leaned over her shoulder and took an appreciative whiff of the steaming plates of food in her hands.

"This smells delicious sweetheart. Do you like to cook?" he asked, taking the plates and placing them on the small table.

"I don't know if I *like* to. Well let me rephrase it. I usually don't have the need to cook. I'm at Imani House most of the time, at least during most of my meal times, and Jorge is such a marvelous cook, I eat there. You know how it is when you're trying to cook for one," she laughed. After she sat down, placing both juice and coffee on the table, she continued with a bittersweet smile, "As a child I did a lot of cooking for Allison and myself."

Mark encouraged her to continue. "Oh really, why was that? Didn't your foster mother know how?"

"It wasn't that she didn't know how. She used to cook for her boyfriend all the time. When it came to cooking for Ally and me, it was up to me, or we'd go without. After a few misses and a few burns, I learned how to make the basics. From there, I experimented and expanded my limited repertoire. I found I liked cooking, and had a knack for it," she said, with a smug smile.

After taking a bite of the egg quiche, he agreed with her assessment, as the cheesy egg confection melted in his mouth.

"Definitely. If this is an example of your cooking, than I'd say you *definitely* have a knack for it." Mark thought back to his conversation with Jordan. "Maya, we've talked about so many things in our lives. But we've never spoken too much about race." He wasn't sure how to start.

"What do you mean?" When she looked at him, he saw a spark of something in her eyes before she looked back down at her plate.

"Well, I know you and Ally were raised in foster care. How was that? Were you treated differently?"

"Because I'm black?" she asked bluntly.

"Yes. Because of that." He didn't shy away from the bald statement.

Maya brought the coffee to her mouth and took a small swallow before answering. "To be honest, Melissa treated us both pretty badly. But I believe she had more issues with me because of my heritage." Even though she wasn't looking at him he could feel the pain come through in her voice.

"Because you're biracial?" he guessed.

She nodded her head, her expression thoughtful as she answered. "She'd make fun of my hair. She was constantly threatening to cut it. She'd call it a nappy nest, all kinds of things. "

"But your hair is beautiful," Mark protested. He reached across the table to finger one of the curls, before letting it fall back into place. Maya's hair was one of the first things he noticed when he first saw her sitting outside the lieutenant's office.

"I hated my hair because of her," she whispered, her voice barely audible. Mark looked away from her hair when he heard the anguish in her tone.

"Do you know what it's like to be raised by someone who hates you, calls you hateful names no child should be called, and makes you feel worthless and ashamed?" She tore her gaze away from her plate and finally looked at him.

The anguish of her past was reflected in her eyes. The soft flaring of her nose and clenched teeth gave testimony to how deeply Melissa's abuse had affected her as a child. And the long lasting affects it obviously had on her as a grown woman.

"When a child is told they're ugly, a burden, or stupid enough times, they start to believe it. Even if they're lies. Just like if you tell them they're wonderful and capable, despite what's going on in their life, they'll believe it as well. It's like food. Give a child healthy food, and they grow up strong and confident, full. Feed them junk, and they're still hungry, looking around trying to find something to satisfy their tummy. Something to fill the void."

"Is that what you did? Tried to 'fill' the void?" he asked, more pieces of the puzzle of Maya falling into place for him.

"I did. I still do." She made no other answer, and after eating for a few minutes she asked, "What about you. Do you cook?"

It took him a moment to adjust to the change of topic as Maya brought the conversation back to his earlier question. He wasn't sure if he should be relieved or disappointed.

"I learned out of necessity too. A little later than you had to," he said around a forkful of food. He decided to return to lighter topics, knowing there would be a time when it would come up again.

"Growing up, neither my brothers nor I had to do any of the cooking. My mother didn't cook too much either. Our housekeeper, Maria, did the cooking and baking." As he spoke, he could feel his smile split his face as her remembered the smell of her baking.

"She made the best deserts I've ever tasted. She would make these cookies she'd call junk cookies, and they must have had everything under the sun in them--all kinds of nuts, candy, chocolate chips. The real kind of chocolate chips, not those fake rubbery kinds," he said with the conviction of a man who knew his cookie ingredients.

"So if you didn't have to cook growing up, when did you learn?"

"When I left home for college. I spent a couple of years in the dorms, and then moved out into my own apartment. My parents lived too far away for me to go home every day to eat. I got tired of PB and J. So I guess I did what you did and experimented and eventually it was palatable. Now I kind of like to cook," he told her with a smile, adding, "something else we have in common."

Although he made light of his ability and why he'd learned, Mark felt ashamed. He'd never looked at his life of privilege as anything but convenient. Working as a cop, he'd seen poverty at its worst, and it had altered his perception of humanity in ways it never would have if he'd joined his father's law firm. Being a part of Maya's life made the issue of poverty and race personal for him.

After they'd finished their meal, she started clearing the table before he put out a hand to stop her. "I can do that for you. It's the least I can do. The food was delicious, Maya," he complimented her.

"Thanks, but it'll only take a minute. I'll put the dishes in the dishwasher. If you'd like to, you could use my shower," she subtly reminded him of state of dress.

With a laugh, he gave her a short fiery kiss and went in search of the shower. In the short time of their acquaintance he had kissed her more than she'd ever been kissed in her life.

Turning her attention back to her work, she put the dishes away and wiped down the counter and breakfast table. Maya thought back to his questions on how she was treated my Melissa. As they'd grown closer, she'd opened up with him more than she had with anyone. She'd shared her feelings on many topics. The one they'd never discussed was race or racism.

With everything else going on, from Allison's murder, running the house, and learning about Mark, she'd never bought the topic up. When he asked her about race, she'd been shocked, and not prepared to talk about it. She found herself doing what she normally did when things came up she didn't want to discuss. Run away.

She inhaled deeply, and breathed out on a long sigh. She was tired of running.

She decided it was a good time to change the sheets as Mark took his shower and left the kitchen to return to the bedroom. As she was pulling the quilt back on the bed, she heard the bathroom door open, and there he stood glorious, naked, and holding one of her bath towels in his large hand.

"Oh Lord, I'm sorry, I thought you were already in the shower." She knew she was stammering and felt ridiculous after the night they shared.

Mark followed and reached behind her when her back touched the doorframe. He closed the door, trapping her between it and his large hard body.

"That's okay, sweetheart. I went into your cabinet to borrow one of your razors so I could shave. Don't be embarrassed, Maya. You've seen my body. There's nothing to be ashamed of. In fact why don't you come in the shower with me? It definitely looks big enough for two in there." As he leaned into her, she felt his hot breath scorch a path down the side of her neck, and his tongue snake out to deliver a wet lick behind her ear.

Turning her neck to the side, giving him better access, she put her hands out in front of her and came into contact with his hard, bared chest. Before she knew it, her hands had traveled up his rock-hard abs and twined around his neck.

She felt the ties of her robe give way as he slid the garment from her shoulders. Beneath the robe she wore skimpy satin tap pants and a matching camisole, and he stopped in his sensual ministrations to look her over from head to toe.

* * * *

The silky shorts outlined her small rounded hips, the white lace hem ended at the top of her thighs. The matching top strained against her full breasts, outlining and pushing the large globes together, the golden tops spilling over the neckline. Maya was so sexy he was afraid he'd come from just looking at her.

"Mark...." she groaned, turning from his gaze, searching for the ties to her robe.

When she moved to turn away, he apologized. "I'm sorry baby. I wanted to get a better look at you. I know I must sound like a broken record, but you're beautiful. I like to look at you. Feel free to return the favor," he told her with a low laugh.

He ached for her to feel comfortable enough to look and enjoy his body, as he did hers. With a helpless groan he brought his head to hers and initiated a kiss that had them both gasping for air.

He remembered the running shower and peeled her sexy underclothes off, picked her up and walked into the steamy bathroom. After he pulled back the shower curtain, Mark lifted her with him into the tub.

"Let me clean you, baby," he said, and placed her small body in front of his.

As he began to wash her, he planted kisses everywhere his hand came into contact with. Mark gently moved her hair aside, and beginning at her neck, soaped down the length of her spine. Her groan of delight let him know how much she was enjoying his water play.

Once he'd washed every area of her body, he placed the soap in her hands. He turned her around to face him and encouraged her to return the favor. Maya had a sultry, tantalizing look in her eyes as he used his hand as a guide over hers. His heart raced.

He allowed her to steer their linked hands over his heaving chest. The sensual torture in Maya's eyes showed him the effects their play was having on her. Their shallow breaths mimicked each other.

When he couldn't take her small caressing hands moving over his body a minute longer, he turned her away from him and lifted her hands to place them on the shower wall. He leaned down and took her hips in his hands. He gathered her close and impaled her from the back. Slowly, he ground into her, manipulating her against his hard cock, as the water streamed on their overheated bodies.

"Oh God, Mark. Oh God please, baby, please, please...." she begged incoherently, as her warm, wet sheath eagerly accepted his thick invasion.

He set a smooth rhythm as he glided his body in and out of hers. The hot length of his cock going in and out of her was nearly unbearable. The pleasure was so intense as he gripped her hips tighter, thrusting harder and harder, so that he felt crazed with the pleasure.

"That feels so good," she keened, her head lowered to her chest as she continued to accept his tight thrusts from behind.

Between the tight feel of her sweet pussy and the way she was grinding herself against his cock, the pleasure rose quick, and he didn't know how long he could hold back coming. He reached between her legs, and using his hand, he played with her small clit.

Maya screamed as her orgasm broke, her body jerking in spasms as her release took over. Replete, her body slumped. With her head dangling and her chin resting on her chest, she inhaled deeply, her body shaky and trembling. Once he was assured she'd been pleasured, Mark reluctantly pulled out at the last minute to complete the mind-blowing orgasm he'd been holding back.

The hot water of the shower steamed up the bathroom, pounding down on them, washing away all evidence of his sperm from her smooth brown back, and allowed him to calm his racing heart as he fought to regain his breath.

"That was incredible. Thank you, Maya." He couldn't find any other words to say after what they shared. Maya nodded her head in response, her body still heaving from the aftershocks of their experience.

He opened the shower door and grabbed the thick white towel hanging on the hook and wrapped it around her before he swiped his body with the matching towel.

When they were reasonably dry he lifted her from the shower to lay with her on the bed, complete after their heart-pounding lovemaking. He gathered her close and listened to their combined heartbeats before he spoke.

* * * *

"Yesterday at dinner I asked why you went into psychology. How did it lead you to Imani House?"

After their heated lovemaking in the shower, it took Maya a moment before she could speak coherently. She cuddled closer to his large frame as she considered his questions. She'd been asked the same question many times by some of her intern students. She'd always given a stock answer that she'd always been interested in the workings of the human psyche. This time, for Mark, she stopped and thought about her reasons before answering.

"I started working at Imani House when it was best labeled a halfway house. It was the type of place women could come to when they had nowhere else to go. It was a very eclectic group of women who'd all come in search of a safe place," she said. As she spoke, his hands kneaded her scalp in a soothing massage.

"I came to the center as I was working on my dissertation. It seemed like a good place to finish my hours to complete my practicum. At the time, the programs the shelter used weren't working. They used limited sources and specific techniques for a wide range of problems. The result was no one received the help they needed to give any long-term change."

"That makes sense. How long had they'd been operating like that? Didn't they have any government funding?"

"If the current political environment is more liberal then typically there's more money available for social services programs. If it's a conservative atmosphere, then pickings are slim, and you learn pretty quick how to be resourceful for your program."

"Not enough government support of their programs was Imani House's problem?"

"That, and they tried to help too broad a range of problems. They should have offered fewer programs and run a smaller but more effective center."

"How did you come to take over and transform it into what it now is?"

"I'd finished my dissertation when I found out the center was closing. Around the same time, I'd inherited a large amount of money and property from my grandmother. When I found out the center was closing, I knew what I wanted to do with the money," she said.

As Maya shared her memories with him as they lay together, Mark knew she was sharing an even deeper part of herself than she had when they'd made love. He tightened his arms around her; thankful she was opening up to him, giving him access into her world.

CHAPTER 17

"What can I do for you, Detective?" the clerk asked as Jordan walked into the evidence room and approached his desk.

The tag around his neck showed the name James Smith. Jordan nodded his head. "I need to take a look at a piece of evidence bagged for Guy Kross."

"No problem, Detective. Give me a minute and I'll get it for you." He retreated to a back room in search of the request.

As he waited for the clerk to return, Jordan took a look around the small room. It was clean and organized. The clerk's workspace didn't have a thing out of place. The only things on his desk were organizational trays, clips and cups and traditional office equipment. Jordan wasn't sure he'd ever seen a man's desk so neat. He laughed out loud at his stereotypical thoughts.

"Here you are, Detective. I've also brought you a pair of gloves so you can handle the evidence." The clerk placed the plastic bag of evidence on the counter and handed the gloves to him with a small pair of tongs.

As the clerk bent over, the chain holding his nametag tangled with the thin gold of a chain he wore beneath his shirt. When Jordan reached to help, he adroitly moved aside and untangled them unassisted.

With a small smile he said, "This happens all the time, ever since they switched from pin name tags to hanging ones. There, I got it." He placed the gold chain back inside his shirt.

"Aren't you one of the detectives on the slayer case?" he asked.

"Yes, Detective Halstan and I have been assigned to work it exclusively," Jordan said, as he put on gloves and opened the evidence bag.

"Detective Halstan. I saw him on the news with that nasty Alicia Somers. She is so irritating; why they let her interview anyone is beyond me. She has the inquisitive skills of a flying gnat." A look of disgust crossed the clerk's pinched features.

"What?!" Jordan asked on a choked laugh.

"Oh nothing, I'm sorry. I don't like that woman at all. She's so pushy."

"Yeah well I think they're all like that. It's the nature of their job,"

Jordan mumbled, his mind on the contents of the bag. After he finished his perusal, he took off the plastic gloves and returned the evidence to the clerk.

"Was there something in particular you were looking for, Detective?"

"Excuse me?"

"Oh nothing. I wanted to know if there was anything else I could help you with?" he asked with a small smile.

"No, that was all, thanks." Jordan said, and left the room.

As soon as the clerk was once again alone in the room, the smile dropped from his face, and was replaced with a frown. He picked up the phone to make a call.

* * * *

"Our girl hit again," Mark said to Jordan as soon as his partner returned to the squad room. He led the way as both shouldered their weapons and left the precinct and headed toward the parking garage.

As soon as they arrived at the taped off area of the murder scene, they were immediately met by one of the crime technicians. "Good afternoon, Detectives. We called as soon as I confirmed it was the slayer."

"This is a little soon, isn't it? It hasn't been quite a month from the last one. Is she escalating?" Jordan asked. Soon after he'd voiced the question, the smell of the dead corpse hit him. The tech stopped walking and handed them both masks before they continued.

"Okay, obviously this one has been around for a while," Mark interjected. As they walked closer to the corpse, they could see parts of the nude man's body had begun to decompose.

"If I had to put a time frame on it, I'd say this one has been around for a few weeks. The coroner can give a more approximate time, but it'll be damn close," Davis told the men as they drew close to the decomposing corpse.

The tech went over the scene with them pointing out the similar patterns. After the team dug the victim out of his shallow grave, they'd been able to see the gun shot point of entry at the back of the skull.

"You can see the victim had been stripped, divested of all clothing and any means of identification. She left the body with the dowel thrown across his face." The tech pointed out the wooden down, bloodied, and splattered with the man's own feces.

Mark hunched down to get a closer look, and with gloved hands, turned the body over. Although the body was beginning to break down, he could see where the assault had taken place.

"Same shit?"

"Same shit, different day," the tech answered in the macabre humor of one who dealt with the more gruesome aspects of humanity, daily.

"How was it uncovered? Any witnesses?"

"No witnesses. Old man out in the park feeding the birds came across this one. Called it in, and our guys uncovered the body."

Jordan and Mark made notes as they catalogued the scene. "Looks like that's it. Let us know if you discover anything else."

"Sure will, Detective," the tech promised.

* * * *

As soon as they returned to the squad room, Lieutenant Hernandez shoved his head out of his office and called out in a strident voice, "Phillips, Halstan, I need you in my office. Now."

"Man, what is *wrong* with him?" Jordan asked, as he unfurled his body from behind his desk.

"This case man, this case. Between it, more murders, and the acting chief breathing down his neck every other damn minute, he's going fuckin' nuts," Mark answered as he followed Jordan into the lieutenant's office.

"Have a seat, men. Before I go into my news, what'd you uncover at the scene?" Lieutenant Hernandez started without preamble, encompassing both men in his query, and Mark gave him a succinct retelling of their discovery.

"All right good enough, good job. The reason I called you in here was to let you know the *acting* chief has decided, over my objections, to bring in the FBI," he told them at the close of their brief.

"Shit! What the hell for? They're not going to uncover anything we haven't already," Jordan exclaimed, running an angry hand across the back of his neck.

"Hell, we've been working our balls off on this case. What the hell else does the guy want from us?" Mark demanded, just as pissed off as Jordan over the new development.

Holding up his hand for silence, the lieutenant continued. "Look, men, I know how you feel, I feel the same way, but it's a fact and we're going to deal with it, and deal with it like professionals. The agent's name is Nicolai Montgomery. His actual title is Special Agent Montgomery. Special Agent Montgomery heads up a subunit of other specialized agents who assist in cases such as this one."

"He arrived from FBI headquarters this morning. In fact, he should be here any minute."

No sooner had he finished speaking, than a knock sounded on his door. "That might be him now. I didn't think he'd make it in so fast."

"Damn, that was quick." Jordan told Mark in a low voice.

As the lieutenant opened his office door, he looked up into the silver eyes of the man who stood there. His gaze took in the FBI identification badge hanging from his neck, and standing aside, he invited the agent in. Hernandez felt the tension rise as the agent entered the room. "Special Agent Montgomery?" he verified.

"Yes, sir," the agent said, as he shook his hand and abruptly released it.

"I'm glad your flight made it in safely, and I'd like to welcome you on board." The lieutenant's glance then stole to his two detectives, as they each stood to extend their hand to the newcomer. As each man shook the other's in a hard grip, he had a moment to do a quick visual of the FBI agent.

Having already taken note of his strange eyes, his gaze took in the inky blackness of his hair. The agent's nose was prominent in his face, hawked and crooked. His chin was squared with a deep cleft, and a discernible shadow covered it.

Although he looked to be under 6 feet in height, he was thick, and the muscles in his chest and legs bulged through his dark, fitted, standard-issue suit and tie. The agent's legs were braced apart, and he'd maneuvered his body to allow his back to face the wall.

"Please Special Agent Montgomery, have a seat," he offered, indicating the available chair.

"I'll stand for now, thank you, Lieutenant Hernandez. If you don't mind, I'd very much appreciate it if we could start. And Agent Montgomery is fine," he said in a deep scratchy voice.

"Start what? What's your role going to be in this case?" Jordan asked.

Turning his head toward Jordan, the agent gave Jordan his direct gaze, his head tilted to the side as though considering his words carefully before answering.

"My role is to assist this department and give aide to this investigation. I emphasize the word assist. I don't know what your experience in the past has been with the FBI, Detective, whether it was positive or negative. Although judging by your hostility, I would guess it wasn't very good," he ventured in a direct manner, a sardonic smile creasing the corners of his hard mouth.

Taking all three men in his gaze, Montgomery continued. "I'm sure you've been running this investigation with skill, experience and expertise. My intent is not to belittle what you've done. I'm here to give you aid, and perhaps add my particular skills, experience, and expertise to the table in the hopes of capturing the perpetrator of these murders." He paused, his mercurial gaze sweeping over each man in the room.

"So where we start is wherever you want to start. I'd like to listen to what you have to tell me about this case and what you know about the offender, and we can go from there."

After he'd finished speaking, he took the proffered seat and waited in quiet expectation for their verdict. Lieutenant Hernandez knew he was waiting for them to either accept his aid or not. Either way it was clear from the agent's demeanor he would do his job, with or without their assistance, or approval.

CHAPTER 18

Over the next few hours Jordan, Mark, and Lieutenant Hernandez alternated giving the agent information as they offered their speculations as well. When they'd completed their brief, the agent remained silent for several minutes, squinting, as though he were trying to figure out a puzzle.

"From what you've told me it appears the offender is displaying some of the more typical characteristics of an organized serial killer. The murders are taking place over an average of a thirty day period, give or take a week, with no escalation."

He took a moment to take a drink of the water at his side. "The offender is methodical and organized, and she takes great pains to hide her victims. You believe she's female so I'll refer to the killer in the feminine gender. However, she doesn't try to hide the abandoned car left at the scene. Keeping constant with her methodical nature, she brings along a rape kit which she uses post mortem on the victims."

Agent Montgomery recanted the information from memory. He'd taken out a small black notebook and had occasionally written a note down. However, he had paid close attention to what each man had to say, as though the way they uttered the words were as important as the words themselves.

"She's smart and allows the police to discover what she wants them to find. She's methodical and organized, and is the most difficult type of serial killer to capture, as I'm sure you men are aware. The more organized the killer, the better their ability to function in society. What further illustrates the nature of her organization is her ability to lure the victim to a location of her choosing. This gives her infinite control. Or she's killing them before driving to a prearranged destination. I'd like to go survey the location of where the *first* victim was discovered."

"Any particular reason?" Lieutenant Hernandez interrupted.

"The first crime is typically committed close to where the offender lives or works. As they become more proficient, they in turn become more confident. As their confidence grows, they venture out further. Yes, Detective?" Agent Montgomery asked, his gaze turning from the lieutenant, to Mark, although Mark hadn't voiced a question out loud.

"You said you were interested in the psychological as well as the physical aspects to the case. In what way do you mean? In the role of a profiler?"

"Of sorts. I belong to a subunit of FBI specialists who, at one time in their career, were strictly profilers. I too was a profiler before moving to the unit."

Montgomery glanced at his watch. "It's been a long day for me, so maybe we can start early tomorrow where we leave off here." The agent began to unfold his thick body from the chair and picked up the small black case he'd carried in with him.

Lieutenant Hernandez had seen Jordan look at his watch and stretch his back before he settled further back into his chair. He'd thought he'd been the only who'd seen the move because he happened to be looking in Jordan's direction, but when Montgomery asked to wrap things up, he realized the observant man had cataloged his movement and responded. Hernandez's estimation of the agent's observational abilities went up a notch.

They set a time to meet the following day. The agent shook hands with Lieutenant Hernandez before shaking hands with Mark and Jordan. This time, none of the men felt compelled to use as much force as before, confident they had a measure of the other's worth established.

After the agent left, those who remained sat down in the chairs they'd risen from. They'd had dealings with the FBI before, and not always good ones. Agent Montgomery seemed different from the others. Mark bluntly put a voice to what they were all feeling.

"He seemed to have a handle on what we've been doing in the investigation."

"He wasn't *too* much of an asshole. He didn't come in telling us what *he* thought we should be doing, he listened and gave good input." Jordan agreed, with reluctance.

"Yes I agree with you both. Agent Montgomery will make a good addition to this investigation, and to this team," Lieutenant Hernandez agreed with both men's assessments.

Turning to Mark he asked, "Could you give Dr. Richardson a call and ask when it would be convenient for her to meet with the agent? I agree it's important for him to meet with her so she can share her knowledge."

"No problem, sir. I'll give her a call tonight and find out what her schedule looks like."

"It can wait until tomorrow, Mark. It's getting late, no need to call her tonight. When you speak with her, tell her she can either come by the station or you can take Agent Montgomery by her center and speak there." He finished and dismissed the men back to their work.

Soon after, Mark and Jordan called it a night and left the office, walking together to the underground parking lot. "How is everything going with you and the doc?" Jordan asked as he stashed his gym bag in the back of his jeep.

Mark had been lifting the back hatch of his Expedition when he caught the question and the subtle difference of inflection in Jordan's voice.

He glanced around the hatch door as he lowered it back into place and answered. "Learning more about one another, typical relationship things. You know."

"I don't know. We haven't talked much lately. Want to go grab a drink at Hooligans?" he asked with studied casualness, referring to their favorite sports bar.

It was a Wednesday night and although he and Maya hadn't made any formal plans, Mark had intended to call her as soon as he left the precinct. Over the course of their relationship he'd gotten into the habit of calling her first thing in the morning to start his day off right, he'd told her with a laugh.

Over the last few days, he hadn't been able to reach her. He'd left several messages, but she hadn't returned his call. Today he and Jordan had worked early in the morning and he'd missed calling her, and he'd left a message with Dalia for Maya to call him when she was free. He tried not to think she was avoiding him. He'd planned to go by the House and see her as soon as he left the precinct. He glanced at his watch and thought he had enough time to grab a beer and still be able to go by Imani House for Maya.

"Man, if you and Maya have plans we can make it for some other time," Jordan said with studied casualness.

"No, we don't have any plans. Tonight is her late night at the House. I'll meet you at Hooligans."

On the drive to the bar, he made a call to Imani House in hopes of speaking with Maya. His luck was with him when she picked up on her private line.

"Imani House, this is Dr. Richardson," she answered on the second ring.

"Hey, sweetheart, it's Mark. Remember me?" A smile of satisfaction crossed his face, in automatic response to hearing her voice.

"Hey you, long time no hear," she lightly teased back.

Mark breathed a sigh of relief. Although he'd picked up a slight hesitancy in her voice, at least she answered her phone.

They'd grown closer, and he was glad she found it easier to open up with him. He cared about her feelings, and he tried to show her at every opportunity. He hoped she was starting to believe him when he told her he'd never felt as he did about her with anyone else. He just had to make sure she believed him.

"I told you about the FBI agent coming on board the investigation," he began.

"He arrived?" she asked.

"Yes, we had our first conference with him and we'd like to have the two of you meet. Whenever you have time in your schedule, I'll arrange it."

"If you can bring him to the House tomorrow, I'll have some time."

"That should be fine. I'll check in the morning and let you know. Are you ready to wrap up for the night? I worry about you driving home so late every night. I thought I'd come by to get you," he turned the conversation away from the investigation.

"Actually I'm done with work for the night. I told you about our major fundraiser we've had for the last two years? Well we're doing it again, and I need to meet with Arlinda to start planning for it." She mentioned the name of her college friend who donated the majority of the clothes for the show.

"Alright, baby. Jordan wants me to go and have a beer with him, and I'd plan to come by afterward. I guess I'll have to wait until tomorrow to see you." Mark didn't try and hide his disappointment.

"I would have liked to see you too," she admitted. "You should go with Jordan and have a beer. Where are the two of you going--to your house?"

He thought about saying yes because although Maya didn't go out to bars she may have heard of Hooligans, and he didn't want her to get the wrong impression. It was a nice bar but had a reputation for being a meat market.

Deciding to compromise with the truth, he told her they were going to a sports bar, without mentioning the name. "I'd better let you go. You be safe, okay? And call me when you get home."

"Don't worry about me, I'll be fine. I'll call you," she promised.

After he hung up the phone, Mark shook his head in mock self-disgust, still amazed with the depth of his growing feelings for her. And although she was affectionate toward him, he still wasn't confident in how deep her feelings ran for him.

He hadn't said the words *I love you*, but they were there; ready to spill. But he held back, frustrated as hell. He knew she wasn't ready to hear them yet.

Maya hung up the phone with a smile lingering. Despite the doubts plaguing her, she'd smiled more than she ever had in her life. The smile was still in place when her office door was slung open.

"Hey girlie! Ready to go out and have some fun?" Her flamboyant friend bounced into Maya's office.

Maya's grin widened as she came around her desk to give her friend a hug. "What are you talking about?" She released her friend and gathered her paperwork.

"Well I was thinking. When was the last time I bullied you into going out dancing with me?" Arlinda asked with a gamine smile and a small shake of her hips.

CHAPTER 19

Maya couldn't help smiling, but Arlinda brought the smile out of most people. Her infectious smile and positive personality drew men to her like a magnet. Neither did it hurt that she was beautiful, Maya thought.

Arlinda also had a mixed heritage, her mother was Puerto Rican, and her father was African. That was where the similarities ended. She and Maya were polar opposites.

Maya was quiet and held her emotional cards close, and Arlinda was flamboyant and outrageous. She would often laugh and joke, making light of life and love with the majority of her friends.

She once shared with Maya that most of the time she was Arlee. Arlee was the pretty girl who laughed and joked and made 'friends' quickly. With women, she played the party girl who was always up for a fun time, with a flippant comment always at the ready. With men, she played the sexy flirt who used her femininity as a shield to hide her intelligence and ability. In the end she shared with no one the complete Arlinda.

With Maya she was Arlinda. Arlinda was the real thing. She laughed and cried and showed she was a woman who was sensitive, and often had her feelings hurt by the selfishness of others, like anyone else.

Arlinda respected the fact Maya didn't party. But once in a while, she'd drag her out with her and make her laugh and by the end of the night, Maya would have to admit she'd had a great time.

"Girl, I already *know* what you're thinking. We're supposed to start organizing and taking care of business, and we will. I have a great idea for the show this year, and we can talk about it at this great sports bar I discovered last week, it'll be fun. They have great music, cool atmosphere, and the men--ooh la la." A broad grin split her pretty face. "Girl, the men are simply *too* fine. Umm. There ought to be a law against 'em! It'll be fun. Come on," Arlinda wheedled.

"Arlinda, I'm not dressed to go out anywhere," Maya protested and laughed at the same time, holding out the floral dress for her friend's inspection.

"What? You fishing for a compliment? You look gorgeous; that dress looks great on you! It really shows off your assets if you know what I mean. If you got it, flaunt it, right? It's a great departure from you normal wear, girlfriend," she teased her friend, as her glance stole over the short floral dress that was simple in design, yet complimented Maya's full curves.

"Okay, it sounds like fun. Let me gather my stuff and I'll follow you," Maya finally agreed, and Arlinda let out a whoop before the women left with Arlinda leading the way. Maya drove and followed Arlinda to the popular bar, located not too far away from Imani House.

"It sure is crowded for a Wednesday night, isn't it?" Maya asked, after they'd been forced to park a few blocks from the bar, as the parking lot was packed.

"No, this place is never short for customers, I hear. Each night of the week they feature something different. You know, like karaoke, line dancing, live bands, and Salsa. Tonight is R&B night," she answered.

"Arlinda, for somebody who recently discovered a place, you sure do know a lot about it." Maya laughed at her.

"Girl, I know. The party girl never stops. I honestly did discover it last week--for real, Maya!" She laughed at Maya's doubtful expression. "But I have been back a few times since," she admitted with a sheepish grin.

Once inside, Arlinda led them through the maze of patrons like a Seeing Eye dog would for a blind woman. After they found a deserted table, they sat down on the high-backed stools. A waitress soon approached them with a large smile and took their drink order.

Maya looked around the bar. It was teaming with noise and activity. They'd lucked out and landed a good table near the dance floor, giving them a bird's eye view of the entire bar.

"So what is this new idea you have for the fundraiser?" Maya's voice rose to compensate for the loud music.

"I was thinking we could include a section for men's fashion. I've been dedicating a small section of the boutique to a new designer who features men's clothes, and I thought we could include some of them in the show." Arlinda spoke over the music, and Maya saw her checking out a few men who'd caught her eye.

"That sounds great, tell me more," Maya spoke over the music.

Sitting back with her drink in hand, Arlinda looked across the table at Maya with a slow smile spreading across her face.

"What? What's that look for?" Maya asked, noticing both the smile and the coy expression on her friend's face.

"Okay, I know we don't get to see one another as often as I'd like to, but in the last month I've seen you--girlfriend, you've changed."

"What do you mean? How've I changed?"

"Can't quite quantify it. Not really tangible or physical. Although I do like the dress, much better than those damn jeans and granny dresses you normally sport. But seriously, I don't quite know what it is, but..." Arlinda insisted, and tapped the end of her nose with her finger. "And if I didn't know better, I'd say it was because of a man."

"Is that your stock answer? Why does the change have to be because of a man?" Maya wasn't sure if she should be offended or not.

"So you admit there's something different going on? If it's not a man, then what's going on? And don't be offended, it's a compliment. Maya you're glowing, I swear to God!"

"I *have* been seeing someone," Maya admitted. She rarely spoke to anyone about her intimate feelings, and even with Arlinda she felt uncomfortable.

"I knew it!" Arlinda returned, before sobering, to put a semi-serious look on her face at Maya's scowl. "Sorry. Well go on--tell me all about it, and don't leave out any juicy details," she demanded, rubbing her hands together and grinning.

"I told you about the detective who's been investigating Allison's murderer?"

"Yes. How's it going? I guess I should say, how are you doing?" Although it was obvious Arlinda wanted to hear the 'juicy parts,' Maya knew her friend was concerned with how she'd been coping with the death of Allison.

"I'm doing a lot better. Mark is the major reason I've been able to handle it all. Arlinda, I think he cares, at least he acts as though he does" she said, with a slight catch in her voice.

"You sound hesitant, what's up?" Arlinda asked bluntly when Maya paused.

"I don't know," Maya admitted with a sigh before continuing. "It seems too good to be true sometimes, Arlinda. It's like I'm constantly waiting for the other shoe to drop, you know?"

"Maya," Arlinda paused on a long sigh.

"What? What is it? You obviously want to say something. You may as well get it out, Arlinda."

"Okay I'm gonna just say it. Stop with the sabotage."

"What sabotage?" Maya asked as she took a sip of her drink.

"Maya girl, you know damn well what I'm talking about. Every time you have a potential for happiness you do this. Admittedly, you rarely let a guy get close, but the few times you have, you find some reason to end it before giving it a chance." Arlinda sat back and crossed her arms over her chest to stare at her friend.

One part of Maya admitted that what Arlinda said was true. The other part of her closed herself off to the possibilities that what her friend was telling her was true. As she contemplated Arlinda's words, she glanced across the room and made eye-contact with the man in question as he danced on the crowded dance floor with a tall blonde.

CHAPTER 20

Mark wasted no time leaving the dance floor, his long stride catching up with Maya as she ran to the women's lounge and was opening the door.

As her arm was reaching out to open the door, his much longer one slammed it shut as he nudged her down the wall. Crowding her body with his, Mark forced her into closer contact with him and captured her hands in his when she tried to push him away.

"Maya, sweetheart, it isn't what I *know* you're thinking." When she looked blank, no expression on her face, he felt desperation claw its way through his gut.

She had twined herself so tightly around his heart, he felt a near physical ache from looking at her. Everything about her he found intoxicating. The way she moved. Her funny expressions. Her presence. Her intelligence. Her dedication to Imani House and the women who depended on her.

Everything.

The thought of her not believing him was intolerable. He tilted her chin back when she wouldn't make eye contact.

"Baby, don't do this," he pleaded. When she refused to make eye contact, he felt anger, frustration, and fear mingle inside his gut.

"Dammit, Maya! Don't do this shit! Don't shut down on me," he demanded. When she continued with that blank look he hated on her face, he felt helpless. "I was only dancing, baby. That's all, he told her in desperation.

"I know," she spoke so low he had to strain his ears to catch her words.

"My first response was to run when I saw you dancing with another woman. It seems like I've been running my whole life."

He felt uneasy. As though something wonderful was slipping from his grasp. In a desperate attempt to stop her from saying something he didn't want to hear, he captured her lips with his. He moved his mouth searchingly over hers; capturing and then releasing her full bottom rim over and over, as his hands shakily caressed her face.

When she didn't respond, he realized he wasn't reaching her. He released her lips and moved slightly away. Afraid, he wanted to get her alone, away from the bar.

"Maya, listen to me sweetheart. Why don't we go somewhere and talk. We can go anywhere you want. I want us to be able to talk somewhere, uninterrupted. Please," he pleaded.

It took her a long time to answer, and when she did, he felt his body sag with relief. "If you'd like, you could come to my house and we could talk."

"I parked in the parking lot right out front. I need to go and tell Jordan I'm leaving, and we can go."

"I came here tonight with a friend and I need to tell her the same."

He guided her back through the throng of people, keeping physical contact with her as his hand settled on the small of her back. When she stopped, he looked down at the pretty woman who had been sipping her drink as they approached.

"What happened to you, Maya? One minute we were talking about your friend, and the next minute you got up and left. Are you all right?" her glance slid off Maya to go to Mark, as his hand rested on her waist.

"I'm sorry ,Arlinda; I'm fine. Mark and I need to talk about some things, so I'm going to have to leave if it's okay with you? I'll call you tomorrow and we can schedule a time to go over the particulars for the fundraiser," Maya answered her friend, her voice solemn.

"Mark, this is my friend Arlinda Nyoni," she introduced.

"Hello, Arlinda. It's nice to meet you." He shook her hand before releasing it to place his arm back around Maya's back.

As Maya picked up her oversized bag, Arlinda watched the man at her side as he took the heavy bag from her hands, his eyes lingering on hers, as she looked up to thank him, and just as quickly, looked away.

Arlinda watched the pair leave and a sigh of longing escaped her lips. She then noticed the man at the table Mark had been sitting with, look across the room her way.

A slow smile spread across Arlee's face and she lightly pat her curls in place, as he unfurled his long body from the table and sauntered over in her direction.

* * * *

In silence they walked to Maya's car. Mark didn't know what was going on in her mind, and that alone put him on edge. His main thought was he needed to be alone with her and reassure her there wasn't any other woman out there for him.

He could think of no other reason for her sudden withdrawal from him. And it scared the hell out of him the way she'd shut down.

When they reached the lot where her car was parked, Mark asked for her keys and opened her door.

"I'll be right behind you, sweetheart." He gave her a quick kiss, closed the door and ran back toward his vehicle.

He followed her as she drove home. When she drove into the garage, he followed suit within seconds. After climbing out of her car, she reached back to retrieve her things and waited for him to join her inside before closing the garage door.

"This door leads directly into my wing." She allowed him to go in first when he gently moved her aside. She followed him as he turned on lights and began to look around, making sure nothing was out of order.

"I know it's getting late, but I think we need to talk." He followed her into the sitting room.

"Do you want anything to drink?"

Picking up on her nervousness, he walked over to her and took both of her hands between his, and then he led her to the overstuffed sofa.

"Maya the two of us have been learning more about the other. I love the fact you're beginning to trust me and grant me access into your world. Baby, I know that's something you don't do easily and I don't want it to change. You've got to know there was nothing going on at the bar."

Mark sat back and pulled her with him to a more comfortable and intimate position on the sofa. He knew it would be easier for her to talk without looking at him. He felt her resistance, and ignored it, forcing her to accept his touch.

"You're right. One part of me knows that. But I guess for me it seems I don't have much luck when it comes to intimate or personal relationships."

Her words caused some of the tension to ease from his body, the fear that she was slipping away from him abating as she spoke.

"I know that, Maya. That's why what we have is so special. Something I wouldn't jeopardize for anything." He closed his eyes and placed a small kiss on her top of her head.

"I had a difficult childhood I guess you could say. It seemed as though I could never do anything right no matter how hard I tried."

Mark knew of her childhood and how she'd been the caregiver for her foster sister from the time she herself was little more than a child.

"I started doing chores and taking care of Ally when I was young, and I thought that was the way it was supposed to be. Although

Ally wasn't much younger than I was, she always *seemed* to be. We settled into the role of mother and daughter. I never did resent it. At least I didn't think I had. In high school, the girl who shared a locker with me was pretty nice. She would invite me to go to the local hangout a lot. I'm sure you know the type."

Mark looked down at her upturned face and placed a small kiss on her forehead. He knew her childhood had been hell, but this was the first time she had gone into details. Lifting his hand, he stroked the side of her face, encouraging her to continue, "I know the type."

"It was a Friday afternoon, and my locker mate issued her standard invitation for me to join them. I don't know who was more surprised, she or I, when I accepted. It was my senior year, and maybe I wanted to hang out for once. I don't know. Feel normal." She said with a laugh that had him tense, not sure what was coming next.

"I went with my locker mate to the mall, and for a couple of hours I forgot my responsibilities, forgot about what I needed to do at home, and had a fun time." Knowing there was a 'but' coming, his breath caught as he waited for her to continue.

"After a while one of the kids suggested we all go somewhere to eat, and I was horrified at how late it was. I got on the first bus that would take me near our apartment, and ran the rest of the way home. I had this awful feeling in the pit of my stomach. I knew something wasn't right."

She paused before continuing with a hitch in her voice. "When I made it home, the door was opened, and I could hear Allison crying. Danny was standing over her. His shirt was open and his pants were around his ankles. I was stunned. I didn't know what to think or do, I felt sort of detached. You know when you feel disconnected with your body somehow?"

Her phrasing and the hesitancy in her voice told Mark she didn't expect an answer. She was caught up in the horror of reliving her sister's rape.

CHAPTER 21

"Mark, I can't begin to tell you how guilty I felt that night. Because of my selfishness, Allison was brutalized and scarred for life. I've always felt responsible." Her voice was thick with unshed tears.

"Maya, I'm sorry Ally was harmed by that asshole. No woman should have to go through that. And because she was a young girl that makes it much worse." He consoled her, hugging her tightly against his chest, refusing to allow her to move away from his comfort.

"But sweetheart what happened wasn't your fault. No, look at me, baby." He said when she tried to turn away from his probing eyes.

"I know I'm not responsible for another person's actions. I know that. But I also know if I had been there, then Allison wouldn't have been harmed," Maya nearly cried her response.

"Baby," Mark paused, and she could hear his frustration. "Maya, because you went out on *one* normal activity in all of your young life and something terrible happened to your sister does *not* mean you're responsible. Had you been there, he may have assaulted both of you. Or he may have come back when you weren't around and still raped Allison. The truth is, you were able to take care of her, and you may have saved her from him hurting her even more. Don't keep beating yourself up for participating in a normal adolescent activity."

"Whether or not you believe I have a place of blame for what happened to Allison doesn't negate the fact my sister was raped and her life was changed. Ally had always been a carefree girl, always found something to laugh about. After she was raped, she was different."

"How so?"

"I told you Ally came to live with me when I left Melissa's house for college."

At his nod she continued, "I'd known she had been experimenting with drugs with some of her friends at school. Whenever I tried to say something to her about it she'd tell me to mind my own business. After what happened with Danny, she also became promiscuous and would come home from school late with no explanation. When I confronted her about it, she admitted she was doing drugs and she didn't always have money for it. I think you can guess how she got the money for her habit."

"I can." He answered and Maya knew in his line of work, he came in constant contact with young people who grew up in the type of neighborhood she'd grown up in. To them, crime was a normal way of life--dealing and taking drugs, gangs, and prostitution. Each was a normal component of their everyday lives.

"Maya, I want you to understand I would never take you for granted. You deserve so much more than to be treated with casual neglect. No, please listen to me. I'm sure Allison loved you. Dalia, I can tell cares a great deal for you. The women at Imani House admire and respect you. I'm not saying no one cares for you. What I see is you give a lot."

It was hard for Maya to listen to what he was telling her. She was comfortable in the role of counselor where she was helping someone to get her life on track; she felt confident of her welcome.

But when it became personal, she wasn't as sure of her reception. She'd learned not to expect much in the way of return affection. To have expectations was a surefire way to disappointment. It was the way she'd learned to cope--not to expect too much. That was the way to avoid heartache.

She hadn't realized it, but with Mark she had been doing the same thing. He was the first man she had shared so much of herself with. He said things to her no one had ever said.

He did things to her body she'd allowed no other man to do.

He seemed to have a genuine interest in her. He asked her about her life, and wanted to explore new things with her.

"When I first saw you dancing, I was upset because all I could see was this woman in your arms, dancing with you. Then I kind of felt it was inevitable.

"What do you mean inevitable? That you would see me with someone else? Baby, I was only dancing with her," Mark said gently.

"I know. I guess I've always waited for the other shoe to drop. That something was bound to happen to end this," she admitted in a low voice.

"I've always been honest with you Maya. I've told you how I feel, and my feelings haven't changed. In fact the opposite has happened. You've invaded my heart," he admitted, and her heart caught at his simple words.

"Sometimes I get a little scared of what's happening, because it seems like it's happening too fast. But it doesn't make it any less real. I'm not walking away from this, and neither will I let you." He hugged her close. As he'd come to the last words, he cleared his throat.

"I'm sure along the way one of us will make a mistake, but it doesn't mean we don't love each other. Or, that our relationship is destined to fall apart. It means we made a mistake, and all we do from there is learn from that mistake, not give up on the relationship. Giving up is too damn easy, Maya."

Maya didn't think it registered on him he mentioned love. She allowed the slip to pass because she didn't want to examine it too closely. What she did examine was his desire to be with her. She was happier than she'd ever been, and she didn't want to sabotage it through her fears. Fears she carried around like the unnecessary, excess baggage they were.

"You're right. I don't want to give up on this. It's natural for me to withdraw when it becomes personal, and it's something I've been working on. But I'll keep trying. That's all I can promise. I'll try," she promised him with a small smile.

"We'll work on it," he corrected her.

When she saw him glance at his watch, she realized how late it was. Lately, she would take one of her weekend days off to spend with him, which meant her Fridays were busy late nights at the house.

When Mark realized she was working later on Fridays and figured out why, he didn't try and talk her out of working late. He simply arrived at Imani House on Friday night when he left the precinct and worked from his laptop or visited with the residents. After Maya finished for the night, they would drive to her house and he would spend the night.

He'd even kept a few of his things in her bedroom over the course of the last few weeks.

"Sweetheart, it's getting late, why don't we go to bed? I'm sure you've got a busy day tomorrow, and so do I with this FBI agent," he told her as he helped her to her feet.

"I know Fridays are kind of hectic for you, so why don't I bring him by Imani House and you can meet him there." Mark wrapped his arms around her waist as she stood in front of her bathroom mirror.

"That's fine. I'll be out of the House for a meeting in the morning, but I'll return in the afternoon for the rest of the day. Call me when you're ready to come by."

As she'd begun to speak, he opened the front of her robe and had insinuated his hands inside. He cupped her breasts as he stared at their dual images reflected in the mirror as he caressed her.

He took her erect nipples between his thumb and forefinger, and lightly pinched it until she arched her back, a moan escaping her parted lips. "Mark…"

She loved when he played with her breasts, and in the mirror she watched him toy with her nipples, making them stand out in stiff peaks as he kissed his way down the side of her throat.

He eased the robe down her shoulders until it pooled in a heap around her feet. Turning her around, he picked her up and strode back into the bedroom where he deposited her on the bed.

He made quick work out of taking off his pants, his eyes never leaving hers. He turned off the bedside light and came to lie beside her on the bed.

"I'm happy you're a part of my life. If you ever are in doubt about anything, please ask me, and we can talk about it. Don't run away from me again or assume the worst--okay?" he pleaded in a voice grown rough with arousal.

"I'm trying," she whispered against his throat. She could barely think with his big hands roaming over her bared skin, his touch electric on her breasts.

"You have to know how serious I am about you," he told her moments before his hot mouth found her breasts. She wrapped both of her arms around his neck, her hands coming to rest at the base of his neck. She tangled her fingers in his sable curls as he continued his intimate torture. "And you also have to know I'm not playing some game with you," he said and pulled away from her heaving breast to look down at her.

"I know you aren't. I feel the same way." She didn't like his distance from her, and sat up, so they were facing one another. She took his face between her hands, her eyes searching his in the dim lit-room; the only light came shining from the moon. But the dimness of the room couldn't hide the way his beautiful dark blue eyes were staring at her with such hot intensity. She had to close her eyes in order to breathe.

When she opened them again, a smile played around the edges of his sensual mouth, and she leaned forward to kiss him.

His mouth immediately took over, fastening on hers in long drugging kisses before he wrapped his arms around her and fell back to the bed with their bodies facing.

Mark was everywhere. Moments before he was gentle and sweet, now his body covered hers as he molded himself to her. She felt his erection on her thigh and moved closer for better access to the long thick length of him.

"Oh God baby, oh God, I can't get enough of you. I need you. Now," he said, and his fingers found her clitoris.

She nearly died on the spot from the feel of him teasing her, making her crazy, wanting, no, needing to have him buried deep inside of her. As she pushed against his hand, he lifted her bottom and impaled her on his engorged penis.

"Mark!" she screamed, her breath ending on a long keen.

"This is the real deal," he grunted, his breathing ragged, as his hands held her still to receive his plunges deep within her body. He took her hard and fast, the time for slow and gentle long passed. The feel of her tight sweet pussy gripping his cock made him grit his teeth, as he buried himself in her as far as he could.

Her velvet walls opened and closed in welcome over him as he pumped relentlessly into her. He pushed them both outside their previous limits, testing to see how far they could go beyond ecstasy. When he felt the first signs of her body rippling, followed by her long keen as she released, it drove his mind and body over the edge.

"Maya!" With a harsh groan he delivered two more tight, hard, corkscrew thrusts as he called her name. He released long and hard, his orgasm so prolonged he knew he'd died from the pleasure.

Mark held them in the same position for long minutes, not ready to give up the spiritual connection their physical connection had given them. Their racing hearts calmed and he stroked a shaking hand gently over her soft curls. "You have to know this isn't a game, Maya," he whispered against her temple, as she lay exhausted in his arms.

CHAPTER 22

Mark had just sat at his desk with a steaming cup of coffee in his hand, when Lieutenant Hernandez called out for him and Jordan.

"Detectives could the two of you meet me in the conference room? And Detective Halstan could you please bring in any notes you've compiled with Dr. Richardson? Thank you, gentlemen," he said before heading toward the conference room ahead of them.

Mark and Jordan filed into the conference room at the end of the hall once they'd gathered their notes. Inside the room, Lieutenant Hernandez sat at one end of the long scarred mahogany table, his back to the door, while Agent Montgomery sat on the other end with his back to the wall facing them as they entered.

Mark noticed, both times he'd seen him, the agent's body had been stationed in a defensive position. Montgomery's back had been close to the wall, his arms held close to his body.

Now, as he looked over at the agent, he took note of the way his legs were braced apart as he sat in the straight back chair. There was an intense quality about him that was hard to define. He had the look of someone who was prepared for anything. Mark wondered what he was preparing for.

He caught Jordan observing the agent also. He knew Jordan held a dislike for the man because he was FBI. He and Jordan once had an ugly run-in with an FBI agent when they'd first worked in the homicide unit. Since then, Jordan had steered away from anyone in the division.

"Detectives, thank you for joining us. I've been in conference with Agent Montgomery, going over some of the particulars of the case. I've also informed him of the valuable insight Dr. Richardson has been providing for us." Lieutenant Hernandez waved Mark and Jordan to the two available seats at the conference table.

"Mark, were you able to reach Dr. Richardson to set up a conference?"

"Yes, sir, I was. She said we could come by Imani House this morning, and she would be able to fit us into her schedule."

"That's great. When we conclude here, why don't you take Montgomery over to meet Dr. Richardson?" The Lieutenant suggested, and after the four men spent time going over the case,

Mark took out the notes he had compiled with Maya over the last month.

"Dr. Richardson's foster sister Allison Hill and Phil Hardcastle were victims five and six in the slayer killings. Ms. Hill was the first female victim, and we believe the slayer felt forced to kill Allison for unknown reasons. However, from the projection of the bullet, and the point of entry into the spinal cavity, it appears Allison had been turning to leave when the bullet tagged her," Mark initiated the brief as he looked over his notes.

"Dr. Richardson. Yes I'm familiar with her," the FBI agent spoke in his low, scratchy voice.

Marked look up from his notes. "Oh? And how is it you know her?"

"Dr. Richardson's work is known, and her publication's are well received in the medical and psychology fields. She's published in JAMA as well as other scientific periodicals. I've read one or two of her articles. I have not had the pleasure of meeting her in person. Yet." A small smile graced his austere features.

"I wasn't aware scientific journals were standard reading fare for FBI agents," Jordan mumbled in an aside to Mark.

"I'm sure there are plenty of things you are unaware of regarding the FBI, Detective Philips." The agent's expression remained neutral when he aimed the comment at Jordan.

"Detective Halstan will take you over to Imani House so you and Dr. Richardson can meet. Maybe you can share insights on the case before you go to the crime scenes," Lieutenant Hernandez said in an attempt to lessen the slight tension that vibrated in the room.

"You want us to head to the crime scenes?" Mark asked in reference to the latter part of the lieutenant's statement.

"Yes. Agent Montgomery has requested he be taken to a few of the crime scenes this afternoon after visiting with Dr. Richardson."

"No problem. The entire team has gone over the scenes with a fine-toothed comb. If we haven't found it, it's not going to be found," Mark said with the complete confidence of a professional.

"I'm not calling anyone's competency into question," Agent Montgomery told all three men. "This is standard procedure for me, as well those in my unit when we're called in on any case."

At the conclusion of the meeting, Jordan was the first out of his chair. "I'm going to start working on those call backs." He was referring to the steady stream of calls they received from citizens who thought they had information on the slayer.

It was the same every time. Whenever there was a high profile case with any media coverage, the department was inundated with calls from people with 'information.' Most of the time they were crackpot calls. They ranged from the nosy neighbor who *knew* something weird was going on with the guy in 2D to the ticked off lover trying to get even. Unfortunately, every lead had to be followed on the off chance it was valid.

"I'll catch up with you when we return," Mark told his partner. He turned to Lieutenant Hernandez before continuing. "We'll head over to Imani House and afterward we'll go to the crime scenes."

"Sure, Mark, that's fine. I'll leave you and Agent Montgomery to decide on the ones you'll visit."

When the two were alone, Mark sat back in his chair and reached down for his notes. Before he took them out, he glanced over at the agent and asked the question that had been on his mind for the last twenty minutes.

"When Jordan made the comment on the scientific journals, he wasn't trying to offend you. He made a comment he thought only I would hear. In fact he said it so low, I barely caught it, and I was sitting next to him."

"Well then, perhaps he should be more careful of what he says," Agent Montgomery answered in his scratchy voice.

"Well maybe he should. But like I said he didn't mean for you to hear him. How could you hear him? Do you read lips?" Mark asked half in jest.

"Yes I do read lips. Quite well."

When no other answer was forthcoming Mark, dropped the subject. However, he knew the agent hadn't been reading Jordan's lips. Jordan had been sitting next to him, and Mark's body had been blocking his partner's face from the man as he whispered his comment.

"Have you had a chance to go over any of the files Lieutenant Hernandez provided for you yesterday?" Mark changed the subject.

"Yes, I've gone over all of them. I read fast, and I retain a great deal of what I read."

"Right. Do you have an idea which ones you'd like to check out first?"

"We're going to Imani House to visit with Dr. Richardson, why don't we start with the site where her sister was found? Depending on how that one goes for me, we'll play it by ear."

"How that one goes for you?" Mark repeated the odd phrasing.

"What I mean is how long it takes to view the scene. Sometimes I can go over a scene easily, and sometimes not."

Mark glanced at his watch. "This is about the time Dr. Richardson is expecting us, so why don't we move out so she has enough time to sit down and talk."

Leaving the conference room, Mark led him through the open bay precinct, toward the area where he and Jordan's desks were. Noting Jordan was on the phone, Mark motioned to him they were leaving before he and Montgomery headed to the elevator.

As they were approaching the doors, they were closing. Reaching out his arm Mark kept them open until he and Agent Montgomery could move inside.

"Sorry, Detective, I saw you coming and tried to keep the doors from closing, but the button stuck," the lone occupant of the elevator said.

Glancing in the direction the voice came, Mark noticed the small man who was punching the defunct open door button on the lit panel. Looking him over, he noticed he wore the distinct hanging badge all government employees wore around his neck.

"These elevators are pretty old. They're long past due for an overhaul," Mark agreed, and turned his attention to the agent. Mark noticed Montgomery was observing the clerk, his head tilted to the side.

"The lieutenant has commented on the help Dr. Richardson has provided for the case. Does she come into the precinct very often?" Montgomery asked, returning his attention to Mark.

"Rarely, although, she and I communicate pretty often. In fact, I go to Imani House every Friday. She has an incredible workload. She goes in early and stays late most nights. She's been working even later on Fridays. That's the best time for me to get a chance to speak with her. When I'm there, it allows me an insider's look into the lives of the women who live there."

"Yes, I could see where it would."

As the elevator came to a stuttering halt, the two men exited as soon as the laboring doors opened without a backward glance.

As soon as the men left the elevator, the man left inside repeatedly stabbed the button to close the doors. The benign smile left his face, and in its place a look of distaste fell upon his small pinched features.

CHAPTER 23

"Dalia, do you have a list of the new volunteer counselors?" Maya called out through the open door as she sat behind her desk, eyes glued to the computer screen.

"Yes I do, Maya. I think the numbers are a little short of what it is you were expecting," Dalia answered. She walked into her office and leaned her rounded hip against the corner of Maya's desk. "I am printing off a copy for you as we speak."

"Where are we short exactly?"

"We could get by with one more counselor for the day sessions. And another one for nights and weekends would not hurt either. Otherwise, you will be working yourself to death, as you usually do."

"I'm fine, Dalia," she said, as she went back to entering figures into her computer, her mind on the monthly budget.

"You know, Maya, it has been nice to see you not work every day and spend more of your time in the pursuit of more pleasurable things," Dalia said with a sly grin. "As you are doing the budget, maybe you should see if we can see our way clear and hire another full-time counselor."

"Actually, that isn't such a bad idea, Dal. I've been thinking another full-time counselor would be nice to have. It would ease the workload, and I could devote the free time to organizing the fundraiser."

Mentioning the fundraiser reminded her she hadn't called Arlinda back. When she'd arrived at work, Arlinda had left her a message with a demand for her to call her ASAP. She'd been busy from the moment she had walked in and hadn't gotten around to calling her friend.

"Would you like for me to place an ad in search of an additional counselor?"

"Yes, Dal, we probably should. You know what we need. Just write up the ad and I'll proof it," she teased her assistant.

Although Dalia's English was accented, and she didn't always use the right euphemisms when she spoke, her written form was perfect, and Maya would often have her proof drafts.

"I will make sure I do," Dalia said, giving her a wink in return.

As Dalia turned to leave the office, she came face to face with Mark, making her take a small step back to avoid bumping into him. She glanced past him and caught sight of the man with him.

"Oh, hello there, Detective. I didn't hear you coming," she said with a smile, her hand going to her chest.

"Hi Dalia. I'm sorry, we didn't mean to sneak up on you."

"Maya, would you like for me to hold your calls?" Dalia asked as she allowed the two men to enter.

"Yes please, Dalia. Could you also start writing the ad for a new counselor?" she asked her departing assistant, and caught Dalia running an admiring glance over the man standing near Mark.

"Maya, this is Special Agent Nicolai Montgomery. Agent Montgomery this is Dr. Maya Richardson." Mark made the introduction as he came around to shake Maya's hand.

"Hello, Agent Montgomery—it's nice to meet you."

"It's nice to meet you, Dr. Richardson," the agent replied.

Not a jealous man by nature, Mark nevertheless didn't like the way the agent was holding on to Maya's hand. Very subtly he maneuvered himself closer, separating them as he guided her back to her chair.

"Please have a seat, gentlemen." When Maya waved a hand in offering for them to sit, Mark wasn't surprised when the agent opted for the chair, which allowed him the best view of the entire office.

"Thank you for taking the time to meet with me, Dr. Richardson. I realize how busy you are. Detective Halstan and I shouldn't have to monopolize much of your time."

"You're welcome, Agent Montgomery. It's not a problem; I've been working with the police for a while, and anything I can do to help find the person responsible for killing my sister is worth my time."

"I'm sorry for your loss."

"Thank you. Detective Halstan says your FBI unit assists in cases like this."

"Yes, ma'am. One of my unit's specialties is serial crime. We're sent to help in cases involving serial killers, rapists, bombers and arsonists."

Mark could tell Nicolai was comfortable with his topic, his usual stiff posture had relaxed as he spoke of his unit.

"I've been with the FBI for over ten years. During much of the time I was a profiler."

"Does your experience as a profiler help you with your work in your unit?" she asked.

"Tremendously. It's my job to understand the how's and why's of the crime and the criminal. A good profiler needs to be able to think and 'see' the way the offender does, in order to capture and prevent further atrocities. As a profiler, you must have the ability to go inside the psyche of the offender."

"I imagine psychology is a part of your training?" Maya hazarded a guess.

"In my unit all of my people are trained in psychology, as well as other areas. As a psychologist, I'm sure you understand the importance of understanding the psyche of the criminal."

"I definitely see the importance psychology plays in trying to capture the offender." Maya, too, had warmed to their topic.

"Yes, ma'am, it does. In profiling the killer, we know that they aren't all cut from the same cloth. They have a myriad of backgrounds and experiences that have brought them to where they are."

"Here at Imani House, the residents have also come from a variety of backgrounds and experiences. I've learned not to try and treat them all with a blanket approach to therapy. It never works. And it also can provide a hindrance to treatment," Maya agreed.

They continued to speak on the importance of psychology in their respective roles as therapist and agent. Mark was surprised at the similarities in their roles. He'd been observing Maya closely as she enthusiastically spoke with the agent, and although he felt a spark of jealousy over their instant rapport, he was proud as she spoke so eloquently on her area of expertise.

That was also one of the things that turned him on about Maya. She was so intelligent, and sometimes reminded him of a nerdy professor when she talked about psychology. A very sexy nerdy professor.

But in bed, the nutty professor turned sultry vixen. The sometimes shy, sometimes distracted, Dr. Richardson turned into a sexy woman who'd learned what she liked and had no problem letting him know what felt good to her. He adjusted his pants and tuned back into the conversation.

"It's been a pleasure meeting you, Agent Montgomery. Thank you for sharing your information with me, and if you have any questions please feel free to contact me, I'm usually here at Imani House."

"It's been a pleasure meeting you, Dr. Richardson. I look forward to working with you." Nicolai held on to her hand a fraction of time longer than necessary before releasing her. He headed toward the door and stood back for Mark to exit in front of him.

"I'll be out in a minute Montgomery--give me a second," Mark said.

As soon as the door closed, he pulled her into his arms and tilted her chin so he could look at her face. The dimple in her cheek let him know she knew what was coming.

"Yes?" she asked, and openly laughed in his face.

"Nothing. Just this." He claimed her lips.

He grabbed her bottom lip and pulled the full rim in his mouth, sucking hard, before releasing it. Recapturing both lips, he opened his mouth wide and thrust his tongue inside.

He kneaded the back of her head, and delved his hands inside the curly mass to dislodge the large pins. As he did so, pins flew in all directions and the springy curls fell, enveloping them both in their own private curtain.

He hitched her body up his and crushed her to his chest. As he was flipping her around to straddle him, a knock sounded on her door. Breaking apart, he rested his forehead against hers, a silent curse on his lips.

"Maya you have a call from one of our sponsor's on line two, are you able to take it?" Dalia asked from behind the closed door.

Maya straightened her clothes. "Give me one minute, Dalia," she told her assistant, clearing her throat.

As he helped her straighten her clothes, she reached her fingers up to wipe the mauve lipstick off the corner of his mouth.

He captured her fingers and pulled them into his mouth, giving them a slow, hot lick before reluctantly releasing them. "Stay away from him," he said and she laughed outright.

CHAPTER 24

Jaime's fingers flew across the keyboard, using the department's formidable search engine in the quest for more information.

Bingo, instant access.

Hmm. Let's see, let's see. It looked like she was in need of help. She was such an angel. From the first time Jaime had seen her, the fact that she was special was obvious. She could do no wrong. She was an absolute doll.

It was a darn shame she had to beg for help from the government to fund her programs when they threw money away on things that really didn't matter. All their help did was help perpetuate the cycle. The dumb asses.

Jaime continued to read the University Press article, thoughts racing. More than anyone else, Jaime knew how the government was always cracking down on something. But when they cracked down, they rarely did a damn thing to help those they were cracking the whip on.

Those upstanding congressmen saw them as the dregs of society. Selling drugs, selling their bodies, it didn't matter. They were all the same in their eyes. No good. When you had an angel like Dr. Richardson trying to help, she had to damn near beg to receive aid.

Jaime continued to scroll down. There. She needed volunteers. It seemed as though she was always in need of volunteers. Poor thing.

Jaime picked up the phone and placed the first call. It was time to call in a favor.

CHAPTER 25

"Imani House. This is Dalia, how may I be of help to you?"

"Hello, ma'am. My name is James Smith and I'm a new graduate student. Dr. Tomas instructed me to call you about an internship."

"This is wonderful. But I thought Dr. Tomas had already left for vacation," Dalia asked the student.

"Yes, ma'am, he left a few weeks ago. I work full time, and this is my first opportunity to give you a call. Will that be a problem?" the student asked.

"No not as long as you have your paperwork." Dalia rushed to assure him.

"Yes, ma'am, I do," he answered eagerly.

"Wonderful. Tell me about yourself. Are you a new graduate student? And what is it you are interested in within the counseling area?" Dalia reached for her pad and pencil.

"I recently transferred to UTSA. I'm interested in working with domestic abuse victims, and my counselor suggested I speak with Dr. Tomas." He mentioned the name of the internship liaison between the University and Imani House.

"Do you want to begin your internship in the fall then?"

"Oh no, ma'am, I'd like to start this summer. Dr. Tomas assured me you had openings for summer interns."

"We do. I thought you were interested in the fall. We are in great need of good counselors at any time. Do you have any experience in this area?" Dalia asked.

"I've done some counseling with my church and also some volunteer counseling with a crisis center in Austin."

"This is good. When are the times you are available?" she asked, jotting notes down as they spoke.

"I work full time, so it would have to be after five o'clock. Would that be okay?"

"Yes, that would work out well. We are currently in need of an evening and weekend counselor. Would you be able to work on the weekends for a few hours?" She asked, mentally crossing her fingers.

"Yes, I could come in as long as you needed me on the weekends."

"When would you be able to come in for an interview?" Dalia asked, elated at their turn of good luck. She gave the student the times that Maya had available to interview him.

"I've heard wonderful things about Dr. Richardson, and I would be grateful for the opportunity to work with her."

"Yes, she is a wonderful person. Would you like to come in today to visit with her? She has two visitors in with her now, but she may be able to see you this evening for a few moments," Dalia volunteered.

"No, I'm sorry, I can't come in today. Ma'am, the only day I *can't* come in, would be Fridays. I have a standing commitment elsewhere. But I could come in tomorrow any time Dr. Richardson has available."

"Dr. Richardson will not be in tomorrow. However, she will be in for a few hours on Sunday. Will that be okay?"

After they had confirmed the time, Dalia hung up the phone with a smile. She liked the sound of the young man, he sounded earnest and excited. Dalia decided to wait to place the ad for a counselor until Maya had a chance to visit with the student. With a smile, she turned back to her computer.

* * * *

"This is where we discovered the two victims' bodies; the female of course, was Dr. Richardson's foster sister Allison Hill," Mark began, as he and Nicolai walked to the sectioned off crime scene.

After they left Imani House they'd driven to the crime scene where Allison had been found, so the agent could survey it. Moving crime scene tape aside, Mark entered the area with Nicolai following close behind him. Turning around he was going to speak when he noticed the intense expression on the agent's face.

"Could you show me where the bodies were buried, Detective?"

"Sure follow me. They were buried close together but in separate shallow graves." Mark led him a few feet to the marked place where the victims had been found. "This is where they were found." He pointed to the two hollowed spots where the bodies had been excavated.

"From the report it says Allison was killed after the male victim. Is this the grave where her body was found?" he asked pointing down to the grave in question.

"Yes, we found the male in the first grave, and Allison in this one next to it."

"Detective Halstan if you don't mind, I would like to be left alone." His silver gaze asked Mark *not* to ask him why.

There was something strange about the agent. Whatever it was, Mark knew it was the reason for his unusual quiet demeanor, and the way he silently observed everything around him.

"No problem. While you're here, I'm going to head back down to the car and check in with Jordan to find out if there's anything new happening. Take your time. Whenever you're done, meet me back at the car."

"Thanks I would appreciate it," he said.

Nicolai waited until the detective was out of sight before turning back to the shallow, dug out graves.

Hunching down low, he allowed his arms to reach out and lightly brush back and forth over the nearest grave. As he was brushing his hands over the dirt mound he closed his eyes with his head bent low, and took deep measured breaths.

As his breathing became regulated, his chest rose and fell, taking on the appearance of one sleeping. With eyes closed, he began to go into a deep concentration, centering his focus inward on the far away pinpoint of light that was becoming larger, as though it were coming from some far away distance.

As the light became brighter and larger, muted sounds began to filter into his consciousness.

The sounds were at first full of static, as though he was trying to find a clear station on the dial of an old AM/FM radio. Nicolai's breathing slowed down even more as he concentrated on his goal, and his hand stilled on the first hollow grave. His concentration became pure and focused, until the first audible sounds filtered into his mind …

"I asked you to stop laughing at me; you should have stopped laughing. I wanted to go home but you wouldn't let me, and now you're the one who won't be going home," the soft high voice sounded out of breath.

There were harsh grunting sounds. "Lay off the donuts, big boy. You're definitely a lot heavier than you look. Okay now let's get to the fun part. Do you want to party? Yes, let's have a party. Isn't that what you asked me? 'Don't you wanna party, little girl?' Sure I want to party."

There were rustling sounds. "Now this won't hurt a bit. Just be quiet and it will be over before you know it. If you relax, you might like it." The soft voice took on a different cadence, uttering a low demented laugh before stopping. "There yes, just like that. See-- doesn't it feel good? Oh yes it feels really good." Coarse sounds of satisfaction were uttered for long moments before they came to an abrupt halt.

"Hey where did ya go? I think ah musta fell asleep for a minute. Shit ahm sorry. I don't usually do that. Did ya have to piss or something? Where the hell are you?" A different voice slurred, the words blending together.

"Oh damn it why didn't she keep her drunk ass knocked out? What do I do now? What do I do now? Damn!" The soft-pitched voice muttered the question to no one in particular.

"Hey who are you?" A rustling sound with a barely audible expletive indicated the newcomer's stumble. The closer the footsteps came, the more clearly the second feminine voice was.

"Oh hell no. I'm not into this freaky shit. No more threesomes for me thank ya very much. Been there, done that, got a freakin' badge. As a matter of fact this is it for me. No more johns. I'm cleaning up my act. I promised my sister," the woman mumbled.

"Unfortunately for you, sweetheart, it's too late. You've interrupted something that was none of your business and I cannot allow you to leave here."

"Oh my God. What are you doing?" Hasty footsteps were heard, and the muffled sounds of two shots from a silenced weapon. An agonized whooshing sound indicated the connection between bullet and flesh.

The sound of heartfelt tears filled the air. *"I'm so sorry, sister. I had to do it. You would have told and I couldn't let that happen. I've only begun. I have a lot more work to do. If you told then all of my fun would be over. I'm not ready for my fun to be over."* There was a brief pause.

"Oh what's this? I remember these necklaces. Someone out there shares your heart, huh? Isn't that sweet? Who has the other piece, little sister?" A snapping noise indicated the break of a chain. *"Well now. I don't think you'll miss this. Why don't I keep it for you--hmm? It's time to hide you both away now. It's getting late and I have an early day tomorrow."*

The once sad voice sounded happy and normal, virtually upbeat, as though the anger, sadness, and heart-wrenching tears had never transpired.

Humming lightly, the only other sound was of a shovel steadily digging up dirt, the sound becoming more and more distant until if faded away completely...

Nicolai's heart began to beat at a faster pace. His heart reached its normal speed, and he lifted his chin from where it rested on his chest, rotating his head from side to side. He opened his eyes, and as they came into focus, he clenched them closed tight and grabbed both sides of his head in anguish.

The predictable pain hit strong and true, not giving him a chance to prepare. He blindly reached inside his jacket pocket and located the small bottle of pills, only to have it fall from his limp hands.

Before he could feel around for them, the cap was opened, and the pills were shaken out into his palm.

* * * *

Mark had completed his phone calls and had made follow up calls before looking at the clock on the dashboard. Thinking the agent had been given enough time to do whatever it was he was doing, he'd headed back to the scene.

When he had first caught site of Agent Montgomery, he'd thought the man had fallen down. As he rushed over, he noticed he was kneeling with his head low on his chest, eyes closed. On closer inspection, he noticed his eyes were moving rapidly back and forth behind closed lids, as though he were sleeping.

Not sure what to do, Mark stood indecisively observing him, as Nicolai's eyes opened.

His eyes looked strange and out of focus, giving them an opaque appearance Mark had never seen on anyone. He watched as the agent clenched them shut and clutched his head.

When Mark saw him reach inside his jacket to pull out the small bottle, he went to his side in time to catch them. After opening the cap, Mark reached down to open the agent's palm and shook out several of the pills.

CHAPTER 26

"Thank you," Nicolai knew who'd given him the pills without opening his eyes.

"Hey, why don't you sit down for a minute? Look, let me give you a hand up. There's a tree over there you can rest against until you feel better." Mark reached down to take the silent man's arm and guided him the short distance to the tree, bearing much of his weight as he did so.

Once there he allowed the agent to slide down the tree and watched as he leaned his head back against the thick trunk with his eyes remaining closed.

Mark turned and walked a few paces away to try and the agent time to regain his composure. Several minutes later, he cleared his throat. Turning back Mark looked over the small distance at the relaxed figure.

"Thanks."

"I don't suppose you'll tell me what that was all about?" Mark asked as he looked down at the agent.

"If I tell you, I'll have to kill you," Nicolai replied with a half smile showing nothing but teeth, giving his face an even more predatory look than ever.

Although he'd said the oft-joked phrase with a grimace he was passing off as a smile, Mark noticed a strange gleam enter his eyes that made him wonder how much the man was joking. Shaking off the notion he walked over to extend his hand.

"Thank you, but I can manage this time," he declined. Mark shrugged his shoulders and walked away when Montgomery reached for his arm.

"Thank you. I sometimes suffer from migraine headaches, and when they hit me, I can't seem to function. But it passes. I have a prescription so I'm usually prepared for them. This one, well, it caught me by surprise," he offered by way of explanation.

Mark nodded his head. "No problem. Glad I was here to help." And the two went down the incline toward their vehicle. Once he was behind the driver's seat, Mark gave the agent his full attention. "Are you up to checking out another scene? You still look a little green around the gills."

"I'm fine. Let's go to the next scene Detective." Nicolai assured him.

"Okay, if you say so." Mark pulled away from the roadside and headed for the second crime scene designation.

As he drove, Mark glanced over at the silent agent, wondering what had happened to wipe him out.

He didn't think he looked ready to go over another scene or do much of anything else. It looked like he could use as a nice soft bed to lie down in.

* * * *

"Maya, I have good news," Dalia said as she ventured into her office.

"Yes and what is that?" Maya asked as she continued to peruse an open file lying on her desk. Pausing in her reading, she looked up at Dalia as she pushed the small wire frames closer to her eyes.

"When you were in your meeting this morning with the detectives, we received a phone call from a graduate student who would like to start an internship with us this summer. Not only is he willing, but would prefer to do his hours in the evening and weekends. Except for Fridays. He said Fridays would not work for him," Dalia told her with an excited look planted on her face.

"Oh that's great, Dalia. Does he have his paperwork from the intern office and from Dr. Tomas?"

"He says he has everything. Dr. Tomas signed his paperwork before he left for vacation and the student...." she looked down at the notebook in her hand before continuing. "James Smith. Yes his name is James Smith. James will be coming on Sunday if it is okay with you? He wanted to come in as soon as possible."

"Yes of course Sunday will be fine, preferably in the morning, Dalia. Arlinda and I are working on the fundraiser in the afternoon."

"I will call him back and set the time for Sunday then," Dalia answered as she left the office. As she was leaving, Maya's direct line rang. Motioning that she'd answer, Maya picked up the phone.

"Imani House this is Dr. Richardson," she answered as she glanced over the file in her hand.

"Hello there Dr. Richardson, this is Detective Halstan. How are you today, sweetheart?"

Maya set the file aside and spun around in her chair to face the open window. A smile automatically creased her face. "Hello back at you. I'm fine, busy but fine. How's it going for you?" she asked as she twirled the pencil she held between two fingers.

"Fine. It's calm around here for once. Agent Montgomery and I finished with the crime scenes a few hours ago. Right now I'm catching up on some paperwork."

"How did it go? At the crime scenes," she clarified before continuing. "Did he have a chance to look over the scene where Ally was found?" she asked with a slight hitch in her voice.

"Yeah, sweetheart, he did. He didn't say anything particularly about it. It was pretty odd what did happen, but I'll tell you about it when I see you."

"Okay," she took a deep breath and continued on a lighter note. "Are you going to be here for dinner? Jorge is making quesadilla and rice," she stretched out the last word, tempting him with Jorge's cooking.

In the weeks Mark had been coming on Fridays he'd often eaten dinner with her at the House.

She would tease in front of Jorge that his cooking was the real reason for Mark's Friday visits. A red flush would stain Jorge's dark cheeks before he would laughingly agree and say although he loved her, the poor detective would starve if he waited for the *bonita doctura* to cook for him.

The majority of the residents had grown used to Mark's presence around Imani House too. This was an added bonus. Most of the residents had been nervous and reluctant in the company of the police due to past encounters.

However they trusted and respected Mark as they too had taken to teasing Maya about him. She took it all in stride, happy they welcomed and trusted Mark, allowing her to feel comfortable incorporating a relationship with her life's work.

"I'm wrapping everything up as we speak," Mark said with relish, the sound of papers rattling, discernible through the telephone.

Maya laughed before turning back around in her chair to face her desk. "Okay I'll see you later then." She returned to her work with renewed energy.

* * * *

"Lieutenant, have you seen Jordan?" Mark asked as Lieutenant Hernandez walked into the open bay and went directly toward the coffee pot.

Unlike Mark, the lieutenant drank coffee around the clock, saying it took mass quantities to affect him.

"He's been in and out most of the afternoon following up on some leads. Did you need something, Detective?" The lieutenant asked as he took a bracing swallow of the thick brew.

"Nothing in particular, just wanted to run a few things by him."

"How'd it go with Agent Montgomery?"

"Fine. After he met with Dr. Richardson we went to the crime scenes he selected. Why? Didn't he talk to you about it?"

"Briefly. I wanted to hear your take," Lieutenant Hernandez said with a searching glance in Mark's direction.

As Mark was answering, Jordan walked into the squad room and headed toward his desk.

"How'd it go today with the *Special* Agent? Did he come up with anything spectacular we amateurs overlooked?" Jordan asked, as he took off his jacket and sat down behind his desk.

Mark didn't know what the agent had discovered, if anything. The incident by the crime scene had left him ill at ease. When they'd arrived at the second scene, the agent had looked in his direction and he'd understood he wanted to be left alone again.

Mark told the agent that when he was ready, he could meet him back at the car, unless he needed him nearby. Montgomery had assured him he'd be fine and immediately turned away to look at the hallowed gravesite.

He waited in the car for thirty minutes before he caught site of the agent walking with measured steps toward the car. He waited to see if he stumbled or gave any indication that he needed help. He didn't notice anything different about him other then the methodical way he made his way toward the car.

Once inside the car, the agent then leaned back in the seat and closed his eyes. His coloring was almost gray, and his features were etched harshly with tension, particularly around his eyes.

When he made no sound or comment, Mark started the engine and headed away from the scene. When they arrived outside of his hotel, Montgomery turned toward him.

"I know that you have questions regarding what happened at the crime scenes. I can't give you any answers. I'm sorry. And I would ask that what happened stay between us."

"I'm not sure what did happen, but whatever it was will stay between us," Mark had told the agent. Now, as he looked across at his partner he wasn't sure what to say so he opted for the safe route. "He went over the scenes and kept any findings to himself, if he had any. I'm sure if he 'finds' anything we'll be the first to know," Mark laughed.

"Yeah, we'll be the first to know." Jordan laughed back with a shake of his head. He glanced at his watch. "I was thinking about heading out early."

"Oh yeah? Got a hot date?" Mark asked, with a knowing look.

"As a matter of fact, I do. She's a friend of Maya's."

"Really? And who's that?" Mark asked with genuine interest.

"Do you remember the woman Maya was sitting with the night at Hooligans? What am I talking about? You were in such a rush to get out of there you don't remember anything else but getting your woman home, right?" Mark's sheepish grin was answer enough.

"Well her name is Arlinda Nyoni--Arlee to her friends. When the two of you abandoned us, I made my way over to the young lady's table and introduced myself. Me being me, I got a date for tonight out of the deal. It ended up being all right that you ditched me, man. I'm sure Miss Arlee will more than make up for it," Jordan finished with a wolfish expression.

"Sorry about that. But listen Jordan about Maya's friend. I'm not sure how close she is to Maya, but uh…" He didn't know how to ask his friend to be a gentleman with the woman. He and Jordan had partied together, and he knew how his best friend operated. How he himself had operated before meeting Maya.

"Don't worry. I won't do anything to her she doesn't want done." Jordan laughed. "You know me, Mark. I like to have fun, and by the way Arlee talked, it's all she wants too. She and Maya may be friends, but I have a feeling they're worlds apart when it comes to having fun." Jordan reached over to slap Mark on the back.

"Try to go easy on her, man," Mark said with a reluctant laugh.

CHAPTER 27

As Mark was raising his hand to knock on the door of Imani House, Dalia was opening it to leave.

"What are you still doing here? No study session tonight?" he asked, steadying her as she stumbled into his chest.

Since he'd begun his Friday evening visits, Dalia left early to meet with other students in one of her summer session classes. Usually when he arrived, Dalia had already left for the day.

"Hello, Mark. Yes I am meeting with a few classmates this evening. I stayed a bit later in the day to help Maya with some paperwork."

"Is Maya in her office?" Mark asked her.

"No, I do not think so. She is somewhere in the House. She may be in the kitchen with Jorge going over the proposed menu for the fundraiser."

"Thanks, Dalia, I'll find her," Mark said to her retreating back. Turning back around, he closed the door and went in search of Maya. He followed the sound of her soft laugh and the delicious aroma. Mark found his quary with her face buried in a covered dish.

She was in the process of peeling back the cloth covering, and eagerly picked up one of the sliced pieces in preparation of taking a bite of the cheesy wrapped tortilla. Walking quietly behind her, he motioned with his finger for Jorge to be quiet and reached out both arms to hug her from the back, his arms crossing in front of her.

Before she could react beyond a startled jump, he'd taken a large bite of the quesadilla from her hand, chewing noisily near her ear. After he'd swallowed, he sucked off the cheese that stuck to her fingers with a loud smack.

"Umm. Delicious," he drew out both words.

"Hey, no fair! Get your own." Laughing, she turned around in his loose embrace and hit him on his chest.

As soon as she turned around, he captured her lips with his and shared the taste of the stolen quesadilla with her. They were so caught up with one another they forgot they weren't alone until Jorge cleared his throat and laughed.

Breaking apart, Mark sheepishly looked over Maya's head to see the wide smile spread across Jorge's small face. Jorge, as well as the others at the house, had occasionally caught him kissing Maya whenever he thought the two of them were alone. In her office, the kitchen, the counseling rooms, or wherever he could try to sneak one in, he never cared where he was when he kissed her.

Mark let her go reluctantly and reached across to pull the cloth back again to take a deep breath himself.

"I will make a plate for the both of you and bring it to your office, Doctor Maya. Now get away from my food and out of my kitchen." The little man shooed Mark, as well as Maya, out of the way.

"You're an angel." Maya kissed him on the cheek before turning to leave the kitchen with Mark.

He gave Jorge a mock growl after Maya kissed him, making the man's dusky cheeks blush at the thought of Mark being jealous of him.

As soon as they reached her office, he closed the door and, leaning her against its solid frame, gave her a sound kiss of greeting to make up for his aborted attempt in the kitchen. He smoothly parted her soft mouth with his and slipped his tongue inside.

Placing his hand at the back of her head, he pulled off the large covered band that held her ponytail. Once loosened, he eagerly buried his hands in her hair and lightly massaged her scalp.

"Jorge will be bringing the food any minute," she mumbled around his kisses. The transfer of flavors from the sample of food he had eaten heightened her senses, and what had started out as a simple kiss, as usual, burned out of control within seconds.

She allowed her eyes to drift closed as she stood on tiptoe in an effort to get closer to him. When he kissed her, he fully engaged himself in the process. His hot mouth and aggressive tongue invaded hers by alternately slipping in and pulling out.

He widened his stance and pulled her tighter against his body. She felt her breasts flatten against his chest, her belly flush against his thick penis as he deepened their kiss.

When he released his hold on her mouth and grazed his lips and teeth down the side of her neck, she groaned. He worked his way down her chest, nuzzling the soft fabric of her blouse apart to gain access to her aching breasts.

He reached between their close fitting bodies with his hands, and unbuttoned her blouse to fully expose her, as he lifted the twin globes in his hands. As soon as he had full access, he alternated between each tight coral-colored nipple, leisurely pulling them into his mouth. She soon was so wet that she felt the moisture ease past the elastic of her panties on to the top of her thighs and down her legs.

"You always make me feel so good," she groaned, as he pulled and tugged on her nipples and she felt the familiar ache, which heralded the coming of an orgasm.

Mark had become in tune to her every sexual need. With little ceremony he grabbed the back of her head with one hand and her round tight butt with the other. He positioned her mound in perfect alignment with the hard seam of his jeans, as he ground his thick cock against her.

She threw her head back with a low moan. "Ohh. Yes … that's good. Right there. Right there, don't move." Maya moved against him feverishly, reveling in the feel of his thick erection riding against her clit. He kept his hand steady against her bottom as he alternately allowed her to ride him, while he in turn kept a tight control over her movements.

She let the sensations ride as the storm gathered inside of her body until she released on a long, keening moan. He lowered his head to hers, his mouth swallowing the sounds of her orgasm, as he too allowed his body to release.

After her body began to quiet down after its turbulent ride, Maya became aware of her surroundings and a slow burn of embarrassment heated her face as she lowered her forehead to his chest. A moment of silence passed between them as she kept her face down and averted from his.

"This is getting to be a habit," she groaned, refusing to make eye contact with him.

"Sweetheart," he laughed huskily. "What's wrong? There's nothing for you to feel bad about. Whatever we share, whenever we share it, is okay because we care for each other and we're in a committed relationship."

Maya was an intensely private person and her newly awakened sexuality was something she was still coming to terms with. More than the awakening of sexuality was the awakening of an intense sexual appetite she had become aware of.

"I know that. It's just…" she stopped when someone knocked on her door.

"Dr. Maya I have brought food for you and Detective Mark," Jorge said from outside the closed door.

"I know, baby. I will make it my solemn duty to make sure at every opportunity I give you as much aid as you need to get used to it," he finished her sentence with a sexy glint in his eye. He moved his eyebrows up and down in comic relief, forcing a reluctant laugh from her.

Mark placed a quick kiss on the top her head and adjusted her clothes before he moved her out of the way to open the door for Jorge.

He had to adjust his pants before he opened the door, but he knew nothing could disguise the large bulge in his pants. Or the small wet spot near his zipper. He did the best he could to hide both by standing behind the door as he accepted the tray from the smiling cook.

Maya walked over to her desk to finish straightening her clothes, as she turned back around she saw he was in the process of placing the food on the small round table. He picked up one of the steaming plates and brought it over to her desk with a smile.

She accepted the plate, and after placing it on her desk, rose on tiptoe to soft kiss the corner of his mouth. "Thank you," she said for both the plate of food and his earlier gift of love.

"You're welcome," he answered for both with a toothy male grin. After they'd finished eating, they settled into their Friday night routine of Maya working at her desk finishing up paperwork, while Mark pulled out his laptop to work.

In companionable silence they worked until she glanced up from her computer as she closed it down.

"All done?" he asked.

"Yep, all done," she said in satisfaction.

Friday nights most of the residents were up watching a movie, playing cards, or board games so the house was noisier than on other nights. As they made their way through the house they said goodnight to those who were still up and to the night guard before they left for the evening.

CHAPTER 28

"Mark, earlier you said something odd happened with Agent Montgomery. What did you mean by that?" Maya asked, as she emerged from her bathroom, her skin underneath her thick cotton robe still moist from the warm shower she'd taken.

She walked into the bedroom where Mark sat on the edge of her bed nude. It was a sight she'd gradually become used to. He was supremely confident in his sexuality and nudity and Maya agreed he had a right to be.

At her approach he stood up to grab her around the waist and pulled her down on the bed with him taking the brush she held in her hand and placing it on the pillow beside them.

As she laughed, he took the small towel in her hand away from her, and took over the job of drying her hair. He placed her in front of him as he did so. She leaned her slight body against his bared chest as he began to dry the excess water from her hair.

"You have such beautiful hair, Maya. It's so curly and soft." He worked his fingers through her curls.

"Umm. That feels good. Growing up, I was teased because of my hair," she said with closed eyes, enjoying the feel of his fingers on her cleaned scalp.

"Who would make fun of your hair? Your hair is beautiful as well as everything else about you." He picked up the soft bristled brush to run it over the soft corkscrew curls.

"How did it go with Agent Montgomery?" she asked him as he continued to work the brush through her hair. She waited for him to speak and enjoyed the feeling of his hands on her hair and scalp.

"Well...." he paused to gather his thoughts. "It was strange to be honest with you, just strange."

"Really? In what way?" She turned her head around to look up into his face.

He shared with her the day's events and played close attention to how he explained the agent kneeling next to the hollowed graves and the intense look on his face, along with the obvious debilitating headache the man had suffered from. After he'd finished telling her she sat quietly for a moment before she said anything.

"That's different. I'm not sure what to make of it either. Did you ask him?"

"I wasn't sure how *to* ask. And besides that, before I could, he told me not to ask."

"So what do you think it means? It sounds odd to me just hearing it, so it must have been really odd for you to see it."

"It was. There was something really strange about the whole thing." He agreed with her before he put it out of his mind and leaned down to kiss the side of her neck.

"Before I forget, Mom has invited us out to the house for a barbeque this weekend. Is that okay?" he asked as he continued to nibble her neck. He stopped his biting caresses when he received no answer from her. "Sweetheart, is that okay?" he repeated.

"This weekend? What day? I have a new intern to interview on Sunday morning, and I need to meet with him. I'm not sure I'll be able to make it," she said and Mark noticed how she studiously avoided his eyes.

"There's no set time. It's really informal; we can work around your schedule. Is that the only reason you don't want to go?"

"What do you mean?"

"Is there any other reason you don't want to go?" he asked again.

"It's not that I don't want to go. I don't know how I feel about it. Maybe I'm a little scared," she admitted with a small laugh.

"There's nothing to be afraid of. It's a first for me, and I'm not afraid."

As they'd been talking Maya had been deftly braiding her hair. She turned her body to fully look at him as she completed the long French braid.

He correctly interpreted her look and clarified. "I've never brought a woman home to meet my parents. Honestly I haven't," he said when she looked at him doubtfully. "My mom has always been interested in who I was dating, but there's never been anyone important enough to meet my family. Until now, Maya. And I'm asking you to come and meet my family, sweetheart. Will you?"

As she looked up into his handsome serious face, all fears and uncertainties temporarily fell away. He pulled her into his arms and allowed the two of them to fall back on the bed.

"Everything will be fine, you'll see. You're going to love my family and they are absolutely going to love you, baby," he reassured her. "Now let's take this granny robe off," he laughed at her favorite robe.

He deftly removed the thick cotton robe from Maya's shoulders and peeled it away from her body. He rolled her underneath his body and caught at her mouth, plunging his tongue deep, tasting her, taking her breath as his own.

As the kiss deepened, his hand closed around her breast squeezing and massaging the plump globe as he groaned deeply into her mouth, swallowing Maya's answering moan.

His hands wandered further down her body, as his mouth traveled south. When he got to her breasts, he opened wide, taking in as much as he could. "I love your breasts. Damn they taste good," he said, lifting his mouth from her nipple with a long pull to look down into her hot gaze.

He languidly licked her again, before he drew the turgid peak back into his mouth, giving it a pull she felt deep down all the way to her toes.

As he continued to suck on her, her frantic movements alerted him that the ache was growing out of control for her.

He'd become adept at gauging her degrees of arousal and knowing she was on the edge of reaching a climax with his tugging at her breast, he swiftly rolled over and landed her on his chest, sitting up so they were facing one another.

He took both sides of her face in his hand and placed tiny kisses all over until he came to rest back on her lips. Simply kissing her made his cock grow to enormous proportions as it nestled snugly between them, twitching toward her belly with a mind of its own.

He reluctantly released her mouth. Mark loved looking at her aroused flushed face, reddened lips, and heaving breasts. Seeing her in this state could make him cum on the spot. He flexed and lifted her small body up and slowly eased her back down to straddle him, guiding himself to her slick portal.

The head of his dick brushed against the dark curly thatch of hair as it slowly made its way deeper within the tight passage. Not wanting to hurt her, Mark inched deeper and deeper, until at last he was seated to the hilt. When he was completely merged within her, he let out a deep, agonizing groan of satisfaction to the accompany sound of her low hiss of relief.

"Yes, baby. Just like that," he moaned as the two of them held the position, neither one moving, enjoying the feel of their bodies united.

He adjusted her slightly. Cupping the mounds of her golden breasts, he began kneading them, her nipples swelling as the dusky color deepened, giving them a purplish hue.

"Do you have any idea how I feel about you?" he asked softly, his voice low and husky in the quiet of the room. "I want you to watch me, baby. No don't look away. I need you to see what I'm doing to you. What you do to me." His heated gaze refused to allow her to look away from the intimacy they were creating together.

"I'm going to kiss this one first." His hands cupped and held her left breast. "Nice and slow. And after that one has been satisfied, if you're a good girl, then I'll take care of the other one," he promised her.

"But I want you to participate in this. Do you think you can do that, baby?" While he'd been talking she had been rotating her hips against him. Wordlessly, she nodded her head in agreement.

"I need to hear you say it. Say you'll help me," he insisted, as he continued fingering her swollen nipples.

"Yes, yes I'll help you," she promised, her voice barely audible, her chest heaving in expectation of what his demands might be.

"Good baby. It's nothing too hard. I want you to hand me one of those big beautiful tits of yours while I take good care of it. Do that for me," he demanded huskily.

He knew her breasts were sensitive. She had once had an orgasm after heavy petting from him playing with her nipples. He watched with heavy lidded eyes as she hefted one of her breasts up to him, as though it were a sacrificial offering.

"Higher. Lift it higher and use both hands, baby. You need to use both hands," he instructed, and she did his bidding, lifting the heavy breast to his eager mouth.

He watched her as his lips opened and closed over the dusky areola. No sooner had his mouth closed around her plump nipple, than she arched her back in instant response and cried out his name.

"Oh, sweetheart, that's good, that's so damned good," he praised, as he roughly licked and lapped her nipple only to tug it back into his mouth.

As she held her breast to his devouring mouth, he grabbed both of her hips with his hands and ground their bodies together as he rode her. He lifted his mouth when he felt her try and hasten their speed. "Give me the other one. Now, while I fuck you nice and easy, give it to me," he demanded roughly.

She reacted to the authority in his tone and dropped the breast he'd been feasting on and offered him the other. He gave one last heated lick before he accepted the second globe from her hands.

As he worked on the next breast, he moved one of his hands from her hips to work its way between them, to finger her clitoris, as his other hand maintained its steadying position on her hip, forcing her to accept the restricting slow grind.

The light feathery touch of his fingers against her clit, and the strong pull of his mouth on her breasts, had her disobeying his edict to look at him and she closed her eyes.

He was so deep he thought he felt her womb, and knew he couldn't hold back, he was dangerously close to orgasm from watching her, not to mention the feeling of her tight hot sheath gripping him like a glove. "Are you ready, baby?" he asked in a tight, breathless whisper.

He had to ask her again, and finally, in a croaking whisper, she answered him. "Yes. I'm ready. Please, Mark, I'm ready," she pleaded.

"You beg so pretty, I think I'll let you come." Finding satisfaction at her desperate heartfelt answer, he opened his mouth on the hardened peak of her nipple and closed, biting down as he did so, and then he watched the contractions shudder through her small frame.

Wanting to increase the intensity of her climax and join her in her release, he gathered her slight body closer and ground his dick as deep as he could into her. He held on tightly to her hips as he stroked her. While his body was pounding into hers, his mouth held on to her breast suckling hungrily, his mouth a frenzy of need and wild desire.

She cried out as the orgasm hit. As it gained power in its intensity, her pussy frantically clamped down and he felt her body grip and clench him. She milked him until he reared his head back and allowed his seed to burst free and erupt over and over, gushing hotly into her, as he yelled her name out hoarsely.

* * * *

Maya clung desperately to his shoulders as the scorching river of semen splashed deeply across her womb, her orgasm so strong and prolonged that she felt weak, her pulse racing out of control and her head dizzy with the effects of the violent release.

When it was over, he rested his forehead against hers, his arms snaking around her waist to gather her close. Lifting a wet tendril of hair away from her forehead, he placed a gentle kiss on her sweaty brow.

She glanced up at him and shakily smiled before muttering, "I can't move. Please don't ask me to."

"I know, baby, neither can I," he agreed, breathing heavily.

Even as he said it, she felt a twitch deep within her body, where his cock still dwelled, and she looked at him with an incredulous stare of disbelief. With a laugh he tumbled her back on the bed.

"Sometimes 'he' doesn't know when to quit," he told her as he withdrew from her body and turned her outward to cuddle spoon fashion.

They lay together for a while, quietly holding on to one another, their combined breathing the only sound in the room until Mark raised a hand to caress the side of her face. "You know with you, Maya, I've experienced a few firsts."

"In what way?" she asked after placing her hands over his where they lay crossed at her midsection.

He rubbed his thumbs caressingly over hers as he answered. "Well for one you're the first person I've ever wanted to meet my family at the ripe old age of 34," he told her laughing at himself. "And Maya what we share sexually and mentally? The connection we have is new to me as well as it is to you. It's not something that happens often, in fact it's never happened for me."

He didn't feel as though he was expressing himself well enough and so he stopped talking. Burying his face in the back of her neck, he rubbed his face slowly back and forth along the length of it, his eyes closed as he tried to think of how to tell her how he felt.

She had recently gone on birth control and no sooner had it been safe to do, than Mark had happily stopped using condoms. As long as he had been sexually active, he had, without fail, used a condom, even if the woman he was involved with was using protection.

His father had long ago ingrained in him as well as his brothers, the need to protect themselves against pregnancy as well as sexually transmitted diseases.

From the first time he and Maya had made love, he resented having to use them, not wanting anything unnatural barring him from the natural feel of her. He wanted nothing to come between them and found ultimate satisfaction when he released himself into her womb.

What he'd also found himself thinking of was what it would be like if she were not on any contraception at all. It was a surprisingly tantalizing thought.

CHAPTER 29

"I feel the same way, Mark. I have to admit I'm glad you feel the same. It's hard for me to understand how that can be, but I'm glad it is."

"In what way?" he asked, as he paused nuzzling her neck.

When he stopped his caresses, she moved her head back and forth in a not so subtle reminder for him to continue his nuzzle. He smiled behind her, and continued.

"I suppose it's hard for me to understand how you've never been close to a woman as you say you have with me. I mean, you've dated a lot." When he remained quiet, she turned her body around to face him and caught the look crossing his face.

"Maya I haven't 'dated' *that* much." Now it was his turn to see the incredulous look cross *her* face.

Amending his statement he continued, "Even if I have, that doesn't mean what I'm saying isn't true. I think it's possible to go your entire life without meeting that one person you connect with on all levels. For whatever reason, God smiled on me and allowed us to meet, for which I will be eternally grateful."

When she smiled that small half smile she favored and placed her arms around his neck, Mark stifled his automatic groan of frustration. He placed his arms around her small body and hugged her tight.

From the beginning, he hadn't shied away from expressing his feelings toward her, yet she continued to hold some small piece of herself back from him.

He knew she cared about him, but he wasn't sure to what level, because she never told him. Her lack of expression in turn prevented him from telling her out right he loved her. Which he did.

Irrevocably. Completely. Overwhelmingly. Loved her.

He never knew he was capable of feeling the way he did for a woman, as he did with Maya. They hadn't been together for two months, yet he was couldn't imagine not being with her, not to have met her. His only wish was to have her express her feelings for him more openly.

A slight sigh emitted from his lips as he kissed the side of her neck before he moved his head back to get a better look at her face.

"I didn't mean to offend you, make light of your feelings, or to suggest I don't believe you. I do Mark, and that makes it special to me. That's all I meant."

He watched as she caught her lower lip with her top teeth and released it, only to pull it back in, repeating the process several times. He caught the slightly full lip with his mouth and gently sucked on it, running his tongue along the inseam.

After he'd released it he looked at the edge made reddened from his ministrations. "I can always tell when you feel uncertain about something or if you're thinking deeply about a subject."

"Oh really? And how is that?"

"You start to pull at your lip. It drives me insane when we're not in a place where I can kiss you, because it's really sexy."

"When I was growing up it would drive my foster mother insane also, but not in the same way as it does you," she admitted with a short laugh.

"That had to be the fastest trip in recorded history," he muttered with a sardonic lift to his lip. "Why did it drive the lovely Melissa insane?" He welcomed every bit of information he could get about Maya. However, it wasn't easy to listen to the cruel and senseless things her foster mother had subjected her to, and he usually forced himself not to cringe when Maya mentioned her name.

"I remember sitting at the kitchen table, and I would *feel* Melissa's glares. I knew better than to look at her, if I did, there was no telling what she'd say or do to me."

Although it was hard to hear Maya speak about the hateful woman who raised her, Mark forced himself to listen, soaking up everything he could to learn more about her.

"She made fun of everything about me. My hair, my body. When I first began to develop she accused me of trying to seduce her lover Danny."

"Jealous bitch," he couldn't refrain from mumbling under his breath in disgust of the woman.

"Melissa didn't like any of my mannerisms, that was one which particularly ticked her off. I wasn't even aware I was doing it until Danny made a comment about it, and Melissa lost it. She ranted and screamed at me for hours. Finally left me alone and all I remember after that is laying my head down on the beat up kitchen table and crying. I have no idea how long I lay like that when I felt Ally pat my back. I looked up and there she was standing in front of me in her favorite Garfield pajamas, tears falling down her little face."

"I found out years later where I inherited that particularly mannerism from," Maya said, returning the conversation to his original question. Although she was looking at him, he had the feeling that she wasn't really seeing him as she began to speak about her grandmother …

"…Maya, I so dearly wished I could have gotten to know you. Your mother and I sent letters to one another and she sent me pictures of my beautiful grandbaby but it wasn't the same. I honestly thought we'd be able to come back together as a family. I suppose I was just kidding myself. Or just being plain old scared and foolish." Elizabeth Rutherford pulled her lower lip into her mouth with her front teeth and stopped herself with a small laugh.

"Your grandfather constantly teased me for that little habit after all of these years. In one of the letters your mama sent me she told me that you and I share that little idiosyncrasy so I suppose it can't be all that bad if my grandbaby does it too.

"Maya I know that nothing can erase the past. There's nothing I can say or do to exonerate my role in not supporting your mother and father better. All I can say is I'm sorry and my life has been devoid of real happiness for a long time.

"My prayer is you have been safe. Had I known you were all alone in this world, there is nothing or no one who would have prevented me from bringing you home. If it meant you and I would have created our own home than so be it. I swear to you, Maya, I would not have left you alone. I've been alone for a long time and it's not a good feeling.

"I've left you everything, Maya. It's the least I can do. Mr. Callahan has been my private solicitor for many years and he knows how important this is for me and he assures me he will find you, darling.

"Along with all of my worldly goods I send you this videotape and all of the contents of this small package."

She held up a container filled with pictures and cards and directed the contents toward the camera.

"These are the correspondences your mother and I exchanged, along with the pictures Lizzy would send to me of you her and your father.

"I love you very much, darling, and please find it in your heart to forgive not only me but your grandfather as well. I love you, Maya…"

* * * *

"Maya you've had a lot of challenges thrown in your path from early in your life and yet you've persevered to become this incredible woman. I can't even imagine having had to do without family like you had to at an early age. I know you had Ally with you, but it's not the same as having loving parents to care for you. I don't want you to think I'm being judgmental, it seems as though life has thrown you as many curve balls as they have for some of the women at Imani House, yet you were able to maneuver around them. I think it shows a lot about your will and determination," he said as he listened to her speak of her deceased grandmother.

Silently acknowledging his words, Maya remained quiet and settled her body closer against his. She thought of the residents of Imani House, the majority women, and how she shared a similar background with many of them.

Mark had led a life of privilege and would never really be able to understand what it was like to be poor and have to struggle to make ends meet. He would never be able to fully understand what it was like for her, as a black woman, who'd grown up in a poverty stricken world, unloved and discarded, to rise above her circumstances and forge a better life for herself than those around her had.

"You're right when you say life has thrown me a lot of curves, more than some, and thankfully a lot less than others. But I'm not sure I can dismiss the will or lack of will of others who've had to deal with adversity as well. I think everyone deals with adversity as well as prosperity in their own unique way. I really believe there's a thin line separating all of us from one another. Accident, fate, or genetics--we all have a story that's brought us to become the person we are as an adult," she began.

"And life is full of coincidences. There's a thin line of coincidence and luck, affecting everything from our DNA to who parents us. Based on that, anyone at anytime, could have a different outcome in life."

"That's true. I guess I don't understand why two people can come from similar backgrounds, with the same opportunities presented to them, and one can end up overcoming their life obstacles and the other doesn't. I'm probably not saying it in a real politically correct kind of way, but I really don't understand."

"I don't think anyone else does. At the same time what's the definition of success? You don't always know what's going on inside the 'successful' person's head. You may think that person has it all together. But on the inside, they are a literal mess. Some people are better able to hide the mess than others," she finished with a half smile.

"What about you, baby? Are you 'hiding the mess'?"

"Oh yeah," she laughed. "Some of it still lingers. I've worked hard, and continue to work hard at cleaning up most of mine. It's a lifelong process for all of us. Some have a head start over others. You wanted to know how my race has affected me in life? How it's altered my perception?" she asked him.

"Yes. You never really bring up the issue. Jordan and I once talked about it, and I realized then, you've never shared with me that part of your life."

Maya could hear the question in his voice. "It's not that I don't want to share my life with you. Being black is who I am, Mark. I can't hide that from anyone, and neither would I want to. I'm proud of my heritage, the good and the bad. Being a black woman in a white male-dominated society has taught me one thing," she said with a humorless laugh.

"What's that?"

"Ultimately, it's up to me to determine my success. I grew up in a poverty stricken area. There were blacks, Hispanics, and whites in my community. I saw the good and bad in each one of them, no matter what race they were. When you're poor and disenfranchised, race will *always* take a back seat to survival. Like I said, we all have mess," she laughed somberly. "What about you? Do you have any mess to hide?"

Mark always considered himself blessed not to have had to deal with most of the crap he came across on a near daily basis in his duty of police officer. He'd come from a 'good' family, had never lacked for anything. He'd gone to private schools and gone to college and law school without worrying about how it was going to be financed.

He'd never had to work while in school like some of his classmates, and had interned at his dad's law firm as his first job. He supposed some would say he'd been born with the proverbial silver spoon in his mouth.

The disappointment of not joining the law firm had caused a separation between him and his dad and brothers. Only his mother understood his need and love to do police work. His grandfather had started his career as a beat cop and had worked his way up to chief of police.

Mark had admired his grandfather, and knew police work and investigation were in his blood. It was all he ever wanted to do.

"Mess, huh?" he mused aloud to her. "Yeah I guess I do. You know my dad and brothers are in practice together." At her nod, he absentmindedly rubbed his hands over her hair before answering.

"Even though I went to law school I never really saw myself in the role of criminal lawyer. I wanted to experience what it was like to actually get both my hands and mind engaged in solving the crime instead of defending the criminal. I respect what my brothers and father do. I don't think that I could separate myself in the same way they do. Needless to say, that didn't go over to well with my dad. He said it said a lot about my character. He thought I lacked follow through skills. I didn't have what it took to be a good criminal defense attorney like my brothers."

"You could if you had to. And besides it wasn't *your* chosen profession, it was your father's."

"You're right it was never my chosen field and I know had I wanted to, I could have gone into practice with my family. I didn't want to. I wanted to be a cop."

"Your father probably knew it as well. His desire for you to join them fueled his more hurtful words."

"Thank you, sweetheart." He pulled her pliant body closer and rested his chin against hers.

His father's disappointment paled in Mark's eyes to insignificant crap when he thought of the obstacles Maya had been forced to overcome to achieve her success. As he closed his eyes and listened to Maya drift into asleep, his mind raced, as the issue of racism and poverty took on new meaning for him.

CHAPTER 30

"How did it go with the family, *Sesute*?"

It was Sunday morning, and Dalia had come to Imani House with Maya. Maya had called her on Saturday morning to nervously ask her what she should wear to a family cookout.

"It went well, surprisingly well."

"Surprisingly?" she repeated questioningly.

"I wasn't sure what to expect, and it went a lot differently than I had imagined, pleasantly so," she answered her with a reminiscent smile.

She'd wakened to Mark's kisses and fully turned her body into his as he began to make love to her in the early morning hour. After they'd made love, he had reminded her of his mother's invitation, and asked her if she would come with him. Reading the hesitation in her eyes, he'd begged her to meet them with such a puppy dog expression that Maya nearly gave in on the spot.

After showering together, they dressed and went into the kitchen. As he made his way around her kitchen, pulling out pans, and taking food from the refrigerator, wearing nothing but an apron barely protecting his essentials from the flying grease from the pan of bacon, Maya couldn't deny her feelings for him.

She knew he was frustrated with her because she'd never expressed her feelings for him. She'd had to bite her tongue lately as they made love, not to shout out her feelings in the heat of the moment.

Never having told a man she loved him was only one of the reasons for keeping her feelings to herself. Another reason was fear. Fear that he wouldn't return the sentiment. Either way she would feel stupid and exposed and that was *not* a feeling she looked forward to experiencing.

However, as she sat at the table watching him deftly crack eggs in the small metal bowl, while maintaining a running commentary on the importance of putting *just* the right amount of sour cream in a Denver omelet, she knew it was an unfounded fear.

His love for her was obvious in his every interaction with her. Maya admitted to herself it was more than fear of meeting his family holding her back, it was the uncertainty of what it would *mean* to him to meet his family.

She came to a decision as she sat at her kitchen table, the sun shining brightly through her pretty yellow curtains. She allowed it all to fall off her like the dead weight it was. She decided instead, to take a chance and believe she was worthy of someone truly loving her. She walked quietly behind him, and placed her arms around his waist and hugged him tight.

"Hey what's that for?" He placed the pan on the back burner before turning around and hugging her in return.

"Nothing. I'm looking forward to meeting your family."

"Oh really? And what brought on the sudden change?"

"No sudden change. Maybe more like a dawning realization."

"Oh yeah? Of what?"

"That I love you, and I'm happy you want me to meet your family," she told with a catch in her voice.

Her declaration of love was met with stunned silence, before Mark let out a loud whoop. Before Maya knew what hit her, he had picked her up and her legs automatically circled his waist.

"Breakfast can wait!" he said, nearly running with his small burden hanging on and laughing at his reaction.

He closed the bedroom door with a resounding thud and gently tossed her on the bed. He landed lightly on top of her, kissing her frantically, as he demonstrated how important her words were to him, taking away any lingering doubts she may have had.

* * * *

"I had a wonderful time with his family, Dal. It was obvious, despite their obvious wealth, they're involved in each other's lives; they really cared about one another."

Maya knew there was a wistfulness in her voice, but she had always longed to be apart of a family like Mark's. One that loved each other, and wanted only the best for the other.

Dalia walked across the room from where she'd been listening to gather her small friend into her arms. "*Sesute*, I am so happy to see you have found love with this man. Of course his family would love you, why would they not? What is there not to love? You are very good for their son, and he is good for my little sister."

No sooner was she releasing Maya from the tight embrace then a knock sounded on Dalia's door. "Hello. Is anyone in there?"

"That may be our new grad student, I will go and see. If so, would you like for me to bring him in?" she asked.

"Please do, Dalia." Maya picked up the file folder that contained the information Dalia had already gathered on the graduate student and skimmed over his resume. Maya could hear Dalia greet the visitor as she walked into her office.

Soon after, Dalia appeared at her door with a young man standing beside her. His head came to Dalia's shoulders, which made him roughly four inches taller than Maya.

As Maya greeted her visitor, she briefly took in his appearance, from the wide smile crossing his small features to the tightly clasped hands he'd placed in front of his body. His large brown eyes were framed by lashes long enough to make any woman envious, and his lips were a natural light shade of pink.

Smiling in return, Maya shook the student's hand. "Hello I'm Dr. Richardson, it's nice to meet you Mr. Smith."

"It's wonderful to meet you Dr. Richardson, and please call me James."

"James it is then," she said with a small nod before continuing. "And please most of my interns, as well as the residents, call me Dr. Maya."

She motioned him to have a seat with a wave of her hand. Seating herself, she looked up from the file she'd picked up to begin their interview.

"James I'd like to start by allowing you to tell me anything about yourself you'd like, including your area of study and what interested you in the social services arena. I don't really conduct these interviews in any type of formal way so please feel free to speak as openly as you feel comfortable in doing," Maya began the interview as she sat back in her chair and reached for her pad and pen.

"Yes, ma'am. I started graduate school a few years ago and had to stop for personal as well as financial reasons, and I've only recently returned." As he began talking, a fleeting look of sadness crossed his face. "I'm currently employed by the police department in human relations. As a state employee not a police officer," he clarified.

"Do you enjoy the work you do with the police department, James?" Maya asked after a short pause.

"Very much so. The people I work with are wonderful, and one of my supervisor's was very supportive of my return to graduate school."

"James, how did you first hear about Imani House, and what interested you in doing your internship with us?"

"I only recently saw you on television speaking about Imani House and the work done here. After I learned more about your programs, I was really impressed. I've always been interested in working with this particular population, and only recently returned to school in order further my education in counseling."

"It's very rewarding for me to work with the men and women at Imani House who benefit from all of our programs, especially those in need of counseling services," Maya agreed. "When I looked over your resume I noted you have some experience in counseling at a teen emergency center, what was that like for you?"

Maya listened as the young man eloquently spoke on what it was like for him to be able to help youth who were experiencing some of the same types of problems he'd experienced as a young person.

Without being prompted he continued to tell Maya how he'd been mistreated as a child and adolescent. "Dr. Richardson, this was one of many reasons I decided to study psychology and counseling."

"Do you feel this is a good reason to go into the field?" Maya asked in a carefully unbiased tone.

James's eyes darted sharply in her direction. Maya caught the disquieting look cross his features before it was as quickly erased; making her wonder if she'd imagined it.

"I don't believe it would be if it were the only reason. However, it's not my only reason. Before I decided this was something I wanted to do as a career, I sought out counseling myself. A professor once advised, before anyone enters into social services, or any counseling profession, they should first receive therapy to help them resolve any issues they have. I took that advice to heart and it helped me a great deal. I have a real desire to help other people who've fallen by the wayside for one reason or another to get back on the right track." With a gentle smile he explained.

Maya smiled in return, and nodded her head in silent agreement with his previous professor. She'd known of a few young counselors and social workers who'd either broken down in front of the client or had been unpleasantly surprised at the feelings a client's issue had stirred within them.

They finished the interview, and Maya was satisfied James would make a nice addition to Imani House. She walked around her desk to extend her hand to him.

"Welcome aboard James, I think you'll enjoy your internship at Imani House just as much as we'll enjoy having you here with us. Dalia will help you to fill out the rest of your packet. Usually Dr. Tomas has helped the student with the University's end of the paperwork. I'm sure he was able to do so before he left for Guatemala for the summer?" she both stated and asked.

At his nod she continued, "Great. Make sure Dalia has all of your paperwork. Once it's filled out, she'll bring it in for me to sign. She'll also set up your schedule. Do you have any questions for me, James?"

At the door he turned toward her. "No Dr. Richardson, I don't have any questions for now. I want to thank you for accepting me as an intern here at Imani House." There was heartfelt gratitude in his voice.

"If you have any, my door is always open. And please feel free to call me Dr. Maya. We're not too formal at the House."

"Thank you, but I'd prefer to call you Dr. Richardson. I admire and respect you, and I wouldn't be comfortable calling you by your first name."

"Whatever you're more comfortable with is fine with me. There are a few residents who call me Dr. Richardson also." Maya had opened the door to her office, and waited for Dalia to hang the phone up before she spoke.

"Dalia, James is joining our intern staff. If you start his paperwork, the two of you can set his schedule."

With that, she left them and returned to her office. As she reopened the door to walk inside out of the corner of her eye she saw the new intern staring intently at her.

Maya raised her eyebrows in silent question, and a wide smile spread across his small face, before he turned his attention to Dalia. Smiling in return, Maya went inside her office and gently closed the door behind her.

CHAPTER 31

"Mark is on the second line. I'm leaving for the night, Maya. Do you need anything before I go?" Dalia called out to Maya through their open connecting door.

"No, I'm fine. Have a good night, Dal," she said, before turning her attention to Mark.

"Hi sweetheart, how did everything go? And are you back in town?" she asked the questions back-to-back and laughed. Mark had been in Austin for the last few days investigating a lead.

"Actually, I walked into my house only a few minutes ago. It seems like we haven't seen each other for a lot longer than the three days," he said with on a sigh. "I tried to call you at home first. What are you still doing at the House? Busy today?"

"Yes you could say that. We have a new resident today and her boyfriend slash pimp didn't take very well to her entering the program and decided to follow her here to 'convince' her to leave."

"What do you mean 'convince' her? Was there trouble? Are you okay? What about the other ladies?" he demanded, his voice more alert.

"It's okay, Mark. Walter and I were able to convince the guy to leave peacefully. Everything's fine. He didn't get farther than the front foyer," she sought to reassure him, mentioning one of the guards she employed for light security at Imani House.

"Damn it. Hold on for a minute," he said and within minutes she heard the slam of a door.

"Mark, what are you doing?" Maya asked in resignation. She knew the answer when the powerful sound of his Expedition engine roared to life moments later.

"You know what I'm doing. I'll be there within twenty minutes. Oh and by the way, my brother called, the one who wasn't at dinner last week. He and his wife have invited us over this weekend for dinner. They want to get the chance to meet the woman dad can't stop talking about."

"Oh really?" Maya asked trying to sound nonchalant with the apparent compliment.

"You made a great impression on dad. And of course Mom raved about how pretty and smart you are. Coming from mom that's no small compliment, because according to her I'm the most handsome and of course smartest man in the world," he boasted.

"Well, yes, of course you are," she answered, tongue -in-cheek, playing along.

"So if I'm the most handsome and smartest man, I would need an equally smart and beautiful woman. Until Saturday, mom didn't think such a woman existed until along came Dr. Maya Richardson on the scene proving her assumption wrong," he finished with mock seriousness.

Finally, Maya laughed out loud. As their laughter had subsided she heard a noise in Dalia's office, and assuming Dalia had returned she asked her to close her door on the way out. When Dalia didn't answer, Maya stood to investigate, when Mark sidetracked her.

"Have I told you today that I love you?"

Sitting back down in her chair, she looked at her watch before she answered. "Not in the last few minutes, no you haven't. I love you too." She automatically smiled.

After initially declaring her feelings to him, she found she enjoyed saying those three simple words. She felt complete in a way she couldn't define whenever they exchanged "I love yous."

She had never given much thought about the emotional connection of being in love with someone. But now she was in love, and the love was returned, she knew she would never be the same again, no matter what happened in the future.

She had gone from being emotionally bereft, to being connected to someone on all major levels; mentally, emotionally, spiritually, and physically, something she never had experienced.

"I love you too, baby. I should be there in short while. Will you be done for the night or do you need to finish up?"

"I'll be ready to leave by the time you get here."

A few more minutes of light-hearted talking between the two lovers occurred, some of which made Maya laugh and blush at the same time before they hung up, both eagerly anticipating seeing the other.

Maya heard another noise in Dalia's office and got up to investigate. She stopped short when she came across the new intern stooping to pick up a manila folder with its contents spread out on the floor.

"James, I didn't know you were in here. Can I help you with something?" She automatically bent to help him pick up the fallen documents.

"Hello Dr. Richardson. I came in to drop off my paperwork for school. I didn't think you were still here, I'm sorry if I scared you."

"No you didn't scare me. I wasn't expecting anyone in Dalia's office, especially at this time of night. How has your first week gone so far? We're scheduled for our one-on-one, tomorrow?" she asked in reference to the once a week mentor session she held with each of her interns.

"Yes, ma'am we do meet tomorrow. Everything has been fine. Dalia has introduced me to everyone, and I'm looking forward to working with the residents."

"That's good. We can speak more in-depth tomorrow during our session, unless you have anything pressing you would like to speak about now?"

"No I can wait until tomorrow," he assured her.

"Okay great. I'll go ahead and take your documents now, and have those ready for you tomorrow okay?" She reached out a hand, ready to accept the papers from him.

The intern looked at the papers in his hand. "You know what Dr. Richardson? I'm afraid I picked up the wrong documents on my way in today. I'll bring in the correct ones tomorrow during our session if that's okay. I can't believe I did that," he told her; his embarrassment turned his normally pale skin a deep shade of red.

"Don't worry about it; it happens to all of us. You can bring them to me tomorrow. I'm going to wait for Detective Halstan and then I'll be leaving."

"Detective Halstan is coming? Is everything okay Dr. Richardson?"

"Yes, everything's fine. He's coming by to pick me up to go home."

A quick look flashed across his features before just as quickly disappearing. "Yes, ma'am I'll see you tomorrow then." With that, he turned around and hurried out of the room. Maya looked at the closed door with a bemused expression, before she headed back to her office.

* * * *

Outside her office door, a very different expression had settled across the intern's face, which cast a baleful glow across his small set features. Holding the folder close, and lightly tapping the contents with a neatly manicured hand, he thought back on the conversation he'd overheard.

He'd thought Dr. Richardson had already left for the evening when he'd approached her door, because moments earlier he'd seen her assistant leave. James had learned that the outer door leading to

Dalia's office was left open on Wednesday's so the senior intern could come in and work. After the intern left for the night, she would make sure both offices were locked, and leave the key with the overnight security guard.

The senior intern had called, saying she wouldn't make it tonight and for the offices to be locked. James had taken the call, and had been on his way to inform the security officer, when he'd walked past the office and heard low talking.

Curious, he quietly opened the door and recognized Dr. Richardson's voice and stood silent, listening to her conversation.

Normally a private person, James knew what he was doing wasn't very ethical, but he found Dr. Richardson utterly fascinating and didn't walk away when he her beautiful laugh trickled out from behind her partially open door.

The mild look of pleasantness on James face passed, and he felt the heat of embarrassment light his cheeks. He could tell from her conversation who she was speaking with, and the intern was surprised at the filthy words that came out of the mild doctor's mouth. Well, perhaps he exaggerated a bit. But still, he couldn't imagine her having sex, much less allow that overgrown ape of a cop to do the things she'd just asked him to do to her. Spinning around to escape hearing any more of her low intimate suggestions for the detective, James had tripped and bumped the corner of Dalia's desk, and the folder of the week's programs had fallen out of his hand and onto the floor.

Cursing his own clumsiness, James had been in the process of picking up the fallen papers when Dr. Richardson's door had opened and he had looked up into her surprised face…

He glanced at his watch. He knew he needed to get out of Imani House as soon as possible, and so he hurried down the hallway, his stride stiff and formal.

CHAPTER 32

"What is going on out here?" Dalia's thunderous voice yelled, over the gathering of women who were protectively circling Imani House's latest resident. Dalia's glance took in the scene and summed up the problem in an instant.

Unfortunately, it wasn't the first time an incident of this nature had occurred. Rocco, an acquaintance of Ruby their new resident, had not taken kindly to one of his women leaving him for Imani House.

He'd originally attempted to get the woman the same day she'd arrived, but had been thwarted by Maya and Walter. This time Maya wasn't at the House, and he obviously thought he could bust in and take her.

When he came for her this time, he had been more resourceful. One of the residents had innocently opened the door after looking through the peephole and seeing the large bouquet of flowers held in his hand. She'd thought someone was getting a nice surprise, and had opened the door. Rocco slammed it completely opened, and the resident was pushed harshly against the wall.

Rocco then proceeded to yell at the top of his lungs for Ruby to 'bring her ass out and quit taking up his valuable time with all this unnecessary bullshit' and strutted through the house like a rooster in a hen house, yelling out Ruby's name.

Dalia wasted no time. Although she'd called out for the guard's assistance, she didn't wait for him to arrive on the scene before she boldly ran toward the circle of women in the middle of the large dining room.

Luckily, the guard was entering the room no sooner than his name was called, along with several of the counselors.

Rocco's normal bracing bravado began to visibly fade as his glance encompassed the angry party advancing on him. Mustering up his courage, he straightened his back and pushed away from the small crowd.

"Look here, I came here to see my woman, I ain't come to start no shit. Maybe she don't want to be here no more. Ruby you ready to come on back home? Ain't you? You know I love you, come on back home, baby." The pimp directed his cold stare at Ruby's small shivering frame.

The security guard was quickly advancing on the posturing man when Ruby Vallejo straightened her narrow shoulders. She stared at the pimp, fearful, yet defiant at the man she'd come to hate and fear.

She knew this sudden show of concern over whether or not she was happy was bullshit. He didn't give a damn about her; he only cared about how much money he'd lose if she didn't go back to selling her body for him.

"Rocco I'm just fine where I am. I ain't going back to being a ho for your ass no more. So you can go on somewhere with that shit." As she said the words to the man who'd controlled her life for years, she felt a curious detachment from her surroundings. She saw the barely discernible flush gather on his dusky cheeks, and the way his thick nostrils flared at her words.

She knew if she had good sense, she should be scared. Maybe she didn't have good sense, because she wasn't afraid. What she felt instead was a taste of freedom. She would stay right where she was, and she damn sure didn't have to let this asshole sell her body or her soul anymore.

"Okay buddy come with me, Ms. Ruby has made her intentions clear and I think it's time for you to go." Rowan roughly grabbed the man by the upper arm and pulled him away from the throng of women and counselors.

"You gone regret this you stupid bitch. Don't worry--your ass a be right back beggin' me to take you in when they find out what a worthless ho you really are. Man, get your damn hands off me," the pimp demanded, as Rowan easily held him within his grasp and shoved him toward the door.

As they left the room, Dalia engulfed the petite woman in her arms, as she reassured her everything was okay. "Although it looks as though you are able to take up for yourself very well Ms. Ruby," Dalia chuckled.

* * * *

"Do things like that happen often?" James asked one of the other counselors as they followed the others out of the room, going back to the session they'd been pulled out of.

"Not often, things are pretty calm around here. Sometimes a pimp will call them, but our residents rarely leave on their own, especially the first few weeks they're here, so it's hard for the pimp to get access to them," she explained.

"What does Dr. Richardson do when that happens?"

"Do? What do you mean?"

"Well does she call the police? Does she reprimand the resident?"

"She certainly doesn't punish the resident. And usually she'll call the police and they put a restraining order on the pimp."

"Oh yes of course of course," he hastily agreed. "That was really awful. I wonder how Ruby is? I think I'll go and check on her," James finished with a smile, changing the subject.

He left the intern and found Ruby. "Hi Ruby, I'm not sure if you remember me. I'm one of the new interns, and I wanted to let you know if you want to talk about anything, I'm here," he began in a sympathetic tone.

"Yes thank you, I remember meeting you. Dr. Maya has already assigned a counselor to me but thanks anyhow. I'm gonna meet with her now. She thought it be good for me to talk about how all what just happened made me feel," Ruby answered with a nervous laugh.

"How did it make you feel? Are you angry about what he did?"

"Angry? Why would I be angry?"

"Well… because here you are, trying to start a new life, and he struts in here like some peacock making you feel worthless and ashamed, telling you you're not good for anything besides being a whore. I mean those are some pretty awful things to say to someone don't you think? People like him shouldn't be able to roam around free. I'm happy for you. You got away from him."

"I guess I could be pissed off, usually I'm scared as shit of him. Today, I wasn't scared so much," her voice was filled with pride. "I saw him as a big, dumb-ass bully that I don't need in my life no more."

Patting her shoulder, James commented, "Good for you Ruby. Well I don't want you to be late for your session. Ruby is that Rocco's real name?" he asked as he turned back toward her.

"Naw, that fool thought Rocco sounded tougher than his real name."

At his raised eyebrows she laughingly told him what his name was. They both shared a laugh as James left her to go to her counseling session and he went to attend to his own duties.

CHAPTER 33

"How about it? Doesn't that sound like fun?" Mark asked Maya as he covered her small naked body with his, and planted kisses along her sensitive neck, making her squirm.

"Mark, I haven't skated since I was fifteen years old and that was only once. Besides, I've never roller bladed." Was her answer to his request they go skating at the park close to her house.

"Come on, baby, it'll be fun. It's a beautiful Saturday morning and we've got our weekend to ourselves for once in a long time and…"

"And you want to show off your prowess as the superior athlete and laugh at poor klutzy Maya. I don't think so," she picked up the end of the sentence, laughing as she rolled away from him on the bed.

"Come on, baby, you know I would never laugh at you. And there's no way in hell you're going to convince me you are in any way klutzy, not with the way you move." His eyes raked her body with a leer. He leaned on one elbow and stared at her. "I'll teach you how--it'll be fun. Come on, Maya."

She looked up into his handsome beguiling face, and couldn't resist responding to the little boy expression, on his very adult features. "I suppose you already have roller blades?" At his nod she continued, "Maybe I'll have to watch you anyway. I don't have any blades," she said with feigned dismay.

"Stay right here." Mark gave her a quick kiss, before jumping out of the bed. He jogged out of the bedroom to return with his gym bag in his hands.

In resignation she watched as he unzipped the bag and withdrew a pair of glitzy pink roller blades with a purple Nike symbol on the side. He approached the bed with a smile and sat down next to her.

"Well what do you think? You like?"

"You're too much! I didn't know Nike made roller blades. When did you get these? And how did you know my shoe size?" Maya accepted the blades from him and turned them over, reluctantly admiring the pretty roller blades.

"I bought them a few days ago and of course I know your shoe size. It's my duty to know everything I can about you, didn't you know that? Do you want to try them on?"

"Like this?" she asked pointing down to her naked body.

"Works for me."

"Funny. I think I can wait until I'm dressed. Do we have time for breakfast first?" she asked as her phone rang. She answered it around Mark's groping hands. "Hi Jordan, sure he's right here."

Mark frowned and accepted the phone. "What's up partner?" Maya moved over to give him room on the edge of the bed. As he listened to his partner, the frown increased on his face and he linked hands with her, rubbing his thumb along the inside of her palm.

"Did you send a couple of uniforms to bring her in?" he asked as rose from the bed. With a slight squeeze to her fingers he released her hand to go search for his clothes.

"Okay great. Hold off for a few minutes and I should be there in the next half hour. All right. Yeah--well it's okay, it goes with the job. I'll be there as soon as I can."

"You need to go in to the station? What happened?" Maya asked, when he handed her the phone.

"Hell is breaking loose as we speak." Mark walked into the bathroom, with Maya close on his heels.

"Jordan took a call from a woman who was traveling along I-10 early this morning around five. She was returning from a road trip with her son when she pulled over to the side of the road."

As he spoke, Mark turned on the shower. He reached for Maya as she leaned against the counter and loped his arms around her back. "We could talk and take a shower at the same time you know. Save time, not to mention water," he suggested with hopeful eyes.

"Such an ecologist. I don't think we have time for that sweetheart," she laughed.

"Yeah you're probably right," he agreed and gave her a quick kiss before stepping inside the shower.

He spoke over the sound of the robust spray. "The witness pulled up behind a small compact car, and as her kid is finished with his business another woman comes out of the bushes looking 'crazy' according to Jordan. Jordan said the traveler noticed the woman had blood on her clothes along with some other details. It prompted her to call the police because of the murders." As he finished speaking and stepped out of the shower, Maya handed him a large towel to dry off.

"Thanks, baby," he said taking the towel from her. "There's more but Jordan gave me the bare details. The techs called in a few minutes ago to report they'd discovered a fresh dug grave and a body. No positive ID on the body. A cruiser was sent to pick up the witness."

Maya had donned a robe and as they left the bedroom to head toward the kitchen. She was in the process of putting coffee on for him when he stopped her.

"None for me sweetheart. I'll grab some at the station." After strapping on his holster, he turned around to face her. "I'm not sure when we'll be done with this. We'll have to postpone the skating for a later date. I know that tears you up inside," he teased.

"I'll get over it," she tossed back with a smile as she walked with him to the front door.

"As soon as this is all over I'll be back home," he promised after giving her a lingering kiss good-bye, unaware he'd called Maya's house, home.

"Okay. Call my cell, because I may go into the House for a few hours to catch up on some work. Or you can come on back home, use this." She reached inside her pocket to withdraw a spare set of keys. With a smile she looked up into his face.

"I've been wanting to give you these for a while now, so here you go."

Mark looked down at her small hand offering him something that held more meaning than opening a door. Taking her hand, he held it within his, and kissed it before he accepted the keys.

"Thank you, Maya," he said simply. "I'll call as soon as I can."

After he reluctantly kissed her good-bye Maya closed the door behind him and went into her bedroom, wondering if it was the slayer who'd struck again.

* * * *

"What do we have, Jordan?" Mark headed to the coffeemaker as soon as he walked into the bay. After taking a bracing swallow, he grimaced before taking another healthy gulp. "Who makes this crap?" he asked, shouldering off his jacket and hanging it on the back of his chair.

"Hell who knows?" Jordan gathered his scribbled notes together. "I've been waiting for you before I went in to brief the lieutenant, so let's roll."

"Gentlemen let's get started on the briefing so you can go out and survey the crime scene. Jordan why don't you brief us on the call and then you guys can leave," Lieutenant Hernandez said as soon as they entered the office.

Jordan turned around, so he'd have eye contact with Mark and the lieutenant. "I came in early this morning and at around seven thirty I received a phone call from a Veronica Wells. She and her son were driving home late, and she pulled over so he could use the bathroom. It was the early hours of the morning, still dark out, so Wells left her headlights on. As her son was finishing, a woman came stumbling out of the brush, and according to Ms. Wells it looked as though she'd just gotten out of a catfight. Wells grabbed her son and rushed back to her vehicle. After she was inside, Ms. Wells tried to get the license plate number off the car but was able to only remember the first three digits. She's willing to come in for further questioning if we need her," Jordan finished.

"It looks like we'll need her. Mark why don't you and Special Agent Montgomery go out and survey the scene and find out if it's our Slayer. Jordan, instead of sending out a cruiser, why don't you go out and talk to the woman personally," Lieutenant Hernandez instructed as they filed out of his office.

As the lieutenant watched them leave, a pensive look settled on his face.

CHAPTER 34

"Well, *Sesute*, it seems as though you have received another bouquet of flowers." Dalia entered the kitchen where Maya was sampling one of Jorge's baked wares.

She was taking a bite of the sugary confection, when Dalia walked in with the simple bouquet in her hands. She placed the remains of the desert on the counter, and dusted her fingertips against the side of her dress. "Is there a card?"

"Yes there is, I have left it in there for you to take out and read yourself. What is the matter?" Dalia was clearly surprised at the cautiousness with which Maya approached the flowers.

Placing the bouquet down, Maya lifted the card. After she'd read it, a puzzled look settled across her face.

"What is it, *Sesute*?" Dalia demanded, and without another word took the plain white card and read it out loud, "*You will not be bothered by that cretin again beautiful lady.*' No signature. What does this mean, Maya? Who is this from?"

"Dalia who delivered the flowers?"

"The new intern brought them into the office. I did not ask him who delivered them. Do you wish for me to go and find him and ask?"

"I'll ask him myself. Where is he?" Maya didn't wait for an answer. She searched for the intern and found him in the staff lounge reading from one of the psychology periodicals on the table.

At her approach, James glanced up in surprise before a pleasant smile crossed his face. "Well hello Dr. Richardson! I didn't know you were here." He immediately rose.

"Please sit down. James, Dalia brought me a bouquet of flowers you accepted delivery for. Could you tell me who the company was that delivered the flowers?"

"No, ma'am, I didn't notice anything. The deliveryman didn't have on a uniform or anything, and I didn't get a look at his truck, so I'm not sure which florist company he was with. I'm sorry. They sure looked lovely. Don't you like them?" His wistful expression was close to reproachful.

"Oh yes of course. They're very beautiful. I wanted to thank whoever sent them to me, but the note was unsigned," she told him diplomatically. "Thank you, James. And by the way, you've been doing a wonderful job, how's everything going for you? I believe we're scheduled to have our one-on- one this Tuesday?"

"Yes we're scheduled for this Tuesday. And everything is wonderful. The residents and the staff are simply divine. It's already turning out to be just what I expected. Everyone is so helpful, particularly you Dr. Richardson." His eyes lit as he complimented her.

"Anytime you need anything, you know where to find me, James. I'm going back to my office. As I said, if you need anything, James, please don't hesitate to ask."

"Of course, thank you so much, Dr. Richardson."

* * * *

Mark and Nicolai had barely arrived at the crime scene, when Alicia Somers, along with her cameraman came barreling in their direction. "Oh hell, this is just what I need now."

Nicolai caught at the odd nuance in Mark's voice, as the determined reporter walked to the taped off barrier, boldly lifting it to duck her head underneath. He walked away from Mark and the approaching reporter to observe from a distance.

"What the hell do you think you're doing Alicia? Get back or I'll have your ass arrested for interfering in a police investigation."

Ducking back under the tape, the woman looked at him with beguiling eyes. "Come on, Mark, tell me what's going on. Is it another slayer victim?" She asked with a near gleeful voice.

"What the hell is wrong with you? And how did you find out about this so soon?"

"I received an anonymous tip from a passerby that the police were congregating here. It's a free country you know, Mark. I have a right to be here if I want to. Can't you tell me anything?" She pleaded.

"Look, I don't know anything myself so there's nothing I can tell you. Except stay out of the way or I'll have you and your cameraman behind bars." He told her and stalked away.

"Old friend?" Nicolai asked in his scratchy voice as soon as he caught up with him.

"Something like that," Mark answered. Although there was no way the agent could have heard his exchange with Alicia, he must have picked up on their mutual animosity from his body language. "Let's go." They walked toward the chief who stood next to the excavated grave.

"Have you had a chance to look it over yet, Davis?" Mark asked, after introducing Agent Montgomery.

"Briefly. I wanted to wait for you before I continued. Has the same MO as our gal's others with the exception of one thing." All three men kneeled down to examine the body. "The victim's car wasn't at the scene."

They went over the entry and exit bullet wounds before carefully turning the naked body over. The evidence was obvious that the victim had been sodomized.

Carefully, they turned the lifeless body, face up. Mark noticed although Montgomery had donned the surgical gloves, he'd refrained from touching the body. As they stood, he made eye contact with the agent before turning to the tech.

"Davis I have a few questions I'd like to ask the officers who discovered the scene, could you go with me?" Mark turned in the opposite direction of the dug out grave, and the victim that lay near it, leading the techs away and giving the agent time to be alone.

As he spoke with the technician and the other uniform officers, Mark told them to finish the scene and walked back toward his vehicle. He was surprised to see Montgomery open the passenger side minutes later. "That was quick. So?"

"So what?"

"Did you learn anything?" Mark barely bit back his annoyance with the agent's non-answers.

"Do you mean anything more than what we observed together?"

When he only looked at him, saying nothing, Nicolai relented, "I thank you for whatever it was you thought you were doing to help me. But I could not, *observe* the scene, as I normally would, with others around. I usually do this alone. But I do thank you for your intent, Detective." Mark swore he heard silent laughter in the austere agent's voice, but as he looked at him, his expression was as bland as usual.

"Okay. Whatever the hell that means. Do you want to come back when the scene is less populated with cops?" As they were leaving the scene, Mark noticed Alicia Somers had finally packed up her camera and left, no doubt frustrated with his refusal to give her any information.

After a few moments of silence Nicolai turned in his seat to face Mark. "Detective Halstan, I know you're curious about what I do and I appreciate your silence on what must seem to you to be extremely odd behavior. I would also like to request you do not notify anyone that I'm observing the scenes alone. It would make my job easier all around if no one knew of this. Including your partner as well as the lieutenant."

Mark agreed to keep silent on the matter although he didn't understand the request or the reasons behind it.

* * * *

"What d'ya find out, partner?" Jordan asked Mark as soon as he and Agent Montgomery entered the squad room.

"Same M.O. We'll know for sure after we get the forensic report. Did you get to interview the witness?" Mark asked as he took a seat at his desk. Looking up he noticed Montgomery leaning against LeDoux's desk. "LeDoux's out for the day, feel free." He motioned for him to use his chair.

"I'm fine thank you, Detective," the agent said quietly and in Mark's opinion predictably.

"Ms. Wells stated that at around 3 a.m. she pulled over to let her son get out to pee after he'd woken up. Right after the kid finishes up with his business, Ms. Wells is putting him back in the car when a woman comes 'falling' out of the bushes," Jordan included Montgomery in his brief.

"The woman's clothes are ripped and it appeared as though she had blood smeared on her face but Ms. Wells wasn't too sure about that. However, what drew her attention more than anything else, were the clothes she was holding bundled in her hands. She says she definitely saw blood on them. Her headlights picked it up pretty clearly. Wells was afraid because the woman looked at her, and she said the look in her eyes was friggin' nuts. She ran back to her vehicle with her son and locked her door before starting her engine. The woman got into her vehicle also and took off in a hurry."

"Damn. Did she get a good description of the woman?" Mark asked in sudden excitement.

"Unfortunately the description was pretty generic. Slightly taller than average, estimated her height to be around five 8 or 9. Dark brown shoulder length hair. Dark colored eyes. She couldn't get a clear description of her features despite her headlights. That was it."

"The height is consistent with what we already know from forensics' projection of the bullets, and the size of the foot impressions they've gathered," Mark interjected.

"The hair too. We've already deduced our slayer is more than likely wearing a wig. The fibers we've found in the victims abandoned cars indicate that. She said the woman appeared to have dark eyes but she couldn't say for sure what color. What she did see, was a small blue compact and she got the first three digits which helps us identify the county."

"Great. What did the lieutenant have to say?"

"He barely waited until I'd made it in, before he hit me with a shit load of questions," Jordan laughed.

"He's anxious to break this case. He's still catching hell from the acting chief. This is one the best leads we've gotten so far," Mark said.

"You're right about that. He was anxious to hear what Ms. Wells had to say, and if there was a possibility of her giving a good description or not." Jordan said. "Besides what Dr. Richardson has helped us with, we haven't got a damn thing yet to tell us who our perp is. That reminds me. You got a call from Maya. She said she tried your cell but got your voice mail instead. Sorry I forgot," Jordan apologized.

"That's okay. The battery ran out on my cell, and I haven't charged it yet. How long ago did she call?"

"Ten minutes before you walked in. She sounded kind of shook up."

Without another word Mark picked up the phone to call her as Nicolai excused himself, and headed toward the lieutenant's office.

"Imani House may I help you?" Maya's voice was subdued as she answered the phone.

"Hi sweetheart, I'm sorry you couldn't reach me. Is everything okay?" The tone of her voice made Mark's heart start to beat faster with worry.

"Hi, Mark. I'm not sure. You didn't send me any flowers by any chance?"

"No I didn't. Why? Did you get flowers again? Who sent them?" Jealousy sprang quickly, and Mark had to force it away.

"Yes I received them this morning. I didn't think you'd sent them to me, and I'm not sure who did. There was a card, but it wasn't signed."

"What did the card say?"

"That I wouldn't be bothered by that cretin again. That was pretty much it."

"Who's guarding the House today, Rowan or Walter?"

"Neither one. It's Miguel today," she told him mentioning the third guard who worked weekends and overnights.

"I'm on my way. I'll be there as soon as I can, baby. And don't let anyone else touch those flowers okay?" He asked as he picked up his jacket and threw it over his shoulder.

"I won't. They're in my office."

After Mark hung up, he turned to Jordan. "I'm going to go and take care of Maya. I'll be back as soon as I can."

"What's going on?"

"Maya received an anonymous gift again," he told his partner and quickly left the squad room.

"Where's Mark on his way to?" Lieutenant Hernandez asked as he and Nicolai were walking out of his office.

"He got a call from Maya and he's on his way to Imani House. Said he'd be back as soon as he takes care of the problem," Jordan informed him as he went back to reviewing his notes from the earlier interview.

"Problem? What type of problem is Dr. Richardson having?" The Lieutenant asked with a sudden worried frown.

"I didn't hear the details but I think she got an unwanted package. Mark's on his way to Imani House to find out what's going on."

"What type of package was it?"

"I'm not sure. I try not to listen too carefully when he and Maya are on the phone just in case it's contagious." Jordan laughed.

"What's contagious?" Nicolai asked in curiosity.

"That *love* bug they caught," Jordan said with a laugh, and Nicolai gave the barest hint of a smile in return.

"Dr. Richardson and Mark?" Lieutenant Hernandez voice had risen in his surprise.

"I thought you knew, boss."

"I guess I didn't know it was very serious. Well good for them. Good for them. Why don't we take a look at what we have so far? No use in being here all day. Agent Montgomery has briefed me on the findings at the sight so why don't you brief the agent on your findings." Lieutenant Hernandez instructed.

Before he spoke, Jordan looked in Agent Montgomery's direction, and caught the FBI agent eerily observing Lieutenant Hernandez. His head was cocked to the side, as though he were in deep concentration.

When he noticed Jordan's look, Montgomery turned in his direction. The agent's gray eyes were opaque, and looked out of focus for a split second before they returned to normal, and Jordan felt the hair on the back of his neck rise before he forced his attention back to his notes.

CHAPTER 35

Mark approached the small parking area at Imani House, and barely missed hitting the small car barreling out of the lot. He honked his horn, and quickly maneuvered out of the way. If he hit the car with his oversized SUV, it wouldn't be a pretty sight. As he parked, the incident swiftly left his mind as he ran up the stairs and entered the House. He was met at the door by the security guard Miguel.

"Hello Detective good to see you again."

Mark swallowed the automatic grimace as the large man pumped his hand vigorously in greeting. The guard was massive, and had aspirations of joining the police force. He'd asked Maya if she would put the good word in with Mark on his behalf.

"Hi Miguel good to see you. How's everything going around here? Where's Dr. Maya?" Mark asked, as the guard released his hand.

"She's in her office sir, waiting for you. I decided to hang out close to the door. Too many odd things have been happening lately, and I want to make sure everyone is safe."

"Thanks Miguel, keep up the good work. I'll go and find her. By the way, I checked on the status of your application and you should be hearing some good news soon."

"Thanks sir, that's great. Thanks a lot for your help." The guard grabbed Mark's hand again, and nearly squeezed his fingers off in his exuberance.

"Miguel you didn't need my good word. Your application was sound and you'll make a great addition to the force." He clapped the big man on the back with his good hand, and unobtrusively checked the other for damage, as he went in search of Maya.

"Maya are you in here?" He never walked into her office without knocking first, because she often held her counseling session with either staff or residents inside.

"Come in, Mark, I'm here."

He opened the door and walked inside. His eye zeroed in on the large bouquet of mixed flowers perched on a side table. He walked directly over to the arrangement to get a closer look. Maya came to stand beside him as he surveyed the flowers.

Turning away from the flowers, he leaned down to kiss her lightly on the lips. "Everything okay? You sounded a little 'off' on the phone."

"I don't like getting anonymous flowers and this is the second one I've received in the last two months," she admitted with a worried look as she pulled at her lower lip with her top teeth.

Whenever she did that, Mark knew she was upset or worried and it didn't sit well with him. "Don't stress, honey, it's probably nothing to worry about."

He reached inside his jacket and pulled out a pair of surgical gloves before he picked up the card nestled between the flowers. After he'd read the card he returned it to its position and carefully pulled out a plastic bag from his pocket, and covered the entire bouquet within it.

"Maya, I want to take these in to have them dusted for fingerprints if that's okay with you."

"Of course it's fine with me, Mark. What are you thinking?" She asked as they both walked to her desk.

When she would have sat down, he lifted her, and sat her down in his lap. She laughed out loud, and he hoped it helped relieve her tension.

"Nothing particularly. I want to see if we can pick up any prints. I noticed the card was a generic one--it didn't advertise the name of the florist. Did you catch the name?" Mark asked, as he lightly caressed the tops of her thighs through her dress.

"No, I didn't accept delivery on the flowers."

"Do you know who did?"

"One of the interns. He said the delivery man didn't have a uniform on, and he didn't look to see if they had a company vehicle when he accepted the delivery."

"That's too bad. Maybe I can talk to him and see if he could give me a description of the delivery person. Where's the intern now?"

Maya glanced at the grandfather clock in the corner of the room. "He normally stays late on the weekends, so he should either be in the lounge, or with one of the residents. Do you want to go and talk to him now?"

"I guess I'd better. Then I'm going to take these back to the precinct." Mark pointed to the flowers. "I'll wrap things up at work, and come back by to pick you up as soon as I can, and we can go home. Before I go, I need to talk to the intern."

The two walked throughout the house but couldn't find James, and finally as they entered the kitchen, Jorge solved the mystery of where the intern had gone.

"You are looking for, James? He came into the kitchen when Miss Dalia and I were talking about the flowers. Miss Dalia said she was leaving to study with her group, and James asked her if it were okay if he left also, because he had a test to study for. Miss Dalia gave him permission to do so."

"When he returns, I need to speak with him." Mark glanced at his watch before he continued, "I'd better go. I should be back in no time." With that he kissed her, and said good-bye to Jorge.

"Okay. I'm sure I'll be finished for the night by the time you return."

As Mark was leaving, he nodded his head and smiled in passing to a resident who'd walked into the kitchen before he picked up the bouquet and left.

"Jorge I'm going back to my office to finish paperwork so I can leave for the night when Mark returns," she told the small chef and turning her attention to the other occupant of the room offered her a smile.

"Ruby how has it gone for you this week? Are you settling in okay? No more problems?" She asked in reference to Ruby's ex-pimp's visit.

"Dr. Maya, everyone has been wonderful to me thank you. I am so glad to be here. Thank you for this opportunity. I won't let you down," she promised in a rush.

Maya laid her hand on the woman's arm and lightly pat it, reassuring her, "we're happy you're here with us Ruby. Take advantage of the program and never feel hesitant to approach me about anything. My door is always open."

"Thank you, Dr. Maya. I will."

After Maya left the kitchen, Ruby had a thoughtful look on her face as she turned to Jorge who was busy stirring the contents in his trademark, black kettle. She'd felt an instant kinship with the small man from the moment they'd met. She had the feeling his personal tale was darker than her own.

"Jorge I wasn't meaning to eavesdrop on their conversation, but did the detective say he wanted a description of the delivery man?"

Jorge turned and picked up a nearby towel and wiped the light perspiration from his eyebrow before answering. "Yes I think so. Why?"

"Because early this morning I was sittin' on the porch in the corner swing and I saw James walk into the House with a pretty bunch of flowers in his hand. Are those the same flowers they're talking about?"

"I'm not sure. Maybe you should tell Dr. Maya what you saw Ruby."

"Do you think I should?'

"Yes Ruby. I think you should. It's probably a misunderstanding or something, but still…" Jorge frowned in concentration.

"Okay I'll tell her Jorge, thanks," she promised.

On her way toward Maya's office, Ruby rethought the situation and decided she must have been mistaken about the flowers, and if she weren't, they probably weren't the same ones Dr. Maya had delivered to her.

She didn't want to stir any trouble by insinuating one of Dr. Maya's people was lying to her. No, she needed to mind her own damn business and try and get her life together.

As she bypassed Maya's office, Ruby was unaware of the grave mistake she'd made by minding her own damn business.

CHAPTER 36

"Come in, the door's open."

James walked into the room, unsure what to expect. He rubbed his hands together in anticipation. It was always exciting to see what treat was in store for him.

"Come on slowpoke, you know I've been waiting to hear all the details." He was chastened by a very high, very soft, voice.

He walked in and saw Jaime's reflection in the mirror, and long brown silky strands of hair were slowly brushed out. Jaime noticed his admiring look, and smiled seductively at him in the mirror. That was all it took for him to nearly cum on the spot, he was so excited by the heated look.

He sat down on the edge of the bed and quickly stood back up, when he was 'tksed' at. He knew Jaime didn't like it when he would sit on the bed in the clothes he'd worn all day. He removed all of his clothes, and self-consciously sat back on the bed. He looked into the mirror to see doe, brown eyes, heavy with mascara, glaring at him, waiting for his report.

"She received her gift."

"And?" The strident voice demanded an elaboration.

"She wasn't sure how to take it I don't think," he answered, afraid of the look in Jaime's eyes.

"What do you mean she didn't know how to take it?"

"I … I … mean at first she umm, didn't know who it was from, and … and … I think it unnerved her a little," he finally spit out the answer.

He wasn't sure how to tell the truth, wasn't sure how it would be taken. Jaime was so unpredictable. That was one of the reasons he was couldn't walk away, no matter how odd their relationship.

"But in the end?"

"She loved them," he lied. He thought of the consequences if he got caught lying, and amended his statement. "When I left she had them in her office."

"You left before Dr. Richardson did? Why?" A hard edge crept into Jaime's voice, making it lose all softness.

"*He* was on his way in. I got out just as he was pulling in and he almost hit me. He barely missed seeing me." To his own ears, his voice had risen to an uncomfortable- sounding squeak.

"*Did* he see you?" Jaime slowly and seductively walked over to him, wearing nothing but a short, see-thru red lacy robe, and matching red spiked heels.

Sitting next to him on the bed, Jaime stroked and fondled him, which made him loose his concentration and not really focus on the questions he was asked.

"Uh no. I don't think so. He was too focused on getting in to see *her.*"

He grimaced in sudden pain and glanced down to see in the middle of stroking him, Jaime's hand tightened on his penis, sinking short manicured nails into the sensitive skin close to his balls.

"Sorry, baby. I'll make it all better."

Jaime kneeled before him and took his stiff penis into a willing red mouth, and proceeded to make it all better, and reaffirmed to James why he stayed in the unusual relationship.

He leaned back with a heartfelt groan, and forgot all about the odd demands and idiosyncrasies of their relationship, and allowed Jaime to do what Jaime did best.

CHAPTER 37

The bedroom door opened and closed, and unafraid, Maya called out, "I don't keep any money in the house, or any jewelry other than the costume variety, so you're wasting your time." She paused, with her brush suspended in mid-air, before she continued to stroke it down the length of her curls as she sat on the small padded stool of her vanity.

There was a pause, and the hiss of the vanilla-scented candle was the only sound in the bathroom for a long time, before he answered, "What *do* you have, that I may find, valuable?"

The overhead lights went out, and the only lighting in her bedroom was given from the glow of the candles she'd lit before she'd stepped into the bath.

Hands came to rest on her shoulders, and leisurely moved down her arms in a sweet caress. He ended at the tips of her fingers only to work his way just as slowly back up. She leaned back in the stool and allowed the brush to fall to the carpeted floor.

Turned around and bodily lifted, she was placed on the bathroom counter. Beneath the sheer robe, her naked bottom came into contact with the cool porcelain. She gave an involuntary shiver, her hands gripping his thick biceps for support.

"Are you cold sweetheart? Do you need me to warm you up?" His hot breath scorched her neck.

Without waiting for her to answer, he spread her legs farther apart as he kneeled between her thighs. Moving the silky fabric of her teddy aside, with reverence, he brushed his hand over the springy hairs guarding the soft V at the top of her legs.

He moved his hands back and forth, avoiding actual contact with that part she desperately needed for him to touch.

Just when she thought she couldn't take his teasing any more, when she was close to begging for his touch, he leaned forward and awarded her with a slow, sure stroke of his tongue.

His hungry gaze traveled the length of her body with such a mixture of possession, lust, and love that she closed her eyes, barely able to handle the heated excitement it created in her.

After spreading her legs further apart, he gently placed them on his shoulders and leaned back in to continue his sensual assault, this time using both tongue and lips. Her body went weak, her breath coming in short puffs of air. He relentlessly continued laving her, his hair tickling the soft sensitive skin of her inner thigh.

"Stop," she breathed. Her voice was barely audible above the hiss of the candles. "Please. I don't think I can take much more."

He reluctantly raised his head. "You can take it. You can take it, and more," he promised and leaned down to kiss her mouth.

He lifted her from the counter, without giving up the connection with her lips, and carried her into the dark bedroom. As her legs untangled from his waist, he pushed aside the sheer robe and placed a hot kiss in the vacated spot near her collarbone.

Standing on tiptoe she pressed her tightly swollen breasts against his chest, and coiled her arms around his head. She ground her body back and forth against his, her body aching, and on fire for his touch.

She excited him beyond anything he'd ever known, her slow grind made his body burn and ache, swelling to proportions that bordered on painful.

With a groan, he grabbed both sides of her hips and lowered her unto his painfully hard cock, penetrating her deeply. After he adjusted her body on his, he let her ride, allowing her to set the pace for their loving.

He could tell when she was nearing her completion. A fine sheen of perspiration coated her light brown skin, pooling into a single drop, perched on the tip of her bow-shaped upper lip.

As her body writhed he encouraged her in a voice gone husky and dry. "Come for me, baby. Let it go and come for me." He captured one of her breasts and tugged relentlessly on the large globe.

With a cry, Maya did as she was told, the orgasm wild and intense, until finally, her body slumped against his. "It's your turn," she told him weakly, in a husky voice, completely out of breath. His cock ached, still buried in her to the hilt.

"I need you on the floor, baby. I want to go deeper than I ever have. I *need* to go deeper, until I can't tell where you leave off, and I begin," he said in a low, rough voice.

He lowered them both to the carpeted floor beside the bed. His hard body carefully covered hers, and he devoured her soft lips with his. He released a heart-felt groan as his tongue delved deep into the recesses of her mouth.

"Now!" He shouted, wrenching his mouth from hers. "I need to be inside of you now. Please," he gentled his plea.

He lifted her small hips, and surged smoothly back into her tight slick vagina, with a long groan of satisfaction. He paused, winding around every part of her he could possibly reach, before setting a burning cadence, with fierce, sure strokes.

Maya looked up at him as his body blanketed hers. She observed the beauty of his face through half closed lids, loving the way the two of them came together in perfect symphony, their bodies in one accord striving to reach the ultimate reward together.

His beautifully carved features stood out in stark relief as he concentrated on what they were doing to one another, the feelings they were generating. The total focus and ecstasy etched on his face gave testimony to the intensity of his feelings.

As he continued to plunge and retreat, going deeper and deeper with each stroke, the friction forced her to lose focus. Instead, she was caught in the pleasure, the power and heat of his body burning steadily within her.

On and on it went, until the rush finally reached them, gathering in intensity like a hurricane encompassing everything in its path, leaving them breathless and incoherent in its wake. Depleted, shudders wracked her body as he gathered her close and she felt him empty deep inside her body.

When Mark caught his breath, he carefully lifted himself away from her, and placed her on the bed. He walked into the bathroom to retrieve a small damp hand towel from the sink. When he turned on the small bedside lamp, he was mortified at what he saw.

Her smooth, brown body held evidence of their lovemaking from her beautiful face, to the creamy skin on her inner thigh.

"Oh, baby, I'm sorry, I didn't mean to mark you like this." He knelt down and gently wiped away the evidence of their lovemaking on her thigh. "And I shouldn't have taken you on the floor like that. I don't know what came over me."

"I'm okay. I enjoyed every minute of it, you didn't hurt me." She sought to reassure him. "And whatever came over you, came over me too. I loved it," she took the towel from him, and wiped the soft tip of his penis, still lying thick and heavy in her hands.

Mark turned off the light and lay next to her. He cradled her in his arms, as her head lay on his chest. He picked up one of her curls and rubbed the lock between his thumb and forefinger absently.

She turned her head to look up into his face in the candlelit room. "What are you thinking about?" She asked into the comfortable silence of the room.

He looked down at her and kissed her forehead before answering. "When I got back to the precinct I took the flowers and the card to the lab guys. It'll be a few days before I hear anything from them."

When he didn't immediately say anything else, she waited for him to continue.

"Maya, these flowers aren't sitting well with me. And not only from the perspective of not wanting some strange guy sending you flowers. It's the second time you've received these anonymously and it makes me feel uncomfortable."

"You think there's a connection between the flowers and the slayer?" She intuitively guessed his thoughts.

Mark realized that although he didn't want to voice out loud his thoughts, she was too intelligent and perceptive not to reason it out for herself.

"Maybe. I'm not sure. But my instincts are telling me yes. Which brings me to another point." He wasn't sure how to give voice to the thoughts that had been swirling in his head throughout most of the day.

"What would you think about moving in with me for a while?" He'd intended to ask her when he'd arrived at her house, but he'd been side tracked when he'd entered her bedroom. Now, his thinking a little more clear, he was able to ask the question. When she didn't respond, he tipped her head up with his finger.

"Did you hear me, baby? What do you think about moving in with me?"

"I heard you. I'm wondering why. Is it for professional or personal reasons?" He felt her body clench, after she asked the question.

"What I meant was do you think I'm unsafe in my home?" She quickly clarified.

"I don't like the feeling I'm getting right now sweetheart, I can't really explain. As for personal reasons, there is nothing that would make me happier than to have you staying with me, Maya, until we've caught this woman," he said, referring to the serial killer.

Even as he said the words, he knew nothing would make him happier than if she were to stay with him on a more permanent basis. But he didn't think she was ready to hear that yet.

"Give me some time, Mark. I love my home, and I hate to have someone scare me away from it. I'll have to give it some serious thought."

The day had started early and lasted long for both of them. Mark turned her around so he could hold her spoon fashion. It wasn't long before they drifted into sleep holding on to one another, each ones body automatically moving and adjusting to accommodate the other, as they fell into a contented sleep.

CHAPTER 38

"Hey Jack, did you find anything for me?" Mark asked the lab tech.

As soon as he'd come to the station that morning, he'd gone by the lab before going to the squad room, hoping the tech's had been able to find prints, fibers, or anything on the floral arrangement. Now he'd returned in hopes that the tech had found some usable print.

"Sorry, Detective. It was clean. There were roughly three or four sets of prints on the vase itself, which is in line with the amount of people who handled it. The only prints on the card were from the samples you provided me. There weren't any others."

The technician remained seated in the high-backed wheeled lab chair and rolled over to a steel gray cabinet. Rolling back, he handed Mark a plastic bag that held the small card and envelope from the arrangement.

"Thanks Jack, I appreciate you taking a look at it for me."

"No problem, Mark. Any time you need anything give me a jingle."

With that, the technician went back to his work and Mark left the lab. With a pensive look on his face, Mark closely looked at the writing on the card he could see clearly through the sheer plastic bag. He made a turn that would lead him into the direction of the evidence room.

"Hello," he called out as he entered the room and found no one at the front counter. "Anyone around? I need to take a look at something," he called out to no one particular. As he was approaching the desk, the clerk came out from behind one of the stacks, and hurried over to the counter.

"I'm sorry, Detective, it's been a busy day and I'm the only one here. I didn't hear you come in," he offered in apology. "How may I help you?"

Mark glanced down at the clerk's badge. "Smith, I need to take a look at a piece of evidence from the slayer case. It should be tagged by itself. It's a small white card."

"What type of card? Do you have the tag number?"

"It's a small white card with a hand-printed message on it. The type of card that goes with floral arrangements. I don't have the number, sorry about that," he explained to the flustered clerk and waited patiently as the man went back into the stacks to retrieve the card. Ten minutes later he emerged with the bagged evidence in his hands.

"Thanks…" Mark thanked him as he scrawled his name across the sheet of paper to check the evidence out.

"Detective, when will you return this? I noticed you didn't indicate a return time."

"I'm not sure. Some time today when I'm done with it," he said, and walked out of the room, missing the way the pleasant smile dropped immediately from the clerk's face as soon as he left the room.

* * * *

Before he returned to the squad room, Mark made one last detour back to the crime lab after taking a look at the message on the first card.

"Jack, is Wanda around today?" He referred to the technician who also was a handwriting expert.

"Yep. Somewhere around here," the tech said before he bellowed, "hey Wanda, you got a visitor!"

"What can I do for you sexy?" Wanda asked with a wink, as she came from behind a partition in the room, which separated each technician's workspace.

Mark watched with a smile as the large woman ambled slowly in his direction. Wanda was old enough to be his mother, but that never stopped her from flirting with him.

Her glasses sat perched on the end of her large nose as she peered at him over the frames. Her nearly wrinkle-free sienna skin was liberally sprinkled with freckles and small moles. Her wide mouth usually carried an infectious grin virtually no one was immune to, even though she was known to tease just as mercilessly as she flirted. However, Wanda was sharp, and when it came to her field of expertise, she was the best.

"Wanda, I want you to take a look at these two cards for me and give me your impressions," he asked.

Mark handed her the two plastic wrapped cards. He watched as she looked around before spying a box of surgical gloves and donned a pair before she removed the cards. She then carefully examined both, her eyes squinting behind her half lenses, before looking back at Mark who was watching her expectantly.

"Well sugah, it looks like the writing may have come from the same hand although there are some differences in the script. You see these two letters?" She pointed a gloved, ringed, pinky to the curve of a letter in one of the cards, before pointing to a similar curve in the letter of the other.

"This is unintentional. This is the natural way the writer makes this particular letter. However, what is intentional is the large 'flowery' script, as though they're trying to disguise their true handwriting," she told him as she continued to carefully look at both cards.

"Can you tell if it's a man or a woman?" He bent his head down close to hers, looking at both cards with her.

"Boo, you smell good! What you wearing? Polo? Armani?" Wanda took a deep whiff off the side of his neck.

Used to the way the older woman teased, Mark absentmindedly answered, "Ralph," as he continued to peruse both cards.

"I need to examine them both a little closer before giving a good 'guess.' This one is tricky, it could be a man or woman. Usually I can tell straight off if it's a woman trying to pass off writing as a man or vice versa, but I'm not sure with this one. Leave it with me for a hot minute, and I'll take it back to my lair and find out for you."

"Thanks Wanda I appreciate it. Give me a ring whenever you finish with it." He gave her peck on the cheek, to her delight, before leaving and heading back to the squad room.

Jordan looked up from his work as Mark sat down at his desk, thinking about the two cards he'd left with Wanda.

"What's up?" Jordan asked, when he didn't greet him.

"Before I came up I went over to the lab. Remember the arrangement I gave them Saturday?"

"The one sent to Maya?"

"Yeah that one. Jack said he couldn't find any prints on the card itself other than Dalia's and Maya's."

"What do you mean?"

"Maya told me only she and Dalia touched the card inside the envelope, so I got a copy of their finger prints and gave it to the Jack. According to him, those were the only two prints that showed. That's strange. It doesn't make any sense." Mark could feel dread lurking in the pit of his stomach as he thought of the ramifications of the tech's discovery.

"Man that's *damn* strange. So whoever sent Maya the flowers, must have been wearing gloves when he handled it. Hmm."

"Or *she* was wearing gloves," Mark stated flatly.

"You think Maya's secret admirer is a woman?"

"I don't know. I don't like the looks of it Jordan."

Mark quickly went through his notebook in search of the message left on the card. After he'd reread it, he leafed backward until he found the earlier entry from the first anonymous floral arrangement she was given.

"I saw you on the news. You were wonderful. I'll bet Alicia Somers will think again before she opens that big trap of hers and tries to make anyone else look foolish!!"

"Same type of cryptic message. I went to the evidence room and looked at the card from the first arrangement. I took both cards over to Wanda to have her take a look at them. She says from a quick observation, they may be from the same person. Anything deeper and she would need to take time to really analyze both of them."

"Good thing you kept that card. What are you thinking?"

"I'm not sure yet, just like I said, I don't like the way this looks. You know, I think I'm going to pick the lieutenant's brain for a minute. Do you know if anyone is in there with him?" Mark asked as he rose from his desk.

"I don't know. I got in a few minutes before you did and his office door was already closed."

Mark walked over to the lieutenant's office and wrapped his knuckles lightly on the partially closed door.

He walked inside and closed the door behind him. He was already inside when he noticed Lieutenant Hernandez was not alone; Special Agent Montgomery was inside with him, his back propped against the wall facing the door.

"Sorry sir, I thought you were alone, I wanted to run something by you."

With a wave of his hand, the lieutenant told him, "We weren't discussing anything confidential. What did you need, Mark?"

"No we weren't," the agent agreed, "in fact I think I will leave you gentlemen to speak in private." Agent Montgomery told them both as he pushed away from the wall.

Mark motioned with his hand for him to stay. "Actually Agent Montgomery I could use your input as well." When the man settled back against the wall with a small nod in agreement, Mark continued.

"Maya received flowers for the second time this weekend from an anonymous 'admirer.' The first time it happened was a few months ago when she was first brought into the investigation. I didn't like it then and I definitely don't like it now. My gut reaction wasn't good either time."

"You didn't like it because…? Is this the professional or personal gut reaction?" Mark looked in surprise at the lieutenant's question.

Although he wasn't trying to keep his relationship with Maya a secret, he was surprised at the lieutenant's obvious knowledge of his feelings for her. His surprise must have shown on his face because Lieutenant Hernandez confirmed his knowledge with his next words.

"Detective Phillips made reference to your relationship in passing recently," he said, "congratulations. Dr. Richardson is as beautiful as she is intelligent. You're a lucky man."

"Thanks sir, I think so too. But in answer to your question, my gut was working in pure professional mode. The wording on the first message was phrased in a damn odd way," Mark started, and was quickly interrupted by the lieutenant.

"You read the message on the first card?" The lieutenant asked, clearly now he was the surprised one.

Mark happened to glance in the direction of the silent FBI agent, and noticed the way his head was tilted in that odd way he had, that signaled he was intently listening, focusing.

"Yes sir. After Maya showed it to me, I brought it in for the lab to take a look."

"Did they find anything?"

"No they didn't find anything on it, no prints; nothing. I put it in the evidence room." He didn't add that he had recently taken it out for Wanda. He thought it best to wait until she'd had a chance to examine it. He turned his head away and noticed the agent now had his gaze unerringly directed on him.

"What do you make of all of this Agent Montgomery?" Lieutenant Hernandez asked.

"I believe there's a strong possibility it's no accident Dr. Richardson has received these two anonymous gifts at the same time the these killings are taking place." Nicolai spoke into the silent room.

"You think it's the slayer?" Mark asked him, a deep frown settling between his dark brows.

"I couldn't, and wouldn't say without further proof, Detective. I simply do not believe it's a coincidence, and I also think Dr. Richardson should be closely watched. Wouldn't you agree?"

"I'm not sure that it's anything more than a beautiful woman receiving an anonymous gift from a secret admirer. She works with a lot of people with whom she's helped a great deal throughout her career. Maybe even one of her students or volunteers, who knows? I'm not sure what one has to do with the other." Lieutenant Hernandez injected, clearly disagreeing with Agent Montgomery's assessment.

"The serial killer will sometimes encounter a person who they idolize or think extremely highly of. For whatever reason they'll put this person on a pedestal. Unfortunately, if this person performs some wrongdoing in the killer's eye they can then 'fall from grace' so to speak." The agent informed them in a low tone with his eyes closed and head back against the wall.

"What could cause this 'fall from grace?'" Mark felt an urgency to know the answer. He didn't like the way it sounded, his fear for Maya escalating.

Nicolai opened his eyes and looked at Mark as he answered his question, his silver gaze direct and unflinching. "Anything. Nothing. It's all subjective, and according to the whims of the offender."

CHAPTER 39

"Dalia, what are you talking about?" Maya laughingly asked her friend as she opened the door from the garage that led directly into her portion of the mansion.

"*Sesute*, it is nothing to be ashamed of. That is what love and good lovemaking is supposed to do to a woman. It is the way you should look. Like a petal on a beautiful rose completely opened, I mean unfolded," she told her young friend tongue-in-cheek as she preceded her into the kitchen.

As Maya turned on the light, Dalia's husky laugh dwindled to a stop, and was replaced with a horrified gasp.

Maya was walking directly behind Dalia and stumbled into her when she stopped, after taking a few steps into the room. Moving around her, Maya felt as though she'd been kicked in the stomach as she surveyed the scene in front of her. Slowly, she walked around Dalia taking the site in.

Drawers and cabinet's gaped open, the items inside spilled out onto the floor and along the counter tops. Nearly every surface of her kitchen was cluttered with cans, food, papers, and dishes. In shock, Maya turned large frightened eyes toward Dalia.

After her initial horrified reaction, Dalia grabbed Maya by the hand. "Come on, Maya, we must leave this place. They may still be in here. Come, let us go."

Without waiting for her assent, Dalia half dragged Maya out of the kitchen. Swift and silent, she closed the door, and took the keys from Maya's nerveless fingers. She hustled her quickly into the passenger seat of her car, before going around to the driver's side.

"Dalia I can't believe what I saw. Who would do something like that?" Maya asked as she came out of her state of shock as they sped away from her burglarized home.

"I do not know, Maya, but I did not want to take the chance to stay in there in case they were still in our home." Dalia took Maya's small clammy hand in hers and gripped it tightly, before she let it go, and placed shaking hands back on the steering wheel. "I think we had better call the police and wait on them before we go back."

"Dalia, I don't understand...." Maya choked out, still in shock.

"We will be okay, *Sesute*. We will call the police," Dalia assured her as she turned into a convenience shop before she pulled out her cell phone and placed the call to the police. After she'd completed the call she turned back to Maya.

"It is going to be okay, Maya, I have given them the address, and they have said they are on their way. They have this number to call when they arrive. Are you alright little one?"

"I'll be okay. Could I use your phone please so I can call, Mark?" She asked, doubting her ability to rummage through her oversized bag and find her small phone.

With shaky fingers, Maya dialed the precinct, and when she got Mark's voice mail, left a message for him to call her. She placed a second call to his cell phone and also received his voice mail. After leaving the second message, she sat back in the seat and leaned her head back against the backrest.

"He's not answering."

"Everything will be fine, you will see." Dalia was in the process of saying when her cell phone rang.

She picked up the phone and spoke for a few moments before she ended the call. "That was the police. They are at the house and say it is okay for us to return. The burglars have already left."

When they drove back to the house, both women noticed several of their neighbors were outside, no doubt wondering why two police cruisers were parked in Maya's driveway. They parked and walked to the front door where two of the officers waited on her porch.

The young black female officer greeted first Maya and then Dalia. "Good evening ladies, I'm Officer Greeley and this is my partner Officer Kelley with the SAPD."

Both officers displayed their badges for the women to see. "It seems as though you've had a break in. Which one of you ladies is Dr. Maya Richardson?" The young officer asked, referring to the name she'd written in her small black notebook.

"I'm Dr. Richardson Officer." Maya stepped forward to shake the woman's hand. "This is my friend and assistant Dalia Draugulis. Ms. Draugulis also lives here, in one of the three units."

"Yes we noticed the house was sectioned into three separate living quarters. We haven't gone into the closed sections and there was no forced entry so it's doubtful the intruder went any further than your living quarters Dr. Richardson. Ma'am if you and Ms. Draugulis would follow us we can go inside and take a look around. Be aware the intruder hasn't been very kind in his search through your home ma'am." The officer warned her.

The young officer warned her, however nothing could prepare Maya for the chaos that greeted her when she'd stepped no further than a few steps into her main living area.

With a sudden sharp intake of breath, Maya surveyed the brightly lit interior, her eyes opened wide, her mouth open as she looked around.

Plants were overturned, books thrown from the mahogany floor-to-ceiling bookshelf, and cushions and pillows lay in a heap in the middle of the floor.

Maya walked silently throughout the house, righting overturned plants and picking the occasional knick-knack up from the floor, and lightly caressing it before she placed it back in its original place. She touched her possessions with shaky fingers, traumatized by what she saw.

She touched her roughly handled possessions here and there, not saying a word to anyone, and Dalia turned worried eyes in the direction of the officers.

"I know this is very difficult to see Dr. Richardson. When you've had a moment to take it all in, we'd like to get a statement from you ma'am." Kelley, the male officer informed her, his voice sounding louder than it actually was in the still of the room.

The officers trailed behind Maya and Dalia as they walked throughout the house, and stepped into her bedroom where they came to a sudden halt inside the door way.

"Oh no. No God, please don't tell me they took it. Not my necklace." Maya was frantically searching her overturned jewelry box. There were a few necklaces and her one pair of real pearl necklace and matching earrings she'd inherited from her late grandmother, but no sign of her necklace from Ally.

Maya crumpled into a heap on the floor and, beat the carpet with clenched fists. She had taken off the necklace and charm attached, with the intention of repairing the loose clasp, but her schedule had been so hectic, she hadn't been able to get to the jeweler.

The small inexpensive necklace, which was short on monetary value, but long on sentimental value, was gone, and Maya felt as though her heart was ripping in two.

CHAPTER 40

Mark walked into Maya's bedroom and saw her on the floor crying so hard he felt as though his heart was breaking in two.

He strode swiftly to her side and motioned Dalia aside as he lifted Maya from the floor. He walked over to the bed to sit down with her, caressing her small head and cradling her close.

He recognized both young officers, and as he looked over Maya's head at them, he silently asked for privacy.

"Detective, why don't we give you time to speak with Dr. Richardson, and when she's ready we can take her statement," the female officer said as she and her partner left the room.

After the two officers left, Dalia placed her hand on top of Maya's shoulder. "I am so sorry some awful bastard took your necklace from Ally, truly, *Sesute*," Dalia said with rare heat in her voice and words. Dalia didn't know what to say to her saddened friend, and trusting Mark could console her, she left them alone in the bedroom.

"Baby I didn't know you'd called until I was pulling into your driveway. Get it all out, Maya, it'll all be okay sweetheart." Her wrenching cries made his heart ache along with hers, as she buried her face deep into his chest.

He'd worked late and was on his way to Maya's when his cell phone beeped signaling he had a message.

Smiling when he recognized the number displayed as Maya's, he had called his voice mail and the smile swiftly fell from his face.

As her halting message ended, Mark had been pulling up into her driveway and parked along side the two cruisers. He showed his badge to the officer outside, before racing into the house.

Although he'd only taken a cursory look around, as he bounded through the house looking for Maya, he was still taken aback by the chaos surrounding him. When he'd heard the cries coming from her bedroom, he had quickly made his way there, only to find Maya on the floor in a crumpled heap crying helplessly with Dalia rubbing her back.

Now, as he continued to hold and attempt to sooth her, he looked around the bedroom through the eyes of a cop. The obviously expensive painting that adorned one wall had been left untouched, along with her small mounted shadow box housing her collection of crystal cats, and doves.

The closet door was open, and a cursory glance told him Maya's clothes had remained untouched, while his few hanging items had been ripped from the hangers and left on the floor.

The same thing went for the bureau drawers, his clothes had been cast ruthlessly aside, while Maya's had remained untouched.

She looked at him with red-rimmed, furious eyes. "You know when I was a kid, I didn't have anything, not one damn thing, that I could call my own." Tears streamed down her blotchy cheeks. The anger and emotion in her voice was tangible and fierce, unlike anything he'd seen from her.

She stopped speaking to close her eyes, small nostrils flaring out slightly as she tried to gain her composure. "When I first received my inheritance from my grandmother I had *real* ambivalent feelings about this house and what it stood for. But after listening to the tapes she left me, and doing a lot of praying about it, I forgave and decided to enjoy and be thankful for what the Creator had provided for me through a woman I never knew."

She paused as Mark handed her a tissue from the bedside table and wiped her tear-washed face. "I love my home now, Mark. I've got wonderful people with whom I share it with and I love it. *It's mine*. I'm comfortable and at peace when I come into my home. I've surrounded my environment with things that reflect who I am, and with what calms *my* spirit at the end of the day. When I come into my house I always feel … oh, I don't know, at peace, renewed … at 'home,'" she finished simply.

"I know, baby." He understood perfectly what she wanted to convey.

"You know just because you have a roof over your head doesn't make it a home," she continued, "I once had a friend say she'd rather live in a shack and be happy, than to live in a mansion and be in hell. From the time I moved out on my own I have done everything I could to live in an environment that makes *me* comfortable. I didn't think this 'mansion' would ever feel like home, but it does. You know? It really does. And for somebody to go through, destroy, and steal my things…" she left the sentence unfinished, too angry to continue the thought.

"And worst of all, they've taken a cheap gold necklace, my only physical link with my murdered sister. Something I've had for twenty years." She visibly held back further tears from falling.

"Damn, Maya. Baby, I'm so sorry." Mark shared her loss over the stolen necklace. He felt helpless, and knew there wasn't a damn thing he could do to right this wrong.

He wanted nothing more than to catch whoever was responsible for trashing her home, and he had a sinking feeling in the pit of his stomach this was no ordinary burglary, that it was connected with the slayer.

"Detective Halstan, we need to get a statement from Dr. Richardson," the female officer asked quietly from the doorway. "As soon as you're able to sir, could you bring Dr. Richardson into the dining room so we can get her statement?"

Mark took a moment to reach over for another tissue and lovingly wiped her face before turning it up to his so he could look directly into her eyes. "Are you ready to face them? I'll make sure their questions are brief and we can get you and Dalia out of here." He watched her carefully. When she nodded her head in assent, he stood with her still held in his arms.

As they walked into the dining room, he noticed this room held little evidence of any disturbance at all. Dalia sat in one of the chairs with a cup of coffee in her hands, while the remaining two officers stood waiting for Maya and Mark to arrive.

Dalia turned anxious, worried eyes in Maya's direction. "Maya would you like coffee little one?"

Maya motioned her back into her seat with a wave of her hand. "I'm fine Dalia, but thanks." As Mark guided her into her seat, she asked, "Dalia have you checked your section? Did the burglar get into your apartment?"

"No *Sesute*. Besides I had my alarm engaged and it would have notified the police if they had tried to force their way in," Dalia told her without mentioning the obvious fact the same would have been true for Maya, had she turned her own alarm on.

"What about the Johnson's? In the upstairs apartment?" she clarified. "Has anyone checked on their apartment?"

"I went with the officers to check with your key while you were with Detective Halstan. Everything was locked up and looked the same as the day they left. They too had their alarm on." Dalia answered the question before the officer's could.

"Dr. Richardson, Ms. Draugulis tells us the couple and their two daughter's who live in the upper wing are away visiting family--is that correct?"

"Yes, they've been gone for a few days. Their scheduled to return sometime next month to give the family, especially the girls, time to settle in before the fall semester begins at the end of August."

The officers stayed and asked her several more brief questions before leaving her with the instructions to call them if she needed anything. Although all understood Mark would take good care of her.

After they'd left, Mark turned to Dalia. "Dalia I'm sure everything is fine, but until we find out more about this burglary I think it would be best if you didn't stay here tonight. Why don't you come with Maya and spend the night at my home, there's plenty of room," he invited her.

"Thank you, but I think I will decline the offer. I have somewhere else I can stay."

"Are you sure Dalia? It's late, where will you go?"

"I have a lab partner who has become a good friend. It will be no problem for me to call her and stay with her for the night. Trust me, Mark, it will be fine. You take care of Maya for me, and I will worry less."

Dalia turned to Maya. "Call my cell, when you come back home and I will meet you here and together we will right your home little sister," she promised.

"Thank you. Dal, I will. Why don't we go with you to get your things you'll need for the night?"

"Sweetheart you go ahead with Dalia, I need to make a phone call."

After Maya and Dalia left, Mark made a call to the precinct to request a phone number. "Hey Officer Meeks how's it going? This is Detective Mark Halstan," he greeted the night officer who picked up the phone after the first ring.

"Slow. Too slow. How can I help you, Detective?"

"I need a number from you. Could you get Special Agent Nicolai Montgomery's hotel phone number for me, or his cell number? Whichever one is available."

"Sure thing, Detective, let me look it up for you. Hold on for a minute."

He placed Mark on hold before coming back on the line to give him the agent's hotel room extension number only. "Sorry, Detective, that's the only one we have available for him."

"That'll work Meeks--thanks." After he'd hung up the phone, he quickly placed a call to the agent.

"Montgomery." The agent answered after one ring.

"Agent Montgomery this is Detective Halstan." On the other end of the extension Mark could hear the rustle of fabric, and after glancing at his watch, realized he'd probably woken him from sleep. "I'm sorry I'm calling you so late, I didn't realize the time," he apologized.

"No problem, Detective, I'm wide awake." As he said so, Mark could swear his tone was mocking.

"Look I'm sorry, I'll catch you in the morning."

"Really, Detective, I wish it weren't so but I was awake. What did you need?" His voice reflected the honesty of his words.

"Maya's home has been broken into. Thankfully she wasn't in at the time, and neither were any of her tenants. It doesn't seem as though anything of value was taken except a gold necklace held sentimental value for Maya alone." Mark filled him in succinctly.

"How is she? You said no one was in the home at the time?"

"No. She's shaken up, mad as hell, but thank God, she's not hurt. They made a real mess of it in Maya's wing, but it's nothing that can't be fixed. I'm taking her home with me and her assistant is staying with a friend. I'm going to be at the precinct early tomorrow and I wanted to give you a head's up."

Mark didn't know how to proceed. He had no idea why, but his first inclination had been to call the FBI agent. Oddly hesitant, he didn't know how to voice his next request.

"Would it be alright if I had a look around? I could do so tonight if you're taking Dr. Richardson with you. I'd like to take a look at everything before it gets straightened back up if I could," Nicolai volunteered.

"I'm sure Maya wouldn't mind Agent Montgomery, but it can wait until the morning, I wasn't suggesting you come now, it's too late." Mark quickly assured him, relieved at the agent's request.

"Actually, Detective, I do my best work at night … alone. If it's okay with Dr. Richardson, I can be there in less than twenty minutes."

"I'm sure it'll be okay. I don't think our prowler will return tonight, but we'll leave the key in the mailbox. When you're done, lock everything back up and bring the key to the precinct tomorrow."

"No problem, I'll be there shortly."

"Thanks Montgomery," Mark said.

The only response was the sound of a phone being disconnected. Mark turned around when Dalia and Maya walked toward him. Maya must have packed her overnight bag as well, because both women held bags in their hands.

"That was Agent Montgomery on the phone. He wants to take a look around. I told him I didn't think you'd mind. Is that okay?"

"No I don't mind. I'll be at Imani House all day, so he can get the key anytime he wants to." She was turning to key in the code on the alarm pad when Mark stayed her hand.

"He's going to check it out tonight. He'll be here in a few minutes. I'll leave my key for him to lock up when he's done," he said, when she looked at him questioningly.

Mark walked Dalia to her Corolla parked in the side garage. "Please take care of Maya, this has been hard on her. I don't know how much more she can take," Dalia told Mark.

"You know I'll take care of her Dalia. Be careful driving," he assured her and closed her car door. As she reversed out of the driveway and drove down the darkened silent street he returned to the house.

"It's been a long night, baby, why don't we leave," he urged her, as soon as he walked back inside.

"Yes. I think that's a good idea," she said on a long sad sigh and followed him out after he locked the door.

Mark stored her bags alongside his gym bag in the back of his Expedition before guiding her to the passenger side. They'd been driving in silence for a while before Maya finally spoke. "Why is Agent Montgomery looking now instead of in the morning? Did you ask him to come tonight?" Her voice sounded hushed and weary in the dark. She turned her head and body toward him.

"I called him when you and Dalia were getting your things together."

"What is it?" she asked when he frowned.

"Nothing concrete." Mark shook his head. "My first instinct whenever I need back-up is normally Jordan." He spoke slowly as though he were contemplating his words carefully before saying them. "This time my first instinct was to call Montgomery."

"And why do you think that is?"

"I'm not sure. I'm not even sure I trust the guy," he said, and immediately recanted. "No, it's not that I don't trust him, I don't understand him."

He thought back on the odd way the agent investigated crime scenes and of his desire to be alone while he did so.

"He's good at what he does. I really believe that he can give us the insight into this burglary that we need. Everything will be fine, Maya," he sought to reassure her as he reached over and took her small hand within his, and kissed her open palm. "Everything will be alright, baby, I promise you."

CHAPTER 41

Nicolai casually walked inside the house, closing the door after he'd let himself in. He took a deep breath, and leaned back against the door's hard surface, as though he could gain strength from the antique wood door. Reluctantly he pushed himself away, and walked throughout the lit house.

The evidence of the burglary was everywhere, from strewn pillows, to overturned drawers. Cabinet doors had been opened and emptied, and food dumped into the middle of the floor in the large bright kitchen.

He took his time going throughout the house, careful not to touch anything until he was ready to 'hear.' Nicolai's gaze stole over the simple, yet beautiful furnishings. Fresh picked daisy's sat unmolested on a side table, and haunting artwork hung framed on warm painted walls, all of which showed the many facets to Dr. Richardson's personality.

Nicolai continued walking methodically through her home, and waited until last to go into her personal sanctuary; her bedroom. Upon entering, he could immediately detect a difference in the atmosphere before he touched anything.

Analyzing the feeling, the best way he could describe it to himself was that the air seemed to have a heavier and more oppressive feel to it. His instincts told him this was where he needed to start. He slowly removed the gloves covering his large, yet sensitive hands.

Unlike the other rooms in the house, this one held little evidence of a burglary with small exception. As he walked into the large walk-in closet, he immediately noticed several articles of clothing obviously belonging to a man, had been ripped from the hangers.

However, among none of the strewn clothing did he see any feminine garments. He closed his eyes and picked up a shirt and held it lightly between his sensitive fingers. Immediately a bolt of lightening shot across his shut eyes, almost blinding in its intensity, and Nicolai was slammed into the auditory vision.

"I CANNOT believe this! His clothes are in her closet-why would she have his clothes in her closet? Is she letting him screw her? I thought she was different. She helps us. She hears our stories, and understands. She knows the truth about men. They only want one

thing-they only want to use you, and keep you their dirty secret and come to you when no one else is around and shove their dirty dicks anywhere they can shove them. Doesn't she know?" The voice grew in intensity with every heated word.

" He's the same way. He's no different than the rest of them. I thought she knew better. Why doesn't she know better?" The angry high-pitched voice ranted in a voice that dropped, the words barely above a whisper.

"Oh what is this? Isn't it lovely? Hello there! How would you like to join your 'sister' little locket? So pretty and sweet. Yes I definitely will take you so you may be with her again. Family reunions are so nice, so special."

Once angry and strident, the voice was upbeat and happy, as though the anger and hostility of moments ago hadn't happened. Humming, the voice slowly began to fade away as though it had never been.

Coming out of his trance, Nicolai found himself standing in front of Maya's bureau looking down at her scattered jewelry. Although he'd come prepared and had taken the high potent pills, his head throbbed relentlessly, blinding him.

With blurred eyes, he reached inside his pocket automatically, and withdrew the pills tucked inside. He sat down in a loose heap with his knees drawn up and his arms hanging loosely over them while he massaged his throbbing temples and thought over what he'd 'heard.' He thought past the debilitating pain, which had become an unwelcome accompaniment to his ability.

The familiar singsong quality as well as the pitch confirmed to Nicolai the slayer and this burglar were one in the same. But there was something else mystifying him about this voice, the cadence and pitch reverberating in his head as he puzzled though what it could be.

CHAPTER 42

"There are several things, besides the obvious, I don't like about this burglary, and one is the timing," Mark said as he paced the circumference of the room. He and Jordan had spent the greater part of the morning piecing together evidence, looking for a pattern after Mark filled Jordan in on the burglary at Maya's.

He stopped his pacing to see Jordan was studying the pieces of evidence from the slayer investigation laid out in front of him. In front of Jordan were the two cards Maya had received from her anonymous admirer.

"According to Wanda, the notes are from the same person. She also came up with some interesting speculation on this admirer." Mark walked around the table and picked up the handwritten notes.

"Like what?" Jordan asked.

"Like the fact that although the language isn't threatening to Maya, it was still written by someone who may have been angry when they wrote the notes, particularly the second one. In my handwriting 101 crash course with Wanda she explained some interesting things. Like how the curves and placement of letters indicate a variety of emotional states." Mark pointed to one of the notes as he explained what he'd learned from the technician.

"I didn't know you could tell so much from the way someone writes. I wonder what she could tell from my writing?" Jordan halfway joked.

"Probably a lot. Wanda said she was free for lunch, why don't you go and ask her yourself?" Mark knew how uncomfortable the older woman made Jordan, and he tried not to laugh as he asked the question.

Wanda flirted with nearly every male she came into contact with, but she flirted especially hard with Jordan. She once told him what she would do with him if she ever had him alone for at least ten minutes, and was ten years younger. That's all she needed, she'd say with a wink, just ten minutes and ten years.

"That's alright. I think I'll pass. I'm not that damn curious." Jordan shivered in disgust, and looked over at Mark. "Funny," he said when he caught Mark laughing, and reached over to punch him as hard as he could on the shoulder.

"Ouch," Mark grimaced as he grabbed his shoulder and laughed at the same time. Jordan reluctantly laughed along with him when there was a knock on the conference door.

"Come in," their deep voices chorused. At the sight of the FBI agent, both men sobered as Nicolai walked soundlessly into the room.

"Good afternoon, Detectives." He nodded to both men before turning his gaze toward the table that held pieces of their investigation. "May I?" He asked after he'd walked to the table.

"Sure go ahead. We're going over the evidence. Instead of getting closer to discovering the perpetrator, the evidence we have seems to contradict each other," Jordan ran frustrated hands over the stubble on his cheeks, the levity of moments ago gone.

Nicolai picked up the two cards Mark placed on the table. His eyes blinked quickly for several seconds as though he were struggling to keep them open. No sooner had it happened then it was over, and he placed the two cards side-by side on the table. He glanced at the two men to see if they'd noticed his reaction.

"The lieutenant is in a meeting with the acting chief this morning, so we haven't been able to fill him in on the burglary at Maya's last night," Mark said to Nicolai.

"These are the cards left with the flowers Dr. Richardson received?" Nicolai asked, motioning to the two cards on the table.

"Yes, I had the handwriting examined by Wanda, one of the crime lab techs. She also has a sub specialty in analyzing script," he explained to the agent before continuing, "she believes the card was written by the same person."

A knock on the door and LeDoux stuck his head inside the room. "Casanova you have a call from a Ms. Arlinda Nyoni. Sounds important--can you take it?"

"Yeah sure tell her to hold on," Jordan told LeDoux, before turning back to Mark. "I'd better take this."

"Well it is too late," LeDoux smirked "she said if you would like to speak to her you know where to find her," he told Jordan gleefully.

"Oh damn I forgot the time. I was supposed to take Arly out to lunch. I need to go and make a call." Jordan hastily gathered the evidence collected on the table.

Mark recognized the name of Maya's college friend, and he had no idea Jordan was still in contact with the woman.

"We can wrap up and take a late lunch if that helps. I'll put this stuff back," he told his partner.

"Yeah okay. Thanks man." Jordan walked quickly out of the room.

No sooner had Jordan left, than Nicolai turn toward Mark with a serious expression on his face. "We may have a problem, Detective," Nicolai said without preamble.

Immediately catching on to what he was referring to, all remaining humor over Jordan's predicament left. "In what way?"

"I believe the person who burglarized Dr. Richardson's home is responsible for the serial killings. And if I had to venture a guess, I would bet the floral arrangement was from the same person." Nicolai told him calmly, with little or no inflection.

"Shit!" With lightening speed, Mark raced out the door with the FBI agent close on his heels. When the agent grabbed his arm, Mark swung around, a fierce expression on his face. "What the hell? I need to get a hold of Maya. Now!"

"Dr. Richardson is safe. If I didn't feel she was, I would have contacted you last night. She's safe," Nicolai calmly reassured him.

"Listen, you can come with me if you want. Or you can stay here. Either way, I'm going to Imani House to check on Maya. If you're coming, then on the way you can tell me how the hell you know this shit." He reached inside his pocket, and took out his cell phone to call Maya.

"Hey Dal, where's Maya?" He asked without preamble, and waited as Dalia transferred the call. He took a deep breath and closed his eyes, and opened them just as quickly when Maya came on the phone,

"Hey, baby, how are you doing?" He listened for a moment before responding. "Good. Sweetheart I want you to do me a favor. Who's working security?"

"Rowan's here today."

"Great. I need for you to stay at the House, and make sure Rowan doesn't let anyone unfamiliar in there until I get there okay?"

"What's going on, Mark?" She asked, her voice fearful.

"There's nothing to worry about, Maya. We need to talk to you. I'm on my way, stay where you are," he told her, trying his best to keep the anxiety out of his voice. After a few moments of talking, he flipped the receiver down on his phone and turned to Montgomery, who'd stood discretely away as he spoke with Maya.

"Well, are you coming? And will you tell me what the hell you do exactly? Who the hell are you?" He demanded.

"I'll tell you on the way to Imani House. Let's go," Montgomery said, and the two men left the precinct together.

CHAPTER 43

"Is either Phillips or Halstan around?" One of the homicide detectives asked LeDoux as he sat at the desk that faced Jordan's.

"No, you just missed them both. Detective Halstan and the FBI Agent left a few minutes after Detective Phillips. Why? Something I can help you with? Leave a message for them?"

"I have a name for their latest John Doe," the detective said, glancing at his notepad. "Leslie Dikes. Dikes was a small-time pimp, one of his 'girls' came in to give us a positive ID"

"Leslie Dikes you say? Not exactly the type of name one would associate with a man of his, well, occupation, eh?" LeDoux said on a laugh.

"No shit." The detective laughed with him. "I think the female who identified him called him Rocky or something like that. He probably thought it was more fitting. At any rate, in the end, his image didn't help him out too much."

"Yes you are right about that one. In the end none of that matters at all, eh?" LeDoux agreed with a Gallic shrug.

* * * *

Mark turned to the agent as soon as he'd put on his seat belt and asked, "how do you get your information? Do you have ESP or something?" He joked, and glanced away as he looked in the rearview mirror, to reverse out of the underground parking garage.

When his comment was met with silence, his glance stole back to Montgomery, as the man looked straight ahead with no expression, and no denial.

"Damn I was just kidding. That's not it. Is that it? ESP? Give me a damn break," Mark laughed in disbelief.

Nicolai saw the astonishment on Mark's face, and a rusty laugh escaped before he knew it.

The double look of surprise on Mark's face at the sound of laughter coming from him, made him laugh even harder. After a few moments, his rustic laughter died out.

"What I am about to tell you is highly confidential and if I thought there was a chance you would break this confidence, I wouldn't tell you. However, if you were to say anything, no one would believe you, and you would find your life not quite as enjoyable as it is now," he warned in a very quiet and very matter of fact tone of voice.

"I was born with a heightened sensitivity to noise," he began. "As a child it was difficult because I grew up in an environment that wasn't exactly, conducive, for my particular sensitivities."

He gave the information to Mark succinctly, in a matter of fact tone of voice, obviously leaving out specific details. "As I grew older certain other abilities began to manifest, and it wasn't too long before I realized I was… different… than others."

Mark glanced sharply at Nicolai, and he caught the faraway look in the man's eyes, as though his mind were somewhere else, journeying to another place and time, before he began to speak again.

"Soon I couldn't hide my peculiar capabilities and I knew I needed to leave the small town where I'd lived my whole life. Most of my life," he amended.

"I joined the Army, Special Forces, at seventeen and forged the permission slip that was needed if you weren't legal age."

Mark listened attentively to the agent speak, realizing as he did so, although the agent was succinct in his narration, giving away as little details as possible, he was learning about something not many people knew.

"I left the Army and trained at the FBI academy and joined their ranks as a field operative. Eventually I headed up a specialized team of highly trained agents, with varying talents."

After several moments had passed with no further answer from Montgomery, Mark asked bluntly, "what exactly can you do?"

"I'm sensitive to vocal vibrations. I am able to pick up on strong emotions through inanimate objects. Most sighted people rely on their sense of sight to guide them and help them make judgments. Those without sight, rely on their other senses, especially their sense of hearing, to guide them. In most instances I rely on my heightened sense of sound to guide me. I'm able to pick up nuances others cannot."

"Like a dog." Mark couldn't keep back.

"Actually my hearing is much better than your average dog's." Nicolai countered and watched Mark's eyebrows rise even higher than they'd been.

Mark remembered what occurred in the conference room with the two cards. "Something happened when you picked up the cards Maya was sent. I saw the way you looked." Mark was anxious to get to Maya, worried of this new threat.

"In answer to your question of control, I have received rigorous training to learn control. I've learned to block out unwanted 'sounds' from coming through. As far as the cards, they simply verified what I knew to be true. They were sent by the slayer," he said simply and didn't elaborate.

"So she's after Maya now."

"She's not going to harm Dr. Richardson. At least not yet," Montgomery amended. "She's placed her on a pedestal. Why, I don't know, but more than likely it's because of what Dr. Richardson does with Imani House. The slayer sees them both as 'protectors.' Dr. Richardson helps them escape a life of prostitution by taking them off the streets; the killer helps them escape by killing those who use their services."

"Why break into her house? Steal nothing but a small necklace with no real monetary value? A trophy?"

"Of sorts. She has the other one, the one that belonged to Dr. Richardson's foster sister. She wants to feel closer to her. She probably wears it now, perhaps both of them. Or she's given one away to a lover or family member so she can always look at it. Most serial criminals do this to enable them to relive the crime."

"What does this mean for Maya?"

"It means the slayer feels a kinship to her. However, if Maya does some perceived wrongdoing in her eyes, then she falls quickly from that erected pedestal and will no doubt become the next target."

"Like what? What wrongdoing could she possibly commit to make this maniac turn on her? You said she sees Maya and herself in similar roles as protectors. What could Maya do to change that view?" Mark asked the agent desperately, as they arrived at Imani House.

CHAPTER 44

"Dalia, the fashion fundraiser is a few weeks away, we just can't cancel it. Imani House relies on the money it generates to fund our programs."

"I am sorry, *Sesute*, but I do not think this is a good time for it. I, as well as you, am aware of how much we rely on this money. But no amount of money is worth one's life."

Mark could hear Maya and Dalia through Maya's partially opened door, as he and Montgomery walked inside after a brief knock.

Both women turned in the direction of the door as the men walked inside. Immediately, Mark walked over to where Maya stood and kissed her, showing no concern for their audience of two.

"Ms. Draugulis would you mind showing me around Imani House while the detective and Dr. Richardson have a moment," Nicolai asked.

"Of course Agent Montgomery." Dalia walked slowly toward the agent, her eyes roaming over his body. Nicolai kept his smile in check as he escorted Maya's statuesque assistant out of the office.

Once the door closed behind the pair, Mark bent down to kiss Maya more slowly and thoroughly, before gradually lifting his head to look down into her upturned face.

"I'm worried sweetheart," he admitted as he led her to one of the oversized chairs, and pulled her down unto his lap.

"Something to do with the burglary and the slayer?"

"Yes. We have reason to believe your anonymous admirer and the slayer are one in the same." He saw her eyes widen, as her hand automatically went to her mouth in disbelief.

"Oh no. How could that be? I mean--how, how do you know? Did you find any fingerprints? Some other evidence?" she asked, her words a jumble as she tried to make sense of this new information.

"Something like that sweetheart." He didn't want to lie to her, but wasn't ready to disclose what Montgomery told him in confidence.

"What does this mean then? The slayer is after me now? Dalia told me she had a bad feeling about this. That it was no ordinary burglary, and she was right. I'm really afraid, Mark." Maya's voice rose as she moved, trying to stand.

"Baby it's going to be okay. Nothing is going to happen to you. The slayer isn't targeting you. She likes you. She feels connected to you." Mark tried calming her, holding her in his arms in a light restrain.

"For now." Maya turned and looked at him, her expression tight. "But Mark, when someone has a personality disorder because of a neurosis, anything can happen to change their feelings, which in turn can change their behaviors. The bad thing about obsessions and mania are they're always changing, and what was once considered pleasing and acceptable to them, can turn to disgusting, and unacceptable overnight."

Mark thought about what she said. Psychology was her area of expertise, and she confirmed what he believed to be true. He knew what he had to do to protect Maya.

"Maya we're close to catching her, I believe it's going to happen soon. However, until we do, I'd like for you to move out of your home, as well as Dalia and the other family you have in the third wing." Her instant look of dismay made his heart ache.

"Where will we all go that's any safer? I don't want to leave my home. I don't want to force Dalia and the Johnson's to have to find somewhere else to go. All of them are in school, and the Johnson's have the children. They couldn't afford anything else for what they pay me, that's decent." Agitated, she moved away from Mark, and paced.

Mark stood up and physically took her by the arms to stop her. "If you listen for a minute I think I can help."

He walked them back to the chair. After he'd sat her down, he sat on the end of her desk and took both of her hands between his before speaking. "You, of course, will stay with me."

When she looked at him with raised eyebrows, he hastily amended his demand. "I'd like for you to stay with me, not only for personal reasons, but because I'd feel better knowing where you were. As far as your tenant's are concerned, my family owns a unit of condominiums and has several vacancies right now. The Johnson's, as well as Dalia, are more than welcome to stay there for the same price they pay you for rent."

Her doubtful expression prompted him to ask, "You do charge rent don't you, Maya?"

"I do," she said. "Dalia and the Johnson's do pay, but I could probably charge more," She admitted.

"What do you do with the money?" Mark intuitively asked.

"For the Johnson's, I put a small amount of their rent in their name, in a college fund for the girls. For Dalia, I place a percentage of the money in an account in her name for a down payment on a house if she wants."

Mark only smiled at her, his head tilted to the side as he observed her almost self-conscious expression. For whatever reason, she wasn't comfortable talking about her private philanthropy so he left it alone.

"Whatever arrangements you have with them and in the same amount will continue," he assured her. "When I walked in you and Dalia were discussing your upcoming fundraiser?"

"Yes, and Dalia thinks we should postpone the event. I suppose you think she's right about putting the fundraiser off until later?"

Mark saw the dejected look, and knew he would do anything in his power to help her continue her fundraiser. He surprised her with his next words.

"As of now I don't see a problem with the fundraiser continuing." When a smile spread across her features, he held up a cautioning hand. "With a few stipulations."

"What type of stipulations?" Maya demanded.

"Not too many. The same ones you're going to have to abide by until we catch the slayer. No more late nights Maya, increased security around Imani House, and a personal security guard assigned to you." He sat back and crossed his arms over his chest, ready for a battle with her.

"Those sound fair, Mark. I'm not sure how I'll be able to lessen my work hours without getting too far behind," she said, thinking out loud. "But I'll try. As far as the security guard is concerned don't you think that's too much?"

"No," he stated emphatically. "That's a non-negotiable stipulation sweetheart, until we catch this killer."

"Well I have a stipulation of my own regarding the guard. I don't want him 'reporting' back to you on my whereabouts every five minutes. I love you, Mark, and I don't have anything to hide, it's the principal of it. I hope you understand."

"I love you too, baby, you know that. And neither am I trying to keep tabs on you. I'm only concerned with your safety. He's *your* guard, there for *your* protection, not to 'report' your activities to me," he reassured her.

"Then I appreciate you protecting me, and will gladly accept a guard. Where do we go from here?"

"Montgomery and I want to interview the staff, and residents. Try and find out who saw what, or anything out of the ordinary. If you could give me a printout of all the staff including volunteers, as well as all of the residents we could get started with the interviewing," Mark asked her as they walked out of her office. As they entered Dalia's office, as Montgomery and Dalia were entering.

"Dalia could you give Mark a print out of all staff and residents? There's evidence that the slayer committed the burglary. Mark and Agent Montgomery are going to start the interviews right away to see if anyone has seen anything that's been overlooked."

"I will go and print out both rosters right away." Dalia moved to her computer and pulled the needed information.

Maya turned her attention to Mark and Nicolai. "While you're talking to the staff members, I'm going to speak with the residents to allay any fears they may have."

She turned back to Dalia, "Dal, could you gather the staff after you provide Mark and Agent Montgomery the list. If you could also call and arrange for the others who aren't here to come in as soon as they're able, I would appreciate it," she instructed.

"Of course. I will start assembling everyone as soon as I print the roster."

"I'll leave you to start your interviews. I'll meet back up with you as soon as I've finished speaking with the women."

* * * *

Mark and Nicolai were inside the conference room, the last staff member was leaving the room as Maya approached. "How did it go with your residents?" Mark asked.

"Fine. I didn't realize the time had gotten away from me. I wanted to make sure the women understood they weren't in danger, and you had questions that would help make sure everyone was safe here at the House. They seemed nervous, but basically everyone was content, not afraid."

"I'm glad you were able to allay their fears. We've interviewed most of the staff. No new information, but we still have a few more counselors coming in later. I also called the station and spoke with Jordan, he's arranging for extra security. We'd better start interviewing the residents. It would be best if you were with us as we interview them Maya," Mark told her.

"Ms. Vallejo was hesitant," Montgomery said to Mark when Maya excused herself from the room, to follow Ruby Vallejo.

"Does she know something?" He'd asked, trusting in Montgomery's odd abilities.

"Maybe. She was uncomfortable, unsure," Montgomery dragged

the last word out, as though weighing it carefully.

Mark went to the door of the conference in time to see Maya and the woman speaking quietly to one another before Maya smiled and placed her arm around Ruby's narrow shoulders, and gave her a light squeeze. The woman hugged Maya tightly before releasing her and striding quickly away. Mark turned away as Maya headed back into the room.

"Ruby told me something she didn't disclose earlier." Maya addressed both men as soon as she reentered the room, but her eyes were on Mark.

"What was that?"

" She'd noticed one of our weekend counselors, James Smith, had brought a vase of flowers in the same morning I received my flowers. At the time, Ruby had been hesitant to say anything."

"Who is this Mr. Smith?" Nicolai asked.

Maya turned in his direction and answered, "James is one of our newest practicum students. He comes in the evening and on the weekend."

With a frown, Mark took out the printouts Dalia had given them, double-checking the names. "James Smith? There's no James Smith on this list." He showed the list to Maya.

"I guess Dalia hasn't updated the roster. And he isn't here until later in the evening. He's not scheduled to come in until the end of the week."

"Why does he come in so late?"

"Our residents are used to being out late night and early morning, and that's a hard habit to break. It's good to have a counselor on duty for them in case they want to talk. I usually have a staff member available, and we lucked out with James needing those particular hours, because of his full-time job."

"We need to speak with him. Do you have his work phone number available?" Mark asked.

"I'm sure it's on file. I'll check with Dalia." Maya left the room and went in search of the phone number.

As she went in search of the information Mark and Nicolai perused the remaining counselors on the list, circling the names of those they still needed to contact.

"If you don't mind I would like to speak with him," Nicolai requested as Maya returned back to the room, phone number in hand.

"We don't have his work phone number but we do have his home and cell numbers." She told them.

"Dr. Richardson could I use your phone please? In case he has caller i.d, it might be better for your phone number to show," he explained.

After she handed him the telephone, he dialed the number, and on the second ring it was picked up with a friendly, "Hello you've reached, James Smith. At the sound of the tone please leave a message. Have a wonderful day!" Nicolai disengaged the phone after leaving a message for him to call Imani House.

With a small shake of his head he said, "I'm sure he'll call back but I don't think you have anything to worry about," he said more to Mark than to Maya.

Maya was confused with the conversation, and realized there was something she was missing, the two men engaging in some sort of silent communication she wasn't privy to. She looked back and forth between them, waiting for an answer.

"We'll follow up with another call, and if he doesn't call back, I'll be here when he comes to work to ask him a few questions."

After speaking to the security guards once more, Mark and Nicolai waited until the two uniform police had arrived before they left.

Mark's call to one of his brothers had produced two plain clothed guards, whose expertise would allow them to go undetected outside guarding Imani House and its occupants. He'd also produced two personal guards who would take turns to provide Maya with 24-hour protection.

Before he reluctantly left, Mark turned to Maya and kissed her lingeringly on the lips. "I'll be back as soon as I can. If I think it's getting too late, I want you to let Mike give you a ride home." He referred to the silent watchful guard who'd discretely given them privacy.

"Mark do you really think all of this is necessary?"

"If I thought all of this was necessary I wouldn't let you out of my sight," he told her grimly. "There's someone out there who has a fixation on you, and until we find her, all of this may not be needed, but it damn sure is required." He kissed her good-bye again before he left.

As Mark and Agent Montgomery strapped on their seat belts, Mark asked, "The counselor? Nothing?"

"No. But it wouldn't hurt to have a talk with him," Nicolai told Mark, and leaned his head against the headrest and closed his eyes.

CHAPTER 45

Late that night as Nicolai lay down on the soft hotel mattress, his mind replayed the soft feminine voice he was becoming more and more intimate with.

There was something definitely 'off' about the voice, something was obvious he was missing. He rubbed his temples wearily; the headaches were getting worse and were interfering with his abilities.

He slowed his breathing, and consciously relaxed each major muscle in his body. He lowered his heart rate, slowly and methodically.

When he'd achieved the cadence and beat he needed, he opened his mind, and drifted into a trancelike awareness. Reaching out across the miles, his dream self reached for, and connected with the only one who could help. *"Dafina. I need you."*

* * * *

"It's not so bad living with me is it?" Mark asked Maya, as she lay in front of him on his king-sized bed.

"No. The last week hasn't been too bad at all. If I can't be in my own home, there's no other place I'd rather be, than with you."

He felt the same. Beneath the dense braid that lay heavily on top of her exposed breasts, his hand found and massaged the heavy orb, his thumb caressed the hard peak.

"The last few weeks we've spent most of our free time in your house, and it's been great, but it feels good having you here."

His other hand traveled down the length of her small curves. He stopped at the small triangle junction at the top of her legs, and stroked the hidden nub.

He delved one of his fingers inside, and withdrew it, saturated with her cream. After he took a small lick, he groaned. "You taste so damn good, baby." He spread the moisture back over her clit, and continued to stroke her.

"I don't want this to end. I can't imagine not being with you, now that you've become a part of my life. When this case is over, I don't want you to leave. If you don't want to stay here, if you want to go back to your house we can do that, as long as we're together. Say we'll stay together," he begged huskily, his throat clogged.

"Yes, Mark, of course I'll stay," she moaned, her head tossing against the front of his chest.

With her agreement, he lifted her up and onto his aching, hard shaft, spearing her deeply from behind. He took both of her hips in his hands and set the pace for their lovemaking. Slow at first he guided her, before the tight wet feel of her, demanded he increase the pace.

He lifted her thigh up and over his leg, as he continued to rock into her from the back. He kissed the side of her neck, her small shell-shaped ear, and her smooth brown throat, down to the back of her shoulders.

"Baby, you feel *so* good. I've never felt like this. Never. No matter how many times we make love, it only gets better. I love you so much," he panted as he leveled her body on his.

He knew it was good for her, and he could easily come in this position, but he knew she needed a little more to achieve her ultimate pleasure. "Push back, baby," he instructed, and applied the right amount of pressure with his hands. When her orgasm broke, he felt his balls tingle, signaling his orgasm struggling to break free.

He flipped her on her back, and covered her body with his. He lifted both of her hands high above her head, as he plunged harder, picking up the pace. His body demanded more as he surged into her. He welcomed the way her slick sheath milked his cock when she orgasmed for the second time.

Throwing his head back, he allowed the orgasm to flood his body, his coarse groans of relief hard and long, as he emptied into her willing body.

Once his heartbeat had returned to semi-normal, Mark lifted his head and stared down at the small woman who held his heart in his hands. Feelings of love and permanence flooded him as he voiced out loud what had been in his mind. "Let's make a baby."

Instantly, Mark felt the change come over her loose-limbed body. Instead of feeling her soft pliant curves, he felt a rigidity invade her limbs.

Rolling away, Maya sat up and tried to get out of the bed. He placed one arm out and easily restrained her. "What? What's wrong? Okay. I know that didn't come out right. But I really would like to talk about it. What's wrong?" He asked worriedly when she said nothing in response. He turned her back around to face him. "Maya what the hell is wrong?"

"I don't know what to say. You took me by surprise. I'm not sure what to think. I've never thought about children and me. I didn't know my parents and I'm not sure if I would know how to care for a child," she nearly stuttered her answer.

"Maya look at me. You are the most caring person I've ever known. You show love and concern to women society has thrown away. You help without thought or a desire for acknowledgment. "

He saw her eyes avert his as he spoke. He wasn't sure if she was listening to him at all.

"Sweetheart, you're hardworking and loyal and it extends to everyone you come in contact with. From an early age you nurtured your foster sister as though she were your child instead of a sibling. No, don't turn away from me," he demanded, his hand gripping her upper arm as he forced her to look at him.

"You were only a few years older than Ally, yet you took on the role of mother and protector for her. You did the best you could for her and she knew that, Maya. But no matter how wonderful a parent you are, God has given everyone free will. Some don't choose wisely, but there is only so much you can do. After you've done all you can, there's nothing else to do, baby." He gathered her in his arms when he saw her eyes tear up.

"Please don't allow the way Allison chose to live her life to influence your belief in your parenting skills. That would be an injustice to you, and our child," he nearly begged.

Maya finally returned his hug. As she held on to him, she didn't say a word, simply hugged him, rubbing her head back and forth against his chest. When his phone rang, he barely stifled a curse.

"Let it ring, it'll go to voice mail."

"But what if it's an emergency? With everything going on...."

Mark groaned but answered, "Hello" he barked into the receiver.

"Thank God you answered Detective Halstan. This is Dalia, is Maya with you?"

"Dalia what's going on? Where are you?"

"I am here at Imani House. I came by to retrieve a document I need to work on at home. I am not sure, but I believe Maya has received another message from that woman."

"What is it exactly?" Mark asked Dalia, while Maya leaned close into his side, trying to hear the conversation.

"When I walked into the office, I noticed the package right away, addressed to Maya."

"Did you open it?"

"Yes I did. I open all mail and that includes packages for Maya as part of my administrative duties. When I opened this one, a 'bouquet' of dead flowers lay inside with a note sitting on top."

"Did you open the note?"

"No, I left everything alone."

"Great Dalia. Here's what I want you to do--leave the office and lock it when you do and then go directly to the security guard. Are you on a cordless phone?" He started putting his clothes on as he spoke, and watched with raised brows as Maya did the same.

"Yes I'm on the cordless."

"Okay, I'm going to stay on the line and when you reach one of the guards I want you to give the phone to him okay Dal?"

"No problem, the guard is outside the office door. I will hand the phone to him now, Mark." Within seconds he was speaking with the private security officer.

"Listen Whitaker, I need you to go and do a check around the House. Make sure everyone is accounted for. Make sure you have the resident and staff roster to verify against. I don't want you to let anyone leave the House under *any* circumstances until I get there. Ms. Draugulis has found a suspicious package and it's imperative everyone in that house stay where they are," he instructed.

Before he hung up the phone, Mark asked to speak to Dalia once more. "Dalia I'll contact the guards outside and one will be instructed to come into the house, while the other checks the perimeters. I'll be there as soon as possible."

"Let's go, I'm ready." Maya was dressed and ready as she gazed at him expectantly.

"I don't suppose there's anyway I could convince you to stay home?" When she only gave him a *look*, one brow arched, he didn't bother arguing with her.

"Fine, but I insist you stay close to me. Dalia didn't read the note, but I don't like the sounds of a dead flower arrangement being sent to you," he told her grimly.

On the way to Imani House he made two calls. The first was to the security he'd hired for her, alerting them to what had transpired and instructing them on what to do.

The second one was to Jordan. "Jordan, Maya has received an anonymous package at Imani House, and it doesn't look good," he said without preamble as soon as his partner picked up the phone with a grumbled 'Hello.'

Jordan's voice lost all traces of sleep quickly. "Where are you?"

"I'm on my way to the House." He looked over at Maya in the passenger seat of his Expedition, and revised his statement, "We're on our way. We should be there in fifteen, twenty minutes tops."

"I'm on my way too. I'll get there as soon as possible."

"Okay partner thanks. I'll see you there."

CHAPTER 46

"I'm sorry sir, but Detective Halstan says everyone needs to stay put until he arrives and that means volunteers as well," the security officer informed James.

"I don't understand why I need to stay; I didn't see anything so I won't be of any help," he told the large guard. He was being forced to stay when he would rather be anywhere else but Imani House when the detective arrived.

"This is ridiculous. Dr. Richardson will not like that you've kept me here, when I really need to *go*." He frantically tried to think of anything would allow him to leave.

Dalia walked into the room as James was beginning to seriously start ranting. "What seems to be the problem Mr. Smith? Officer Rodriguez?" She asked.

"Mr. Smith insists he needs to leave, after I've informed him that Detective Halstan has given me strict instructions *no one* is cleared to go before he arrives."

"I didn't *insist*," he insisted. "Something has come up unexpectedly and I would like to be able to leave to take care of it."

"James I'm sure Detective Halstan and Maya are on their way. I called and they will soon be here," she told him, glancing at her watch as she said so.

"Why do *I* need to stay? As I was telling *this man* here, I didn't see anything. I've only been here for a couple of hours and in that time I've been in session with two of the residents. I don't know what help I could be to anyone," he nearly wailed in his agitation.

"Well that does not matter Mr. Smith," Dalia told him, and turned her attention away when the front door opened and Mark, Maya, and Jordan entered the house.

"Maya, Detectives, I am glad you are here." She went to Maya's side and gave her friend a hug in greeting.

"I'm sorry it took so long to come inside, but Jordan and I received a report from the guard who's been surveying the perimeter," Mark explained.

He turned his attention to Rodriguez; "I'm assuming everything is fine in here?"

"Yes sir." The guard retrieved his notebook from his pocket and briefed Mark and Jordan. After he'd briefed them, the officer turned to where the counselor had been standing, only to find him gone.

"There is only one counselor on duty sir, and he insists he needs to leave right away. He's been instructed to wait until you've had the opportunity to question him before he's cleared to go."

Mark dismissed the guard and looked at Dalia as Maya asked, "James?"

"Yes. He says he didn't see anything and he needs to leave in order to take care of some important business. We told him he must wait," Dalia told Maya with frown on her face.

"What's wrong Dalia?"

"Nothing really. James didn't seem to be himself. He seemed very anxious," she told them and then shook her head slightly. "I'm sure it is nothing. As he said, he has an emergency."

"Let's take a look at the package." Mark led them out of the foyer and into the House.

"Why don't I go and question this counselor and I'll meet back up with you when I'm done. I'll keep him around if it's necessary," Jordan volunteered and left the trio in search of James Smith.

When they reached the office, Dalia unlocked the door and turned on the light. Mark pulled the gloves on his hands before he picked up the boxed arrangement. He extracted the small note inside and read the contents out loud.

"Dr. Richardson I admire you and what you do for our fallen sisters. I am also sorry about your sister that was not supposed to happen; however it did bring us together. Unfortunately she didn't keep the best of company and sometimes--bad things happen when we don't keep good company. This is something you should be aware of. Be careful Maya, before something unfortunate happens to you. That would be a total waste. An unfortunate total waste."

"Damn it," Mark cursed and glanced at Maya, the fear in her eyes made him curse again. He placed the note back in the package and gathered her in his arms. "It's going to be okay. Really it is." He was at a loss for words, as anger and frustration warred for dominance.

"You really are starting to sound like a broken record." Her laugh sounded forced.

"How's that?"

"You've said those exact words more times than I care to count. I'm fine, and I know it's going to be okay. I'll just be glad when this is over," she took a deep breath. "My question is how did it get here? And more importantly, are my residents as or staff at risk?"

Maya frowned at him, as she asked the question.

"I don't know how it got here Maya but we *will* find out. And as far as everyone's safety, if I have to stay here myself until this case is solved, no one will be left unprotected. I promise you, baby."

Jordan entered the office after a brief knock, and Mark showed him Maya's package.

"Damn," he said bluntly, echoing Mark's earlier sentiment after he read the accompanying note.

"Did you speak with the counselor?" Mark asked after Jordan looked over the note and flowers.

"Yeah. He didn't arrive until after seven in the evening. He says he was in session with two of the residents immediately after his arrival."

"Were you able to confirm that information with anyone?"

"Sure did. I spoke to the resident he was counseling, and she confirmed the time. Another resident reported Ruby Vallejo accepted the package from the carrier."

Mark sighed. He'd hoped Jordan could have found out more. He looked at Maya and Dalia and asked, "why don't the two of you follow us. Jordan and I need to question Ms. Vallejo, and I'd like to talk to your intern before he leaves."

They questioned the residents and staff, trying to determine if anyone had any valuable information, and were markedly disappointed when no one did.

Mark spoke with James as the counselor was leaving and agreed with Jordan that he knew nothing that could help them. In the end they found the only one with any helpful information was Ruby Vallejo.

Late that afternoon, Ruby had accepted the mail, and the small brown package was among the varied pieces. She knew neither Dalia nor Maya were at the House, and so she left the package and mail in the basket outside Dalia's locked office door.

"No postage, and of course no return of address. Damn." Frustrated, Mark slammed his hand against the wall.

"Shit's heatin' up for real man. What do you make of it?"

"Jordan I don't know what to make of this crap. One thing I don't like is the wording in the note. It's clearly a warning. Although covert, it's still a warning. We need to tell the lieutenant, as well as Agent Montgomery as soon as possible."

"Will Maya go into protective custody?"

"No. She agreed to work only during the day and do as much work as she can from home, but other than that, I can't make her go to a safe house. But at least she's going to do most of her work from my house."

"Where I'm assuming you'll have the place guarded to the hilt?" Jordan asked, with a knowing smile.

"Like Fort Knox. Man I hope I'm not making a mistake by not forcing the issue." Mark ran a nervous hand down his face. "I've got to catch this bitch before she sets her sights higher, and decides it time for Maya to be eliminated." Mark told his partner grimly.

CHAPTER 47

"Arlinda says Maya is disappointed over the decision to postpone the fundraiser," Jordan told Mark, around a mouthful of a massive ham sandwich. "Actually, what she *said*, is 'Maya is pissed the hell off that she had to postpone the fundraiser,'" he amended.

Over the last few nights, they had stayed late into the night working on the investigation, and tonight both men had stayed even later, trying to find overlooked clues, or missing angles.

"Yeah I know it was really hard for her. This fundraiser one of her main sources of revenue for her programs and you know how important Imani House is to her."

"Man as loaded as your family is, you should be able to write a check that would carry the tab for her programs. Don't you have a trust fund or something?" Jordan laughed as he went over to the small refrigerator in the corner of the precinct, and withdrew two cold drinks, and tossed one to Mark.

"I've thought about it believe me, I'm not sure how to ask without offending her. Imani House means everything to her. One of the main things she strives to teach the residents, is self-sufficiency, so I don't know what she'd say if I offered her the proverbial blank check." Wearily rubbing the back of his neck, Mark raised the drink to his mouth and took a long swallow.

"Imani House means so much to her, and all of her staff and residents are incredibly loyal to her. That's one of the main reasons I have *some* comfort in her working there, and not locked away somewhere in a safe house."

"That and the small army you've hired to protect her," Jordan reminded him.

"Well yeah that too," he admitted sheepishly. "But seriously, they look out for each other which is a rare quality. You know I've met all of her staff and they all seem to genuinely care about Maya's vision for Imani House."

As he thought back to her staff, the conversation he had with the new counselor surfaced to the forefront of his brain. There was something that nagged him, something familiar about the man he couldn't put his finger on.

"The only one I'm not too sure of is that new guy--what's his name … James. James Smith, shit shit shit!" Mark exclaimed, dropping his sandwich and throwing the empty soda in the trash.

"Man what is it? What is it?" Jordan asked as Mark picked up the phone and dialed his home number.

"Damn it! She's not fucking there." Frantically he dialed another set of digits and waited for Maya to answer, and felt himself nearly pass out with relief when she did.

"Imani House this is Dr. Richardson."

"Maya what the *hell* are you doing at the House? You promised me you would stay the hell away from that place at night. What in the hell are you doing?" He yelled into the phone.

"Why in the *'hell'* are you yelling at me? I know what I promised you, but I need to go over the House budget and since we're putting off the fundraiser. I have to see where we are fiscally in case I have to supplement some of our programs myself. And let me tell you something, I don't appreciate being cursed out, I…"

"Baby I'm sorry but this is really important that you do what I ask. Is James Smith working tonight?" He impatiently cut in the middle of her tirade.

"No he's taking the night off because of his job." She took a deep breath into the phone, and he tried to calm his racing heart.

"Where's your personal guard-please tell me the man is there with you," Mark both asked and pleaded. He hoped she hadn't somehow convinced the guard he didn't have to go with her to Imani House.

"He's right here. Well, actually he's waiting in Dalia's office for me."

Mark let out a sigh. "Baby could you put him on the phone?" He asked and waited for the guard to pick up the receiver before he spoke again.

"We think we have a suspect in the case. Under no circumstances are you to leave Maya alone. And neither are you to allow James Smith to enter Imani House under any circumstances," his instructed the guard. "The police will be there shortly." After he'd received the guard's word, he asked to speak to Maya once again.

"Okay, Maya, this is really important. I want you to stay put. I need for you to basically shut Imani House down until I send reinforcements."

"You're scaring me what's going on?"

"There is *nothing* for you to be afraid of. I'm taking every precaution I can, and you're safe. I think we may have a suspect."

Mark didn't want to voice out loud his gut belief that her counselor James Smith, and the evidence room clerk J. Smith were one in the same, and both personas were connected with the *San Antonio Slayer*.

"You stay there with the guards and you'll be fine sweetheart."

"You think the counselor and the slayer are connected?" Jordan asked, as soon as Mark said good-bye to Maya.

"I'd bet money on it being a real possibility." As he spoke, Mark placed a call to the department operator. After giving the operator his name and badge number, he requested to be transferred to the evidence room.

"Detective Halstan? It's me Jack." The operator identified himself.

"Hi Jack." After the operator said his name, Mark instantly placed the retired officer, and asked for information on James Smith.

"Just a little info, if you need to reach that clerk, he's working the late shift and should still be in the evidence room. The supervisor is having them all rotate shifts for the next week to prepare for their upcoming inspection." The retired officer made it a point to be as knowledgeable of each department's business as he could. Mark was thankful for the man's nosiness in this instance.

"Thanks Jack I appreciate the tip, keep up the good work."

"The counselor and the evidence clerk are one in the same. He's in the evidence room working late. Let's go," Mark told Jordan without preamble, and the two men leaped from their desks.

Lieutenant Hernandez came out of his office as they were racing out of the squad room. "What's going on?" He yelled, temporarily halting them in their tracks.

"We may have a suspect lieutenant. We're on our way to question him."

"*Him?*"

"Yeah I'll explain later. Sir, could you have a chaser sent to Imani House. Maya is working late and I don't like it." Mark requested, anxious to get to the clerk.

"Of course, you two go. I'll take care of it," he reassured both men.

Turning, with a pensive look on his face, Lieutenant Hernandez closed his office door and locked it after Mark and Jordan raced from the room.

When he walked past the night dispatcher, the man looked up and asked if the lieutenant needed him to have a car sent over to Imani House.

"No thanks Lou, I'll take care of it. I'll take care of everything," he said with a broad grin, and left the squad room.

* * * *

As he'd spoken to the lieutenant, Lou noticed a thin gold chain around his neck, with a small jagged charm attached. He normally wouldn't have noticed such a small thing, but it looked out of place on him, because he had never seen him wear jewelry of any kind.

The lieutenant must have loosened his tie and forgotten about it. His collar had been partially opened, and the small gold chain had been in clear view. Mentally shrugging his shoulders, Lou went back to the crossword puzzle that had been giving him hell trying to solve for the better part of the last hour.

* * * *

Mark and Jordan burst into the evidence room without knocking, and startled James who was standing before a tall, gray metal government-issue file cabinet. The look of surprise on his face was soon followed by apprehension. "What can I do for you, Detectives?"

"We have questions that need to be answered now. I suggest you call someone in to take over for you, or we can close the evidence room down until someone arrives." Mark barely held himself in check. He didn't give a damn if the room was left wide open, but he gave the man the chance to come on his own recognizance.

"What … what is this concerning?" James was clearly taken aback by their presence.

"It's concerning you and some anonymous gifts you've been sending Dr. Richardson. And let's not forget to add in a whole slew of murders over the last six months."

"I don't know what you're talking about. I haven't sent any gifts and I definitely haven't killed anyone," James said in a rush, with a distinct quiver in his voice.

Both men noted the clerk's reaction. "Let's go Smith," Jordan told him as he reached around to take the man by the arm, and lead him out from behind his counter. "'You have the right to remain silent, anything you say, can, and will be held against you in a court of law…'" Jordan began reciting the man's Miranda rights to him as they led him out of the office.

* * * *

Humming lightly, Jaime Hernandez calmly put the key into the ignition and started the vehicle, before he calmly reversed out of his reserved space. As he drove down along the highway, he remembered that day over twenty years ago, when his schoolmate followed him as they left detention together with his tongue swirling outside of his mouth, making his nasty comments.

"Everybody knows all about you Jaime. What--you only give it up for money? I got a few ends for you to do what you do best." Eric said, walking backwards, facing Jaime as he taunted him.

"Eric, why don't you go away? I don't know what you're talking about. And don't you have a *girlfriend* anyway?" he'd asked, trying unsuccessfully to escape Eric's groping hand.

"Leave my girlfriend out of it you damn freak. I asked you a question. Is the only way you'll do it, is if you get paid?" Eric had grabbed him by the arm and pulled him tight against his chest.

"Why would you want to do anything with me anyway-Aren't you the *big man* on campus? Why try and get some from a 'freak'?" Jaime remembered how his heart thumped irregularly against his then frail chest, and he'd tried desperately to pull away from Eric, scared after he realized how isolated the two of them were in the corridor.

"What the hell you tryin' to say? Oh, you paying for that you goddamn queer." Eric had pushed him to the floor, and unbuttoned his jeans. "When I'm done with you, you'll know *when*, and *how*, to use that dumb mouth."

With a grim smile Jaime e turned on the radio, as a hasty revision of his original plan quickly formed in his mind.

"All good things must eventually end, and unfortunately, now is the time for this good thing to end," he spoke out loud, and to no one in particular.

As he hummed along to the music, he turned up the volume and sang in tune with Shania Twain, with carefree abandon. "Man, I feel like a woman oh oh oh...." he laughed out loud, tickling himself over *his* version of the song.

CHAPTER 48

"Why did you start volunteering at Imani House? Was it to get closer to Dr. Richardson?" Jordan asked, as soon as they shoved the clerk into the stiff metal chair in the interrogation room. He examined the cuff of his shirt as he asked, as though they were talking about nothing more important than the weather.

"Yes it's true I do volunteer at Imani House. But that's not a crime the last time I checked, Detective." His arms were tightly crossed over his frail chest, and his upper lip drew back in a sneer when he addressed Jordan.

"No that's not a crime, James, but what is a crime is sending threatening letters and murder. Yeah, mother fucker. Murder's a crime the last time I checked," Mark nearly exploded as he stared at the little man, holding back the urge to pick his ass up and throw him across the room.

"I told you--I do *not* know what you're talking about. I think Dr. Richardson is a wonderful, dedicated woman, even if her taste in men does *suck*." He insolently drew out the last word.

"We're betting you do know what we're talking about asshole," Jordan countered.

As Jordan spoke, Mark had moved to stand behind the clerk, and it was then he noticed the thin gold chain around his neck. He walked around to face James and grabbed the small medallion that hung attached to the chain.

"What the hell is this then?" Mark didn't want to break the small delicate chain because he knew how much it meant to Maya, "Take it off mother fucker," he growled, and barely refrained from tearing it from his neck.

With shaking hands, the clerk hastily did as he was instructed and handed it to Mark. "It was a gift, a gift from my sister," he stuttered as Mark turned the small half-moon charm over in his hand, and read the inscription.

Mark grabbed the small clerk by his collar, and with little effort, hoisted him up, muscles bulging, as he held James inches away from his face.

"You've got less than two seconds to start telling me the goddamn truth, you little son-of-a-bitch, or I will rip your ass apart," he said between gritted teeth, enunciating each word slowly.

James quickly spoke, "It really was a gift. Okay. Okay not from my sister," he admitted quickly, his teeth rattling when Mark shook him once in warning. "It was from my lover."

Jordan and Mark looked at the man and simultaneously shouted, "What goddamn lover?"

Although still afraid, the clerk stared defiantly at the two detectives, and then said a name that made both men's eyes widen, and jaws drop in morbid disbelief, leaving a stunned, comical look on their faces, before they sprung into action.

* * * *

The hotel room was dark and quiet. The only audible sound came from the warm San Antonio air as it wafted into the opened windows, accompanied with the natural sounds of the night.

No sound came from the man who lay still on the bed. His eyes were closed, seemingly in sleep. He tilted his head slightly to the side, as though listening carefully, in silent communication with some unseen person.

Nicolai eyes opened wide, and a name escaped, from tightly clenched lips; Jaime Hernandez. Picking up his cell, Nic quickly dialed, before leaping into action.

CHAPTER 49

"Where's Lieutenant Hernandez?" Mark asked the night officer.

Lou looked up from his crossword puzzle and answered, "He left around the same time you and Detective Phillips left the squad room."

"Shit," in unison Mark and Jordan spoke, knowing without being told, where he was headed, the next words coming from the night officer confirmed their fears.

"He said he was headed over to Imani House and he'd take care of everything."

"Send back up right away to Imani House Lou, we have a dangerous situation. And inform the officers that Lieutenant Hernandez is considered armed and dangerous," Mark yelled out as he and Jordan ran, top speed, out of the precinct.

"Lieutenant Hernandez? Armed and dangerous? What the hell?" Lou asked their retreating backs.

Mark picked up his cell phone with trembling fingers, and dialed Maya's personal line at Imani House, frantically praying she would answer the phone. He jumped inside the passenger seat as Jordan got behind the driver's seat. He impatiently waited for Maya to pick up the phone. When she answered in her normal voice, he almost wept with relief.

"Maya I'm not sure how much time we have, but you have got to get out of there sweetheart. Where's your guard?" He didn't take the time out to greet her, fear making his voice tremble.

"My guard is right outside Dalia's office. I've been working in here since we got off the phone and I haven't seen him, but I'm sure he's still there. What's going on, Mark? You're scaring me."

"Maya get out of there and have the guard take you to my parent's house. He knows the address, now Maya," he yelled, a sick feeling in the pit of his stomach.

"Okay I am. I'm going to my door now," she didn't question him. A knock on her door came within seconds of her reply.

"Maya ask who it is-- Don't..." It was too late. Mark could hear her open the door.

"Lieutenant Hernandez what are you doing here?" Mark could hear her ask.

"Maya listen, the lieutenant is very dangerous, get out of there, baby, and go to the guard right away, Maya … Maya…" Looking down at his cell phone, he saw the call had been disconnected.

He turned to Jordan, blinded with tears, and said in a hoarse voice, "He's there. He's with her."

"Man we'll get to her, we'll get to her." Jordan drove as fast as the sedan could go, stretching his driving skills to the limit, as they sped along the San Antonio streets, frantically trying to reach Maya before it was too late.

* * * *

After pressing the end button on the wireless phone, Lieutenant Hernandez calmly pushed Maya back into her office, and closed the door, the sound of the lock piercing, in the quiet of the room.

"Was that your *boyfriend* on the line Dr. Richardson?" His voice was pleasant as he guided her to her seat and took the chair facing her, sitting down and casually crossing his legs as though nothing were out of the ordinary.

Before he took the phone from her, Maya heard Mark say the lieutenant was dangerous. However, had she not heard him tell her that, she would have already known. Although he appeared calm and relaxed, his eyes were glazed, and his benign smile was eerily fixed, giving him a demonic façade.

Maya had worked with people with a variety of mental illnesses and she recognized he was mentally unstable; a split had fractured his personality completely in half.

She also knew how intelligent he was, and although her first inclination was to calm him, he wasn't one of her residents. He didn't come here for a counseling session, he had come to kill her.

Smiling at him in a negligent manner she said, "I'm not quite sure I would call him my boyfriend, I feel a little too old to use that term, but he serves his purpose." She gave him a conspirator's wink.

Clearly surprised at her answer, she noticed his posture relaxed naturally, and although his voice remained soft and high, the glazed look started to fade from his eyes.

"You know I'm really sorry about Allison." He spoke as though they had already been discussing her sister. His words instantly confirmed everything, and it was all she could do to maintain a neutral expression and not jump up and strangle him.

Putting on a cloak of nonchalance she asked with casual curiosity, "and why is that lieutenant?"

"Please call me Jaime," he smilingly invited before continuing.

"Thank you. I will," Maya smiled back as though they were two old friends.

"Those idiots were right when they said she was drunk. She was in the back of his car passed out when he picked me up. I had him drive to an area *I* chose and he parked the car. He started on me right away, it wasn't easy to convince him that it would be better outside." He mentioned the victim found with Allison, with remembered disgust. "But in the end for a piece of ass they all follow." Jaime philosophically shrugged his shoulders.

"What happened? How did Ally get involved? Did she wake up and witness what you did?" Maya didn't try and disguise the sadness in her voice.

He reached across the small space that separated them and gently ran his hand down her face, only to drop it when she recoiled from his touch.

His face hardened as he continued. "Had she kept her drunk ass in the car she would have lived to whore another day. How 'bout that?"

Maya didn't want to anger him. She knew Mark was on his way and she needed to keep him talking as long as possible, so she changed the subject. "What's your connection with James? What role does he play in all of this?"

For a moment he only stared at her, his face twisting in a parody of a smile before he answered. "So you know about Mr. Smith? Umm. Well he definitely served *his* purpose. In more ways than one, he served his purpose." Jaime mimicked her earlier wink.

"However, once again, most men, including fags, will do anything for a piece of ass. James came in handy several times for me. I met him at a bar where he was moaning about how he couldn't finish graduate school and he didn't have a job, yada yada yada, and I saw an opportunity to 'help.' You see we're not so different, we both like to help those in need." A maddening look of conciliation graced his lean face.

Maya didn't know if he really believed that or not, so she was quiet when he paused, not wanting to give him the wrong feedback.

When she said nothing, he continued. "I helped him get a job, *and* I helped him get back into school. But I told him nothing came free," he said, stringing the last word out in a sing songy voice. "One day soon I would need his help. We were 'friends' for a while as I began to formulate my plans, and then I called in my favor. He had no idea what I was doing when he would help me park my car and drop me off in some different location."

"He didn't think that it was odd? The way you were dressed?"

She ventured a guess.

"Oh that? Nooo." He giggled lightly. "I often played 'dress-up' for him. I imagine he got a real kick out of seeing the 'Lieutenant' all dolled-up. I would even let him take pictures of us, it gave him a sense of power, *leverage* over me. Or so his sorry ass thought," Jaime told her, and laughed out loud at the idea.

"You had no plans to keep him around did you?"

Jaime's laughter came to an abrupt end. "Well aren't you the smart one." A look of hatred entered his eyes before quickly leaving, replaced with one of his irritating small smiles.

"No, I didn't. Why not let the fool think whatever he wanted. I knew *I* held the power, not him, and *I* was calling the shots," he answered emphatically, anger tightening his features. "He didn't have a clue when I had him deliver the flowers to you. Although, I think he was a bit jealous, thinking my interest in you was not so platonic." Jaime giggled again.

"James was the one who brought the flowers in to me after all. How did he bring in the last package? One of the ladies said she accepted them from the postman." Maya tried to refocus his attention.

"Oh that." With a negligible wave of his hand he continued, "that wasn't at all hard to accomplish. He didn't make that delivery, your friendly mail carrier did. Do you know how easy it is to give a government employee a few dollars to perform a small service? Not such a difficult task at all."

From the restless way he was crossing and recrossing his legs Maya knew he was growing agitated. She didn't want to reenergize his true reason for visiting, so she asked him a personal question, her language and voice friendly and causal as though they were two friends chatting.

"You know when I was a child, actually throughout my childhood and adolescence," she amended her statement, "I was always treated as though I were an inconvenience, as though my mere presence was repugnant to my foster mother."

As she started speaking, the honesty of her words caught him, and he eased back into his chair, all signs of agitation evaporating as though it never were. His attention remained raptly on her.

"I never felt as though I fit in. I was always lonely and set apart from my peers. I had the responsibility of raising my foster sister."

Although Maya referred to Allison, she knew she couldn't say her name and keep it together in front of the man who'd killed her. "I never knew what it was like to be an average kid. I cooked, cleaned, and cared for my sister and there wasn't much room for anything else. My dad was black and my mother was white. My foster mother would say all types of hateful things about my dual heritage. She would call me names an animal shouldn't be called, let alone a child. It was beyond hateful."

"I grew up with my Aunt Meg." Eyes straight ahead, with no discernible expression, Jaime related to Maya his childhood, a childhood fraught with neglect, humiliation, and abuse. "I was small because I didn't eat the healthy amount of food as a child. The doctors said I was malnourished. I just knew I was hungry all the time," he told her in a voice devoid of emotion.

"It didn't help that my aunt spent as little money on me as possible. She'd get my clothes from thrift stores, church basements, wherever she could get them. Sometimes they were clothes for boys, and sometimes not. She didn't care. The kids at school would call me fag, queer, whatever, because I was so small, and because of the clothes I wore."

"Sometimes children can be as hurtful as any adult. Or worst."

"Yes," he agreed simply, "they can. Like you, I was a product of a racial mix." He made eye contact with her at this point, a small sad smile playing around his mouth.

"My father was Hispanic, and my mother was white. He didn't claim me. According to Aunt Meg, he didn't believe I was his. He was a prominent man in the community, with a family of his own, and would 'visit' my mother occasionally. When she told him she was pregnant, he refused to believe I was his, since he wasn't her only 'visitor.'"

"Is that why you killed them, Jaime?"

"Those men? Those men who wanted to get their rocks off and leave? Without a care in the world about a life they were destroying? Those fucking pillars of society?" His voice rose, becoming more and more strident with each question.

Standing up he nearly toppled the chair over and advanced toward Maya before coming to a halt. He moved quickly across to the other end of the room.

Once he'd gotten himself back under control, visibly taking deep breaths, he squint his eyes and pursed his lips looking steadily at Maya, as he lightly stroked his chin with his thumb and forefinger.

Under his unerring gaze she kept herself still, displaying none of the fear and uncertainty churning in her belly. She knew he was teetering on the edge of full mental breakdown, and one false move from her, could push him completely over edge.

"Partly. I guess that was part of the reason why I made them pay," he finally agreed after taking deep breaths.

"Aunt Meg followed in her big sister's footsteps in her 'career choice' so to speak. She also shared my mother's lousy taste in men. My first sexual experience was performed at the hands of Aunt Meg's sometimes live in boyfriend Rick. I was only fourteen and it wasn't consensual," he said with blunt honesty, and a faraway look in his eyes.

"Rick decided it was time for me to earn my keep, and he turned me out. He thought it was funny. Always making jokes about keeping it all in the family. Aunt Meg was too damn weak to break away even though she knew what was going on."

Maya was horrified by Jaime's story. Unable to stop the tears from falling, she made no attempt to wipe them away as he told her of his subsequent rape by a schoolmate.

"That was the last time. That was the last time anyone, especially a man, hurt or humiliated me. *I* started taking control. I left Meg as soon as I finished high school. And I took classes in law enforcement. I also took self-defense and martial arts. No one was going to hurt me again. No one damn it," he said fiercely, no longer looking at her. His eyes focused on some long ago image, his face looking tortured as tears streamed, unnoticed.

"I applied to the police academy. I worked long and hard, and made rank. I did well. But I could never quite forget. Images would appear in my mind and I couldn't get them to leave." He placed his hands over his eyes, and began to rub at them stringently, as though he were trying to scrub the images away.

"Eventually I knew what I had to do. I had to make them pay. That was the only way to make the faces go away, it was the only way I could get peace." He reached inside his jacket and withdrew the small, pearl handled .22 and lifted it. He leisurely caressed the polished, gleaming chrome plate.

He looked at Maya with a smile on his face, before turning his attention back to the gun. "Isn't she beautiful? So small yet so deadly." With a low manic chuckle, Lieutenant Jaime Hernandez stroked the handle of the gun and pointed it directly at Maya's head.

CHAPTER 50

Time was running out. She had to do something quick before she became this pitiful creature's next victim. Maya tried unobtrusively to reach her bag where it lay near the chair leg. She didn't believe in guns and refused to take the lessons Mark wanted her to take, but she had a can of mace attached to her key chain.

The keys sat on top of her bag, and she casually reached over the small distance to capture them, along with the mace, as Jaime stroked the small weapon.

When he glanced over as she was bringing her hand back into her lap, his eyes narrowed, and he slowly advanced on her.

He stood less than a foot away, when shouts outside the locked door made him snap his head in the direction the noise originated from, and Maya wasted no time. She unsnapped the leather top and stood up, knocking her chair backward as she did, and sprayed the contents directly into his face.

Most of the spray landed in his mouth and nose, however enough reached his eyes so that he yelled out in surprise and pain. Maya reached for the gun in his hand, and although he was in obvious pain, Jaime maintained his hold. As they struggled over the gun, it went off, and the sound of two gunshots exploded.

* * * *

"He's down, but he's breathing!" Jordan shouted. He bent over the second fallen guard, this one laying on the porch.

"You two go inside, I'll wait for the paramedics," he said to Mark and Nicolai, when the approaching sounds of sirens rent the air with their wailing cry.

Mark and Nicolai burst inside the house, looking around as many of the women stood clutching their robes in fear. The sound of two gunshots polarized the men into action.

With a primal cry of denial, Mark bolted toward Maya's office with Nicolai close on his heels, both men drawing their weapons as they ran. The door of the anteroom, which served as Dalia's office was closed and locked, yet was no real barrier for Mark.

With the amount of adrenaline coursing through his body, he broke the door open with little effort, and rushed into the room. His long strides took him to Maya's closed door, and once again, he shattered the door open.

He stood still for one heart agonizing nanosecond, transfixed for that brief moment in time. Maya lay still on the floor beneath Lieutenant Hernandez and blood was covering both of their bodies.

"No, baby, no. God please not Maya." He rushed forward, roughly moving the lieutenant's body off Maya's, and knelt down to cradle her head in his lap, tears streaming down his face.

Mark frantically felt for her pulse and nearly fainted in relief when he felt the strong steady beat signaling life in her small helpless body. He moved his hands gently over her body, and searched for injury. He inadvertently came into contact with her injury, and her eyes fluttered, trying to open as a moan escaped her closed lips.

"You're okay, baby. Oh God you're okay, Maya." He gently hugged her, kissing her on the top of her head as the tears continued to flow unashamedly down his face.

* * * *

Nicolai rushed into the room followed by two paramedics, and immediately came to stand beside them. Looking down at the hole in the center of the lieutenant's forehead, he already knew the man's fate, yet he squat down and felt for a pulse.

"Please get her to emergency, she has a gunshot wound above her breast," Mark demanded in a barely recognizable voice, his throat clogged with tears.

The paramedic reassured him, and Mark was moved aside so they could reach the small hurt woman in his arms. Maya was placed on the stretcher with an oxygen mask over her nose and mouth, "We'll come back for him." The paramedic said, referring to Lieutenant Hernandez.

"He's dead." Nicolai turned toward Mark, "You go ahead and I'll meet up with you at the hospital."

Nicolai watched them leave, before turning his attention to the man who lay dead on the floor, tissue and gray matter on the carpet beside his bloodied head.

CHAPTER 51

"How're you doing?" Nicolai asked Maya, as he walked into her hospital room with a box of chocolates tucked under his arm.

When he reached her bedside, he placed the candy on the table. "I thought you would prefer chocolate to flowers."

"Thank you. I'm doing fine Agent Montgomery. I'm sure I look a lot worse than I feel." She laughed hoarsely. "And chocolate is always preferable over flowers. At least they are to me," she smiled.

"You look wonderful. I don't think it's possible for you to look anything else but beautiful," he complimented her.

"Thank you, and please sit down Agent Montgomery." She invited, motioning for him to sit in one of the small chairs near her bed.

"I can't stay long," he said, turning down the offer to sit. "I wanted to come by and say good-bye before I leave tomorrow morning."

"So soon?"

"Yes. I need to return to base now that the case is over. My team is waiting for me. I admire who you are, and what you do Dr. Richardson. It takes someone very special to work with those who are overlooked by 'polite' society."

"Thank you, Agent Montgomery. I used to believe the reason I worked with the women and men of Imani House was because of Allison. But now I know what keeps me going is how Imani House changes lives. In Swahili, Imani means faith or belief. I want the residents of Imani House to have faith that they can overcome any obstacle life places before them."

She thought of Lieutenant Hernandez, and how his lack of power from childhood shaped him into the man he eventually became; unable to overcome the injustices perpetrated against him, and therefore sought revenge against those he saw as users.

"Those of us who know what it was like to have control taken away, understand the feeling of hopelessness," Nicolai spoke in his quiet manner.

In the depths of his slashing gray eyes, Maya saw a look of overwhelming sadness that made her breath hitch, before he turned his face away, and broke their eye contact. When he turned his head back in her direction, his austere face was once again serene, his mercury colored eyes bland, as though the cheerless expression of moments ago had not been.

"Yes we do don't we?" Maya said and reached her hand out to cover his.

* * * *

"Detective Halstan?"

Mark turned away from the door at the doctor's approach and held out his hand in greeting. "Yes, hello Dr. Mayes," he addressed Maya's attending physician. "I was going in to see Maya, is everything okay?"

Mark couldn't quell the anxiety that still rode him, the vision of her laying in a pool of blood still lingering in his mind.

"Yes everything is okay. In fact I informed Dr. Richardson she's cleared to check out tomorrow morning." The doctor reassured him. "I wanted to make sure she had someone to look after her when she goes home."

"She's coming with me, or I'll go home with her. Either way, she'll be taken care of."

During the three days she'd been in the hospital he'd worked hard with Jordan to clean up the loose ends and had given all the statements necessary regarding Lieutenant Hernandez. Now, he could take the next couple of weeks off, and take care of Maya.

"Great. The nurse will give the two of you her discharge papers tomorrow morning with full instructions for her care. And of course, if you have any questions feel free to call me."

Mark thanked him, and knocked lightly on the hospital door. Opening the door he peeked inside with a wide smile on his face before walking in. He wasn't surprised to see Montgomery inside, and after he walked over to place a kiss on her forehead softly, he turned and greeted him.

"I'm leaving, but before I go I want you to take this." The agent handed a card to Maya. "If you ever need to reach me for anything you can call this number and I'll be contacted." As he handed her the card, Mark raised his eyebrows.

"Of course the number is for the both of you. Don't share it with anyone. If I'm unavailable then, ask for Dafina." He picked up her hand and gave it a small kiss.

"Thank you for all your help Montgomery." Although the agent had helped him and Jordan tie up loose ends, he hadn't had the opportunity to thank him for his help.

Maya too said good-bye, and they watched him walked out the door. Left alone, Maya turned loving eyes in Mark's direction, and patted the bed for him to sit next to her.

Maya and the lieutenant had struggled over the gun, and it had gone off hitting her high on the right side of her chest. After the lieutenant had seen what he'd done, he had pointed the gun at his head and fired the shot that ended his life. Maya had passed out from the utter shock and terror of the situation and the loss of blood.

Mark carefully looked her over. The blue hospital gown covered the bandage on her chest , which kept the chest tube in place in her body.

The bullet had entered into her right chest and made a clean exit out of her armpit. The doctors had inserted a chest tube because the bullet had punctured the right middle lobe of her lung.

The doctor explained to Mark that the chest tube, along with the three-chambered drainage device, would remove the air and fluid that had escaped from her collapsed lung.

When he'd first seen her after surgery, he'd been filled with terror at the sight of her with so many tubes running from her body, even though they'd assured him she hadn't been severely wounded.

Words like collapsed lung, chest tubes, and draining devices, scared the hell out of him. He didn't have the same casual attitude of the doctors and nurses, who on a daily basis saw far more brutal cases than Maya's.

"How're you feeling sweetheart?" He asked her after he pressed soft kisses on the palm of her hand.

"I feel fine. I'll be glad when I can leave. Dr. Mayes says I can go home tomorrow," she said with a tired smile.

"He said the same to me, before I came inside. I was able to finish up the case so I can stay home with you."

"I imagine there was a lot to do, a lot of explanations. How is everyone handling it?"

Mark had been at her bedside as long as he could, only leaving when she was asleep to go to the precinct. Today was first day they'd spoken about the case.

She'd wondered what happened to the guards that night, why no one was around. Mark told her how the lieutenant had distracted the two guards outside before knocking them unconscious.

Her personal guard he'd relieved of duty, telling the man he would take care of Maya, and as soon as he'd turned away, he'd knocked him out and moved his body into one of the closets.

"To say everyone is surprised; shocked, is putting it *way* too mildly. No one understands why, there are a lot of unanswered questions. Once you're feeling better you'll be able to help them understand the lieutenant's motives."

Unable to stop the detectives assigned to the case from questioning her, Mark insisted on being in the room when they came by to take her statement. Maya was the last one Lieutenant Hernandez had spoken with and she had been the one to whom he'd confessed his crimes. The interview had been brief due to her injury, however, when she was feeling better it was understood she would need to give a more formal statement.

What she'd been able to tell them explained how the lieutenant was able to work effectively as an officer of the law, and how he was able to effectively slip into the female persona of 'Jaime,' and commit the murders. And how, in the end, when he had spoken to her, the two personas finally, fatally, collided.

"I know what he did was awful, killing those men. And he took my sister from me. But there's a part of me that feels nothing but sadness for him, and others just like him. He and I, our lives, at least our childhoods, were so similar." She mused, carefully weighing her words. "Neither one of us was wanted, neither one of us had a decent childhood, and yet mercifully, my upbringing didn't tarnish my psyche in the same way it did Jaime's."

"No it didn't. You're a strong person, Maya. I know you don't want to hear that, but it's true. You've dealt with adversity and overcome it. You didn't allow it to become a part of who you are. To dictate who you'd become."

"Thank you. I know you love me and you believe only the best about me. But Jaime suffered from a mental illness that was brought on by his childhood traumas. I don't suffer from some of his psychological issues, but that doesn't mean I don't *have* issues," she admitted with a small laugh.

"I try not to wonder too deeply how I keep it together and enjoy life, I just do. And I thank God I'm able to do so, without allowing the past to continually dictate my present; my future." She thought of Jaime's last words to her.

They were both momentarily silent, their thoughts on the man who brought them together, who now lay dead from his own hand.

Wanting to alleviate the sadness that clung to her like a dismal cloak, he tilted her face toward him. "You know as I recall before this last bout of insanity, you and I were having a very serious discussion," he said around the small hand he was delivering soft kisses to.

The bright overhead light, caught the reflection of the new thick gold chain he wore around his neck, and attached pendant, which matched the one he had placed around hers as soon as she'd gotten out of surgery.

A smile blossomed on her face. "Oh yes, I think I recall something about a baby?" She squint her eyes, as though she couldn't recall the exact topic.

"Yeah. A baby. But you know I think I jumped the gun a bit."

"Oh? And how did you do that?" Her confusion quickly turned to surprise, and finally joy, as he reached into his pocket to pull out a small black velvet box.

Going down on the proverbial one knee, he opened the box and took out a beautiful princess cut flawless emerald and took her left hand in his.

"I know this is probably not the best of timing, but I've learned life is too short and too uncertain to wait," he began. "Maya you are an amazing woman, so full of life and love and compassion. I could not, nor would I want to, imagine my life without you. Would you do me the honor of being my wife?" Mark's voice had grown rough with emotion, toward the end.

"Yes. Yes, of course I'll marry you." Maya hugged him as tightly as her restrictions allowed.

She allowed the tears to run down her cheeks, as she marveled at the way life and coincidence had brought the two of them together under the worst possible circumstances, and love had forged a bond between them that broken down all other barriers.

PART III
EPILOGUE

Jerked awake, sweat poured down his face as he picked up the ringing phone and answered in a voice deepened further with sleep, "*As-salamu-alaykum*. Princess, did I wake you?"

Nicolai knew who was on the other end without hearing her voice, and therefore greeted her in *one* of her languages. Even though she'd been the one to call him, he knew it was he, who'd called out to her in his distress as he'd dreamed, who had awakened her.

Her soft, trickling, laugh cascaded over him like a lover's sweet caress, as she answered, in her deceptively mild voice, "*Alaykum s-salam*. Now you know I do not *really* sleep, Chief. *Kayf haluk*? The case is settled then," she more stated then asked as she in turned asked him how he was.

"*Shukran. Al-hamdu li-lah*," he gave the obligatory answer before continuing. "Yeah. It's settled. It could have ended a lot differently 'Fina," he told her as they both settled into their respective beds.

Dafina was one of the few people Nicolai allowed anywhere close to his heart. He had never expressed his feelings to her verbally, and doubted he ever would. Nicolai trusted his teammates; yet it was Dafina he shared his deepest thoughts with. It was Dafina he showed *some* of his vulnerabilities.

"I missed easy clues 'Fina. I don't know the last time I couldn't tell a male from a female voice, even disguised. The headaches are getting worse; they're interfering with my ability. Thanks to you I could 'hear' more clearly. But it was nearly too late, and my mistake could have cost another innocent woman her life," he said, anguish filling his gut as he remembered.

"We will find out how to ease these headaches. You know we have at our disposal the best doctors money can buy," she reminded him with a sardonic laugh.

"And besides you do not simply listen to the voice, you hear what they project. Jaime projected as a female, and not as a male. In that persona, he connected too strongly with the feminine facet of his personality for you to pick up anything else. And as you know, the feminine is the true strength," she subtly reminded him of her